No Place

Katharine D'Souza

To Amanda
Thank you for
inviting me to Barford
Katharine D'S

ISBN-13: 978-1535306379
ISBN-10: 1535306378

Chapter One

For two years it'd been wall-to-wall red, white and blue at home. Royal wedding, Team GB, Diamond Jubilee: any excuse to fly the bunting. Not just bunting either. Mugs. Cushion covers. Bath mat and hand towel set. Dadda did things properly. The ultimate patriot, more British than fish and chips.

Tanya didn't get it. Britain might be home, but there was a world out there and staying put meant missing out.

At least the three colours revealed as the man in front of her rolled up his sleeve belonged to the stars and stripes of the American flag, and the tattoo adorning his bicep gave her a conversational opening. She liked to chat with the patients sent to the radiology clinic. It encouraged them to relax and helped dispel any nerves brought on by her uniform and the hazard stickers marking the equipment she controlled.

'We don't see many Americans,' she said as she turned to read the details of his injury on his notes.

She'd noticed his accent immediately, but you couldn't always be sure. He might have been Canadian. She'd assumed a New Zealander was Australian once and the offence taken led to a lecture on the various ways in which

1

New Zealand was superior to Australia which ended with her promising the patient she would definitely visit his homeland, if she ever got to leave her own. She couldn't empathise with that kind of nationalistic pride, but had no desire to repeat her mistake.

'I guess not,' the man replied and smiled at her. 'Plenty of broken wrists though, right?'

Tanya scrutinised his expression. Uncommon for someone in pain to be so cheerful, but not unheard of. They'd have given him painkillers down in A&E.

'Injuries are all different,' she said and swung the arm of the X-ray machine over the table beside him. 'And we don't yet know what's wrong with your wrist. That's what I'm going to find out.'

'Happy to be in your hands, ma'am.'

She made eye contact and just managed to stop herself returning his smile. Plenty of men flirted with her; something about the hospital environment brought it out in them. Not many were her near own age though. Fantasies about doctors and nurses seemed to be more popular among older men. She decided it was more likely this patient was just being friendly and turned back to his paperwork before starting the job. Both the fact he'd listed his mum as next-of-kin and the lack of a ring on his injured hand suggested he wasn't married, though she mentally reprimanded herself for looking. Patients needed treatment, that was all. Even charming patients from interesting places.

'Can you confirm your name and date of birth, please?' she said.

'William O'Brien, though you should call me Will. Three, fifteen, eighty-four. And you, Dr Gill?'

It wasn't only his accent which was interesting. His voice was resonant and warm-toned. She shook her head, translated the date into UK format and double-checked the details against those her assistant technician had already reviewed. Tanya forced herself to keep her own voice neutral as she said, 'Sorry to disappoint you, I'm not a doctor.'

Nor was she an astronaut, ice dancer, or any of the other careers she'd aspired to when younger. Childhood dreams had no place among the responsibilities of real life and right now her role was to help work out what was wrong with this man's wrist.

'Can you place your hand here? Palm down.'

She pointed to the plate fixed to the surface of the table. A definite flinch twisted his face as he lifted his left arm to comply with her instruction.

'What do I call you then?' he said.

The referring doctor had noted some soft tissue swelling below his little finger. Tanya could see it too. His broad wrist with its freckles and fine, dark hairs was distorted to one side with a puffiness that indicated a potential triquetrum fracture. Not easy to get a clear image of that. The anatomy of the wrist was complex; the carpal bones overlapped. More than one X-ray would be needed and she paused to consider the angles to take.

It was her job to find the damaged parts of patients and play her role in fixing them because underneath it all, everyone ought to be similar - their fundamental human physiology standard, regardless of skin colour, body shape, piercings or tattoo ink.

'Go on,' he said and used his undamaged hand to point at the ID badge strung on a lanyard round her neck. 'I won't tell. What does the T stand for?'

Distracted by her thoughts, she failed to fob him off. 'Tanya,' she said.

He repeated the word, his flat, elongated vowels making her name sound foreign to her own ears. That didn't often happen. It was a name which could pass for British. It generally did. Only her dark skin and hair gave away that her heritage came from elsewhere, but she felt as little connection with India as she did with Britain. This patient was welcome to brand himself with red, white and blue if he chose to fly a flag. Tanya's allegiances belonged to no country. She didn't look at him again as she made final adjustments to the machine.

'I need you to stay absolutely still, please. I'll be back in a moment.'

In the safety of the cubicle off the X-ray room, she tapped settings into the computer terminal which controlled the machine before looking through the window to make sure his wrist was still positioned correctly. It was. He caught her eye with an expression she couldn't interpret. She pressed the button to release the second-long burst of radiation which would capture an image of his bones and, not for the first time, wished the pictures also revealed thoughts. Of course she'd never expose her own. Patients were out of bounds.

She broke the eye contact and bent to the screen. The image was clear with all eight wrist bones positioned and spaced as expected. There were no immediately obvious dislocations or fractures. While always relieved to see a textbook example of normal human anatomy with no suspicious clouding, unexpected masses or alarming breakages, Tanya knew her job wasn't done. This man was in pain.

'I need a second image,' she said as she returned to the main room. 'Would it be too difficult to turn your wrist like this?' She demonstrated with her own arm, pushing her watch back to be sure he could see the positioning.

'Yeah, I can do that.' He grimaced as he moved though. 'Nice watch you've got there, Tanya. Mine broke when I fell. Smashed the glass and it sounds like something's loose inside.'

'I'm sorry to hear that,' she said and touched her own wrist to make sure her watch was secure. It hadn't occurred to her to fear losing or breaking it before. To do so would be a trauma worse than any broken bone, but a recollection of the voice of the radiographer she'd done her training with saying 'treat the patient, not the X-ray' brought her back to the present. Will's obvious distress as he turned his wrist to allow her equipment a clear view of the lateral plane was really all the guidance she needed. 'Just hold still a moment longer. I'm sorry if it hurts.'

She repeated the procedure. This time, as she assessed the details in the black and white image, she could see the problem. Without the overlapping bone obscuring the detail, a clear fracture was visible. She didn't doubt it was painful but once the bones were realigned and immobilised his wrist would mend. Not everyone she took images of was that lucky.

'OK, that's all. You can rest your hand now.'

'Cool, I thought we'd never be through.' He cradled his wrist close to his body.

'I'm sorry, it's just ...'

'I'm teasing. You Brits are always apologising. It's my fault for being a doofus and falling over, not yours for doing your job.'

'Oh, OK. Right, well I'll send the images and my notes to your doctor so if you head back to the clinic they'll see you again shortly.' Tanya scribbled her initials and closed his file before standing to help him collect his possessions.

'Do I get to see you again?' he asked as he leaned close to let her drape his jacket over his left arm.

She looked at his face and couldn't resist returning his smile before stepping backwards to put a more appropriate distance between them. She'd been nothing but professional and was almost certain she hadn't revealed her attraction to him, but, unlike his wrist and his watch, his confidence was undented. She straightened her back and spoke briskly. The waiting room outside was full.

'Unlikely I'm afraid. If you need another X-ray you'll see whoever's on duty. So I'll just say get well soon. Oh, and your watch, there's a good repairer in a shop by Bournville Green, do you know it?'

He nodded. 'Bournville's why I'm over here. I'm working at the chocolate factory so thanks, I'll check that shop out.'

She began to reset the equipment as the door closed behind him. Will would need all of that charm if he wanted to be popular at work then. Her own Dadda, who'd stopped working at the chocolate factory a few years earlier, had strong opinions about the American takeover of what had been a British company with a proud heritage. In her own opinion though, a little international experience could only be a good thing.

Will's pronunciation of her name remained on her mind, the unusual stress on the syllables giving it an exotic rhythm. The only other person who pronounced the word Tanya with a similar cadence was Dadda himself. He hadn't lost his Indian accent despite nearly thirty years living in Birmingham and being in every other way as English as afternoon tea.

Her own accent gave little away. Though born and bred in Birmingham, her pronunciation bore little Brummie twang. The constant changes of register - from home to school to university to work - had wiped away most of the characteristics. Yes, she was British; she just didn't feel it. The diverse backgrounds of the patients she treated and other hospital staff meant she felt no sense of belonging. It was as though they shared no common ground. Other people seemed to have an attitude, an ease within their own skin, which she'd always lacked. Tanya had no idea where she fitted in.

Will had immediately assumed she was British though; not all white people did that. Still, she resented the label, and the fact that he remained on her mind. There were many more patients queueing for her attention and she was on first name terms with none of them. Professional distance, she reminded herself and stood to call the next one through.

*

It was getting dark as Tanya drove home after her shift. She parked the car on the drive in front of their semi-detached house and noticed that a heap of fallen leaves had been swept by the wind to obscure the step up to the front door. It was unusual that Dadda hadn't immediately cleared them on his return from work. He'd complain about it, but autumn remained his favourite season.

Intending to tease him for slacking on his chores, Tanya walked up to the front door but was surprised again to find she only needed the key for the Yale lock to open it. The deadlock was unfastened. Dadda always kept it locked, even during the day, even if everyone was in.

He'd once seen a crime drama in which a burglar had easily broken in to a house whose door was secured only by a Yale and, since then, added it to his measures to ensure total security at all times. Tanya found it easiest to go along with the rules, not that her younger sister always did the same.

'Dadda? I'm home,' she called as she bent to remove her shoes. His bunch of keys linked by their Union Jack fob lay on the surface of the hall table rather than hidden in their usual location inside the drawer. She frowned as she yanked out the band holding her hair back into a ponytail and turned to push open the living room door where she came immediately face-to-face with their neighbour who'd opened it from the other side.

'Oops. Mary, I'm sorry, I didn't expect you,' Tanya said.

The older woman reached out to squeeze Tanya's shoulder. 'I'm so glad you're here, bab. I wanted to call you but your dad wouldn't disturb you at work.'

Alarmed, Tanya pushed past her and rushed towards Dadda's armchair as she asked, 'What's wrong?'

Despite being in his usual chair, her dad did not look normal. His back was not straight, his eyes were not lively and, while he'd removed his shoes, he was not wearing his slippers.

'Tanya,' he said. 'I'm glad you're safely home.'

'What's happened?'

He opened his mouth, but didn't speak. Instead he lifted one hand and placed his fingertips to his lips as though to hold the words in. While he hesitated, Mary spoke for him. 'He's had a run in with some nasty lads. Just boys by the sound of it, and idiots too. You mustn't mind them, Jagtar,' she said as she bent to pat his shoulder. 'You mustn't take it personally.'

Tanya knelt by the side of his chair. 'Dadda? Are you OK? Did they hurt you?' She scanned his face, touched his limbs, her heart pounding as she assessed for signs of injury. The recent news story of an Asian man who'd been attacked, murdered - stabbed in the back as he left early morning prayers at his mosque – leapt to her mind. And other stories: the gunshots, slash wounds and beatings frequently reported on the local news. The city was a dangerous place.

He dropped his hand from his mouth and patted her arm. 'No, they didn't hurt me. They only spoke cruel words.'

'Racists,' Tanya said. It wasn't a question because what other reason could there be? Jagtar Gill was no threat to anyone. He was polite, quiet: utterly ordinary. He'd have done nothing to cause a confrontation. 'What happened, Dadda?'

He closed his eyes and let his head fall back against the upholstery. 'I was on the bus, usual bus home. These boys got on - white boys talking like black boys, perhaps five of them, or six. There were very few other people upstairs.'

'Oh, Dadda. I've asked you not to sit upstairs.'

'And why shouldn't I? I'm not a geriatric, not too doddery to climb stairs.'

Tanya squeezed his hand. 'Of course not. Then what happened?'

'They were showing off. Playing about. Pushing each other and one boy fell against me. His friends laughed and said he should watch out in case I set off my bomb, in case I turned "all jihad" on him.'

Mary tutted. 'You've got to ignore them; they're ignorant fools. I don't know why they assumed you're a Muslim, but that just proves what idiots they are. Anyway, now Tanya's here, I'll get home. You call if you need me though. Bang on the wall.'

She smiled at him as she gestured towards the adjoining wall between their houses, but tilted her head as she looked at Tanya to indicate she had more to say. Once they were out in the hall, Mary spoke softly, 'I found him sitting in the bus stop at the bottom of the road when I was coming home. I guess he got off the bus and just stopped. You'll look after him, won't you? He's taken it pretty badly.'

'Of course,' Tanya said. 'Thank you.' She held the front door open for Mary then double-locked it behind her before going back to the living room where she knelt on the floor in front of her dad.

'Did you hear what Mary didn't say?' he asked.

'Didn't say?'

'She didn't say that not all Muslims are terrorists. She didn't say that it's only the extremists, the distorted fanaticists who use terrorism.'

Tanya shook her head. 'How is that relevant? We're not Muslim.'

'It just shows what these people really think.'

'These people? Mary's been our next-door neighbour for ever. She's always been friendly. Are you accusing her of being racist too, or just anti-Muslim?'

He shook his head. 'It wasn't only what those boys said this afternoon. I stood up to move away from them and a man blocked my way by putting his leg across the aisle. I said "Excuse me" and the woman he was with, they were both older, perhaps Mary's age, she looked at me with such hatred and said "Go back where you came from". As I went down the stairs, the man leant over and spat on me.' He wiped his hand over his head as though there was still something to be removed, then grimaced at his palm.

'Oh, Dadda.' Tanya reached to touch him. 'What horrible people.'

'I didn't tell Mary, but I was afraid to leave the bus stop. Those boys followed me off the bus, shouting and jeering. I wanted to stay near traffic and crowds. I wanted witnesses.'

'They followed you?' Tanya's voice pitched high in alarm and she gripped his arm. 'What happened? What did they do?'

'Nothing, nothing. They pushed and shoved and knocked into me, but they moved on. They were shouting, they were ...'

'But they didn't hurt you, not physically?'

'No,' he said and pointed to the busy road which passed outside their bay window. 'They came this way.'

'Did you recognise any of them?' Tanya asked. There were often gangs of lads hanging around at the park up the road, but they'd never seemed threatening before now.

He shook his head. 'They had hoods, they slouched, and I didn't want to look at their faces. This country, this city has always appeared tolerant, but today I saw that it only goes skin deep.'

Tanya shook her head. 'You don't believe that. I don't believe that.' She stared at the carpet where a worn patch in front of Dadda's armchair was evidence of how many hours he'd sat there over the decades in which he'd lived in this country. Hideous though the people sounded, they'd heard worse incidents reported on the news on an almost daily basis and, while what happened would have distressed anyone, she couldn't bear hearing him speak like this. He was a man who loved Britain, a man fully integrated into British culture. It was appalling that strangers had suggested he didn't belong here, but worse if he was losing trust in people. She said what she thought he needed to hear. 'We're British, Dadda. Geena and I were born here and you have citizenship. This is where our family belongs.'

He sat up straighter in his chair and, with his eyes focused on a point somewhere far beyond their living room, nodded. 'We're not safe here, though. The city's too violent. We should move to the countryside, somewhere quieter, more civilised.'

Tanya pressed her lips together. She could guess what he'd be imagining: a thatched cottage on a village green - the emblem of an England which no longer existed. They'd spent every family holiday of her childhood chasing that dream of his, driving down hedge-shrouded country lanes with Dadda convinced the 1950s would be around the next corner. They never were.

All that happened was Tanya and her sister, Geena, bickered in the back of the car while their parents admired everything they saw but never quite found perfection. Since their mum died, the holidays had stopped. Despite having been old enough to holiday alone or with friends for many years, Tanya had never fulfilled her own dreams of international travel. She had a responsibility for Dadda and Geena. She couldn't leave them home alone.

This wasn't about holidays though, this was him suggesting they left the only home she'd ever known to retreat to his idea of a sanctuary.

'I have my job here, so does Geena. We're settled, Dadda. Birmingham is where we're from,' she said.

He shook his head. 'When there was rioting in the city centre I knew things were changing. Now I'm abused on a bus here, so close to my own home. The danger is in our street,' he said, pointing again at the window. 'If I can't keep my family safe, it's time to leave.'

His reaction to the 2011 riots had alarmed Tanya. Instead of expressing shock and anger towards the televised images of gangs rampaging across the city centre and looting shops, he'd become fearful. He'd attempted to set curfews for his daughters which had led to arguments with Geena. It was as though he couldn't accept that his girls had grown up. While they stayed under his roof, he wanted to control their actions and influence their decisions.

Tanya had always been happy to stay with him, she'd promised her mum she'd do as much, but to follow Dadda into a rural seclusion would be going too far. Her own dreams had no borders. If she left Birmingham it would be to travel beyond British shores.

He clutched at her hand. 'Where is Geena?' he asked.

'She's fine, Dadda. Probably out with her friends.' Typical Geena. Never there when she was actually needed.

'What time will she be home?'

Tanya shrugged and stood to close the faded velvet curtains across the darkness outside the bay window, pausing as she did so to make sure there was no-one there. Car headlights swept up the road and illuminated the empty pavements. Everything was normal.

She'd made no other plans for the evening and sat with him, sharing his horror at what had happened, providing tea and a sympathetic ear and, convinced he'd bounce back from the incident, refused to discuss moving. When he'd finally gone to bed she went up to her own room, powered up her laptop and logged in to her favourite website.

Social networking held no appeal for her. Instead the screen filled with a map centred on Birmingham. Symbols indicating the real-time positions of aeroplanes flickered and moved through the airspace. She clicked on a few to identify them from the information which popped up under the cursor. A Ryanair flight from Dublin made its final approach to Birmingham's runway while, coming in from the east, a Swiss plane was arriving from Zurich. Out to the west a smaller, private jet listed only its flight code, its destination concealed.

Tanya zoomed the map out and let her eyes lose focus so it became a shimmering image of activity in the skies above and around her, stretching out for hundreds of miles in each direction. She imagined the people inside each plane travelling on business or for pleasure, leaving family, friends or colleagues behind, or heading towards them.

Unlike the X-ray pictures she'd been studying all day, the fine detail was irrelevant here. The individuals didn't matter. What this screen showed was the potential the world offered. It proved anyone could go anywhere. Well, almost anyone.

Planes were up there on their way to JFK, to LAX. The three simple letters of an airport code held such promise. Tanya could imagine the glamour of an international airport, the drama of arriving in a foreign city - how the differences in climate, in architecture, in language would underline the exoticism of being abroad. How different it would be from Birmingham.

She bit her lip.

Although the potential was out there, although she knew other people were up in the skies, that those symbols of aeroplanes represented anything from two to hundreds of people, she couldn't imagine herself one of them.

The science made sense. The evidence of many thousands of planes taking off and landing safely on a daily basis could not be disputed. But the idea of boarding a plane herself terrified her.

Chapter Two

Geena slouched against the glass counter and regarded the closest of the synchronously ticking clocks lining the walls around her. Five past twelve. Twenty-five minutes until Mr Davis would say, 'I'll leave you in charge then,' and go for his lunch break. The same words. Twelve thirty. Every day.

She didn't mind being left in charge; she wished he'd give her more responsibility, because under her management the shop would be unrecognisable. She'd expand the stock, refresh the displays, develop a website, perhaps she could even take commissions. The customers would have to know she was a jeweller of course, not only a sales assistant in the most old-fashioned of all the traditional jewellery shops in Birmingham. And there were plenty of those.

Ten past twelve. She rubbed the side of her index finger with her thumb, itching to pick up a pencil and return to the sketches she'd begun that morning. The ideas weren't ready to share yet but she couldn't wait for a moment of privacy when she could grab her sketchbook from her bag and set down her newest thoughts for an earring design.

She was certain the concept was original, although until she tried it out in the materials she had in mind, she couldn't be sure how it would work. Ideas bloomed in her mind, growing beyond the elements of her original inspiration and almost tangible.

As she thought, she twisted the set of thin bangles adorning her wrist. The jangling as they knocked against each other had been the soundtrack to her life for as long as she could remember. The rich-toned Indian gold with regular grooves etched into their top surfaces was unlike anything for sale in this shop. Most of their stock was in sterling silver and nine carat gold, eighteen carat for a few select items. Geena's bangles were the real deal, brought by her mum from India in another lifetime and now Geena's most treasured possession.

Sixteen clocks chimed the quarter hour in unison. Almost as melodic as the forty-eight bells of the carillon across Bournville Green. She liked it when they practised or played tunes there. She wouldn't admit it to her family or friends, but that traditional peal of a church bell intensified by the scale of the carillon caught at something in her. Something she would never openly admit that she possessed. Patriotic spirit, Dadda would probably call it. Though perhaps he'd lose some of his after the way those idiots on the bus had treated him.

She sniffed, annoyed that neither he nor Tanya had told her the full story about what had happened, or listened to her opinions over breakfast that morning. Trying to protect her as usual. And Tanya had no right to be pissed off when she hadn't bothered to call to say something had happened. She couldn't be annoyed that Geena hadn't helped when Geena was unaware that help was required. Anyway, Tanya and Dadda were probably overreacting. As usual.

Geena stood up straight and placed her hands on the counter as the tinny ding of the shop door opening provided a welcome distraction. Customers on a weekday were a rare treat. Cute male customers rarer still.

'Hi, I've been told I might be able to get my watch mended here?' the man said.

Geena flicked her hair back and smiled. 'Of course. What seems to be the problem?' A hot, young, American customer deserved US standards of service after all.

He stared at her for a beat too long before replying. 'Pretty much everything, I think. Look.'

He produced an envelope from his jacket pocket and placed it on the counter, indicating that she should open it because, with his left arm in a sling, he couldn't. She unstuck the flap and extracted an old analogue watch with a brown leather strap. Not what she'd have guessed he'd own.

You could tell a lot about a person from the watch or jewellery they chose and she'd assumed he'd have something designer, something slick and expensive to match his suit. This was an older man's watch, a much older man's, and it was very damaged. The glass from the face was shattered, the case dented and the hour hand twisted.

'What happened?' she asked.

'I guess it took the full force of what could have happened to my wrist. A disagreement between me and one of your sidewalks. You know the paving's not exactly smooth out there?'

She smiled. 'I'm sorry. Is your wrist OK?'

'Yeah, it will be. Basically I wasn't looking and tripped into some steps. What about the watch though; can it be fixed? It belonged to my Gramps and I'd hate to lose it.'

That explained why he wore such an old watch rather than something more suited to his otherwise modern image.

'We'll have to ask Mr Davis,' she said and glanced at the time. Twenty-seven minutes past. Mr Davis hated interruptions to his routine, but an interesting timepiece might be the one thing he'd forgive.

As if he'd sensed its presence, Mr Davis came through from the workroom behind the shop, glanced at the customer and immediately turned his attention to the wounded watch on the counter. He lifted it as though it were a baby bird and examined it from all angles. Neither Geena nor the customer said anything. The sixteen clocks chimed the half hour and, when they'd finished, Mr Davis spoke.

'Sentimental value,' he said.

Geena looked at the customer who replied, 'Yes. Very much so.'

Mr Davis nodded. 'I'll need to look properly at the internal damage. Miss Gill will take your details then she can call you when I know more.' He took the watch with him back into the workroom.

'I'm sorry,' Geena said, 'are you OK to leave it with us? He is very good, I promise. And reasonably priced.'

The man smiled. 'Of course. I just want it working again, and now I see why you look familiar, Miss Gill. It must have been your sister who sent me here. You look very like her.'

'Tanya? Oh, of course,' she glanced at his sling, 'at the hospital. Well it's nice to know she recommends us.' Geena reached for the receipt book and riffled its thin paper to move the carbon copy sheet to a new page. 'Can I take your name?'

She wrote Will's contact details along with a description of the watch onto the slip of paper before folding and tearing the perforation to hand the top copy to him.

'Pretty old-fashioned way of doing things,' he said.

'It works,' she said, surprising herself with how defensive she sounded.

'Sure. It just amuses me how you Brits cling to your traditions. Maybe not your sister with her hi-tech equipment, but here and down at the factory,' he gestured toward the chocolate factory behind the parade of shops, 'not everything's moved with the times, has it?'

Geena frowned. It was OK for her to be critical of Mr Davis' shop, but this man had some cheek to say the same things. No wonder the takeover of the factory by a big American corporation was the subject of so much muttering in the area if this is what they were like.

'Hey, I didn't mean to offend. I mean, you've got some well-established and successful businesses here. I just think modern techniques can help. You know, some streamlining and updating. The world's changed. Business has to move with it.'

'Yeah. I agree with you.' Geena glanced behind her to make sure the door to the workroom was closed. 'I'd like to shake things up a bit in this place, but, well, it's his business. I just work here.'

Will nodded. 'Listen, can I ask you something? Does your sister have a boyfriend?'

Typical, Geena thought, hottest guy I've met in ages and he fancies my geeky sister. 'Tanya? No, she's single.'

'Me too,' he replied. 'So, you're Brummies, right?'

'Born and bred. Where are you from?'

'Chicago - your twin city. Far from identical twins though. Can't believe I've landed somewhere like this.' He looked out the window towards Bournville Green where mature trees punctuated lawns strewn with colourful fallen leaves and lights illuminated the leaded windows of the Rest House. 'This is like something you'd see on the History Channel.'

Geena followed his gaze, trying to see the familiar scene through his eyes.

'Hmm. So you're here to work at the factory then? Just a temporary thing I suppose?'

'The project I'm on is for a year. It'll take that long and I expect I'll be around for most of it. I'm hoping to visit Ireland while I'm here - it's where my family were originally from. Have you been?'

Geena shook her head. 'Ireland? No.' She'd met a few Irish people but it had never occurred to her it was a place people went. She thought it was somewhere they left.

'Where are your family from?' Will asked.

'Um, India. But I've never been,' she said, pre-empting his next question.

'No? So how did you all end up here?'

She frowned. Another thing she'd never considered. Or never questioned, at any rate. 'My mum worked at the hospital. I guess she and my dad came over for the jobs. Dadda used to work at your factory.'

'Oh. I see.' Will nodded as though he understood something more than she'd said. 'It's a big thing, isn't it? The chocolate factory? There's this sense of it belonging to the city somehow when, you know, it is a private business. Speaking of which, I guess I should get back to my job and let you get on with yours. You'll be in touch when you know more about my watch, right?'

'Of course.'

He smiled. 'Remember me to your sister, won't you? It was good to meet you both.'

The bell above the door dinged again as he left and Geena slouched back against the counter. No matter if this guy hadn't shown any interest in her; she had other prospects, Sami, for one. OK, so he'd just split up with her friend Jules, but there was a very good reason for staying in touch with him.

She walked across the shop to wipe a smear she'd noticed on the cabinet displaying jewellery adorned with Celtic designs. Very popular with people with Irish roots, those. She should have tried to sell something to Will.

He was right that British businesses could be old-fashioned, she only had to look around her for proof of that, but Sami's family had bigger ideas. His uncle owned a chain of shops selling products imported from India, mostly through small units in the suburbs with big Asian communities. They had plans to expand further though, to break into the mainstream and go up market. And Geena had expansion plans of her own. Her Indian-influenced jewellery designs could fit very nicely into their desire to upgrade their stock, and Sami was too hot to stay single. Jules would regret letting him go.

*

19

A nurse in green military uniform opened the door to the radiology room and asked, 'Are you ready for us?'

Tanya nodded. As suggested, she'd used screens to shield some of the diagnostic equipment from view and cleared every surface so no distractions were visible. The nurse pushed the door open and, with assistance from a porter, steered a wheeled bed inside. Tanya stepped forward so the patient could see her. He twisted his neck to stare at her through wide eyes.

She smiled and said, 'Hi Rob, I'm Tanya. I'll be taking your X-rays today.'

The man gave a single brief nod and turned his head to scan the rest of the room. The movement revealed a tattoo of a roaring lion's head on the side of his neck; a strange contrast with the fear in his eyes. The nurse finished checking the line to his drip and then said, 'Everything's OK.'

Tanya was glad that Deb, from the defence medicine department based at the hospital, had been to brief her before bringing the patient down. Rob was a twenty-year-old soldier, injured by a bomb while on what should have been a routine patrol in Afghanistan. A bomb which had killed both a local boy and the solider walking two yards ahead, while Rob's own left arm and leg below the knee were so badly damaged both had already been amputated. The dead soldier had been Rob's best friend.

Less than forty-eight hours after the incident, the medical evacuation team delivered Rob to the armed forces medical staff in Birmingham and his physical condition was now stable. His mental state was more fragile and Tanya was keen to do anything she could to minimise his distress.

The missing limbs were an obvious sign of what had happened, but Tanya's involvement was to assess the blast damage which wasn't immediately visible. Her X-rays of his chest would show the effects from the blast pressure on his lungs. As she prepared him for the procedure, Tanya observed that Rob's breathing was shallow and fast. It might not be a symptom; he was under stress and she didn't rush him to follow her instructions.

Once everything was set up, she and Deb retreated to the cubicle which housed the controls.

Tanya spoke quietly. 'OK?' she asked.

'Brilliant. Thank you,' Deb replied, although she kept her eyes fixed on her patient through the observation window. She'd explained to Tanya that he'd had a panic attack while a consultant examined him earlier that morning. He'd torn off the bandages at the amputation sites and ripped the cannula from his arm.

Tanya asked Rob to hold his breath, took the X-ray then nodded to Deb to indicate she could go back to his side. The image of his chest was crisp, but it didn't reveal good news. Tanya wrote up her notes and added them to his file.

As she went back into the main room, she noticed how the young soldier looked constantly to Deb for guidance, as if her presence reassured him. Tanya wondered if it was a response to the trauma, or his military training; if he was so used to taking orders that he particularly needed them now he found himself hurt and helpless. Deb probably didn't outrank him, but her calm words and confident movements exuded competence and trustworthiness. Her manner was practical and kind, almost maternal.

If your world had been blown apart, if both a friend and a child had been killed in front of you, then Deb was exactly the kind of person you'd want to come to your aid.

Tanya stood aside as Deb made sure Rob was comfortable before they moved his bed. He didn't ask what she'd seen on the X-ray. Not many people were so passive, most wanted details of what had happened, what would happen next. Perhaps it was stoicism in his case. Perhaps he understood that events were entirely out of his control and maybe his training meant he accepted that.

She forced herself to smile at him. His injuries were life-changing and recovery would be tough.

Deb rested a hand on his right shoulder and turned to say, 'Thanks so much, Tanya. On with our travels then.'

Tanya held the door for them as Deb and the porter steered Rob's bed through. She watched their progress down the corridor and realised that Deb's perky attitude and willingness to do anything she could for someone else reminded her of something. It triggered memories of her mum, a nurse herself although Tanya had rarely seen her at work. If nursing was a caring vocation, her mum had brought that care to every area of her life.

Deb's interaction with Rob reminded Tanya very much of the way her mum had been with Dadda. Not that Tanya had ever considered him weak or passive before now, but his experience on the bus had changed that.

She put everything in the room back to normal for the radiographer who'd be in on the next shift and powered all the equipment down. Barring emergency call outs, she'd be back in the clinic herself in less than a day's time. One day off wasn't long enough.

She couldn't remember the last proper holiday she'd had and, while Afghanistan didn't feature on her list of dream destinations, meeting that American patient the day before had reinvigorated her desire to travel, to leave Birmingham, to see something new. For now though, in her mum's absence, Dadda had to be Tanya's top priority.

She turned off the lights and went out to her car.

*

As she waited in the queue of traffic which had built up outside the hospital, impatient to get home and see him, Tanya realised that Dadda had always been not just the driver, but the driving force behind their family holidays. She had clear memories of him at the wheel of their family car with its precision-packed boot, navigating his way along the roads of Britain every summer to bring his family to out of the way attractions and beauty spots. From Cornwall to the Highlands, he'd led their expeditions across his adopted country's landscape and demanded that they admire its geographical features, appreciate its history.

Geena had thrown a tantrum once - wouldn't even undo her seatbelt in the car park of yet another National Trust property. Tanya couldn't remember which, they'd merged into what felt like a never-ending montage of how upper class white people used to live.

'I'm not going in,' ten-year-old Geena had stated with her arms folded high across her chest.

At thirteen, Tanya should have been the difficult one, but Geena had always been more dramatic. Dadda's anger was instant. No cajoling, no bribes, just an instant accusation.

'You don't know how lucky you are,' he'd said. 'At your age I was working and didn't know what leisure meant.'

'I don't know what leisure is,' Geena screamed back. 'This is worse than school. At least at school I've got my friends. We have fun.' This she said with a glare at Tanya who said nothing. She didn't want to side with her parents, but really wanted Geena to shut up and give in so the whole thing could be over as soon as possible. Other families were staring at them.

It was bad enough being practically the only Asians there without Geena making them stand out as the troublemakers as well. Tanya dug her hands into her pockets and stared at the churned up grass of the overflow car park so that curtains of hair fell to shield her face.

'And who says we won't have fun?' Their mum reached into the open door to hand Geena the anorak she'd refused to put on when they left the bed and breakfast place that morning. 'I don't know what we'll find in here, but there's bound to be something. Why are all these people here otherwise?' She gestured at the hundreds of parked cars around them.

'Because they're boring,' Geena muttered.

'Because they're interested in their heritage,' Dadda replied.

His wife smiled. 'Because there's a story to hear, and beautiful things to see, and a quiz to do, and maybe even an ice cream. Come on,' she said and squeezed Geena's arm, 'let's go and find out.'

Geena took her time unbuckling the seatbelt then fumbled with the zip on her coat to make her continued reluctance known. Dadda locked the car and led the way towards the house, his wife's hand clasped in his.

'Hurry up,' Tanya told Geena.

'Like you care. I'm only coming cos I don't want to upset Mum.'

'Me neither. So, come on.'

Geena grimaced. 'This is going to be so dull.'

Tanya elbowed her. 'They love it,' she said, nodding towards their parents. 'Can't get enough of this stuff. Like the civil war, or Henry the eighth or the Norman invasion matters any more. It's not even their history, anyway. These people are nothing to do with us.'

They'd caught up with their parents in the queue to pay for entry to the site. 'Who's that?' Tanya's mum asked her. 'Whose history isn't it?'

Tanya lifted her hand to her mouth and chewed the edge of her thumbnail. She agreed with Geena, the last thing either of them ever wanted was to upset their mum. Her good example was impossible to live up to though.

'Um, ours?' Tanya said, hoping that including herself made the criticism less hurtful.

'Of course this is our history; we're British,' Dadda said.

There was so much wrong with his statement Tanya didn't know what to say. She glanced at the others in the queue, all the pale-skinned, middle-class people patiently waiting their turn and giving no sign they'd heard his statement, no indication of whether they'd like to dispute it.

At least they did stay silent. Not like the teachers at school who, on an almost annual basis, expected Tanya to be able to explain the origins behind the Vaisakhi festival to the rest of the class during religious studies lessons. Her response that her family weren't practising Sikhs was met with incomprehension.

It was fine for the white kids to think Christmas was about Santa and Easter about bunnies laden with baskets of chocolate eggs, but all the other Asians in her class came from devout families, regardless of which religion their parents were devoted to. Holi and Eid al-Fitr were discussed in detail. When Tanya asked her mum about their lack of religion, she'd been told to ask Dadda.

When she did ask, he only said, 'We are British now.' It wasn't an answer which helped her fit in.

Standing in the queue to enter the stately home, Dadda looked around the family group and expanded on his point. 'I may not have grown up here but I want to know this country; I want you girls to understand your home and I want us all to learn about it together. Now, come on.' He paid the admission fee and led the way up a wide, tree-lined road towards the Regency mansion.

Tanya lagged behind and watched as Geena slipped her hand into their mum's. Dadda's theory was all very well as an idea, but in practice it meant that Tanya's own emerging desires - to experience European culture, to laze on tropical beaches, to go shopping in New York and other ideas inspired by what her white friends talked about - would never be fulfilled until Dadda knew everything there was to know about Britain. While her view from the back seat of the car suggested Britain was a big place, it didn't excite her. It certainly didn't feel like home.

Even now she was an adult, it still didn't. As she accelerated away from the junction responsible for the hold up and turned towards their post-war suburban house in Selly Oak, Tanya still felt that urge to escape. Perhaps she could put a positive spin on what had happened. Perhaps even Dadda might agree that it was time to get away for a while.

Chapter Three

'What do you think Mum would've done?' Geena asked as she took a plate from the draining rack and held it for the suds to slip off before giving it a brief swipe with the tea towel.

While it was great that Tanya finally wanted to talk to her about what had happened to Dadda on the bus, Geena was struggling to know what to suggest. She'd have yelled at the idiots, but Dadda's reaction to the incident was worrying.

There was a pause before Tanya replied, 'I honestly don't know.'

'We can't just ignore it though.' Geena moved around the table to push the kitchen door closed with her foot, leaving a trail of drips across the tiled floor as she dried a glass. The sound of the laughter track from the TV programme Dadda was watching in the living room was muted and she returned to Tanya's side. 'He's not himself. It's been a couple of days now and he's not getting over it.'

'I know, but he won't report it to the police and there's no physical damage we can bully him to see a doctor about. He's decided he wants to put his head in the sand, not deal with the situation. I have no idea how to persuade him otherwise.'

Silence fell as they both considered this. They carried on clearing up after the evening meal, their routine familiar and established. Unlike Dadda's odd behaviour during the meal. He'd told Geena she shouldn't stay out so late at night and she refused to feel guilty that she'd answered him back, snapping that what she did was none of his business. He'd put his knife and fork down, stood up and walked away from the table, something he'd never done before. That you finished everything on your plate was one of the family's unbreakable rules.

Eventually, Geena said, 'Mum would have known what to do.' She placed the mugs into the cupboard above the kettle registering that one was of the art deco rose design which had been their mum's favourite. 'She knew best about everything.'

She paused, wondering what her mum would have had to say about her most recent late night which had started with her meeting Sami the evening before to pitch him her ideas about how his family firm could stock her jewellery range, and ended many hours later with him dropping her home in his BMW, the windows of which were pretty steamed up. Tanya pulled the plug to let the dishwater drain out of the sink and said nothing. The gurgle of water brought Geena back to reality.

'She wouldn't have stood for that redundancy thing at the factory. He hasn't really been the same since then,' she said.

Tanya shook her head. 'How could Mum have done anything about that? It's a business. They make decisions based on finances, not feelings.'

Geena frowned. If Tanya wanted to be so practical about things then the least she could do would be to come up with a solution. 'I guess Mum always did too much for us. We don't know how to solve anything without her.'

Tanya peeled off the rubber gloves and shook them over the sink. 'You could try having some ideas for once,' she said.

27

'I have ideas,' Geena said. 'I have ideas all the time at work. Speaking of which ...' She paused until the brightened tone of her voice forced Tanya to pay attention.

'What?'

'I made a call today. Spoke to someone interesting.' Geena folded the damp tea towel into neat thirds and draped it over the handle of the oven door as she smiled to herself. It wasn't only her love life that had a bit of spice in it.

Tanya slumped into a chair at the kitchen table and rubbed her eyes. 'Really? I diagnosed five broken bones, identified some osteoarthritis and assisted in reconstructive surgery. No wonder I'm tired.'

'Don't be stroppy. I've done you a favour.' Geena took the seat opposite her sister and tapped a drum roll on the pine table.

'You've done me a favour? I can't imagine how.'

'Well, I was returning the favour. You recommended us to a hot American guy who wanted his watch fixed?' Geena paused, waiting to assess Tanya's reaction. She shifted in her chair and a flicker across her lips indicated she remembered, even if the rest of her expression remained blank. Geena went on, 'I had a nice chat to him when he brought it in. He was ever so complimentary about you. So when I called today to let him know the estimate for the work and he asked after you again, I passed your number on. Told him he should ask after your health for himself.'

Tanya's mouth fell open. 'You did what?'

'Tried to get you a date. A little bit of gratitude would be nice.' Geena stood up and ran the tap to pour herself a glass of water.

'You gave my phone number to a stranger?' Tanya's voice sounded tight and hard.

Geena sipped at the drink. Perhaps she had been carried away by Will's charm when she spoke to him earlier, but really, it was just a phone number and after her own evening with Sami, she'd been inclined to match make. 'Hardly a stranger,' she said. 'We've both met him, he's nice. And come on, he's cute.'

'He's a patient. I meet millions of patients. I don't give my phone number to any of them.' The legs of the chair Tanya had been sitting on screeched across the floor as she stood up. 'You can't go round telling people they can get in touch with me. Who knows what kind of nutter he might turn out to be?' She stomped out of the room.

Geena tutted and, with a jangle of bracelets, wiped down all the work surfaces and wished she hadn't bothered generously encouraging Will's interest in her elder sister. She had enough to do with working out how to respond to Jules's texts asking why Geena hadn't been out with the girls last night. Obviously the truth wasn't fit for purpose.

Tanya should be pleased someone was taking an interest, anyway. Some people had no idea how to be grateful. Or how to have fun. Regardless of Dadda's ideas about going out, she planned to see Sami again the next evening and, if she happened to be late home because things got interesting again, well Dadda would just have to live with that.

*

Once out of the kitchen, Tanya paused and unclenched her fists. Perhaps she'd overreacted. Geena was only being her usual frivolous self; she probably hadn't thought twice about her sister's privacy or whether it was appropriate to put a former patient in touch with her. Tanya sighed.

As she looked into the dimly-lit living room, she could see light from the TV screen as it flickered over the lenses of Dadda's glasses. He sat motionless with no indication of whether he was awake or aware of her presence. In no mood for a difficult conversation about why he'd been so hard on Geena, she turned away and climbed the stairs, grabbing her handbag on the way.

It had begun as a standard evening in the Gill household: she and Geena always took turns to cook and then shared the clearing up; Dadda joined them at the kitchen table for the meal before returning to the TV. The routine adjusted when she worked late shifts or on the many occasions when Geena went out. But Dadda's abrupt departure from the table this evening, and his evasiveness earlier when she'd asked how he was feeling, had Tanya worried.

She was glad Geena was at least staying in tonight, so an immediate confrontation between the two of them had been avoided; they were experts in winding each other up. It was unlikely Tanya herself would ever be the source of friction. She rarely went out these days anyway, which was depressing in itself.

The invitations from school friends to cinema trips, restaurants, even parties had begun to dry up during that year when everything changed for all of them. Once they turned eighteen and went their separate ways to universities around the country, collecting new friends and expanding their horizons, there was less time to keep the old friendships alive.

Tanya's horizons didn't expand as far as she'd hoped. She'd had to abandon the plans she'd made to go travelling with friends before taking up a place to study physics at university in London, and instead stayed home and accepted a place on a radiology degree at a college in Birmingham so she could be there as her mum's illness worsened.

She didn't regret it. The practical application of scientific skills to ease suffering supplied a job satisfaction she doubted she'd find elsewhere and she'd enjoyed the course, made a few new friends, even had a couple of boyfriends, though none as serious as the relationship which had ended just before college started. None of the other students bore the responsibility of keeping a home running smoothly for a sister struggling with her GCSEs and a dad unable to accept that he was losing his wife to cancer. The new friendships weren't deep.

Tanya sat on the edge of her bed, then flopped onto her back to stare at the ceiling. She could never have fitted in or built a social life when each evening after lectures or days at her hospital placement she came back to this house not knowing what she'd find. She'd open the front door and attempt to sense the atmosphere: could she hear conversation, were the curtains still drawn? Each detail bore evidence of whether it had been a good day.

Sometimes her mum had been able to sit up in bed, talk a little, even smile. Other days she'd been too weak, unable to respond to Dadda's desperate encouragement. The worst day was the one when Tanya had opened the door to find Geena hunched halfway down the stairs, her school shirt sodden with tears, her red eyes staring at nothing and her mouth clamped closed.

Tanya pushed past her and rushed into her parent's darkened bedroom. She froze just inside the door. Dadda sat in the armchair by the bed with his head in his hands. Only the slightest movement of the sheets showed that her mum was still breathing, the breaths infrequent and shuddering.

Dadda looked up. 'Tanya,' he said. 'It won't be long now. The nurse will come again soon with more pain relief.' He stood up, putting a hand to his back as he did so. 'They expect she'll slip away.'

Tanya bit the inside of her cheek and nodded. He didn't need to spell it out. The morphine would soothe, sedate and remove all sensation from the cancer patient, but do entirely the opposite to her family.

He crossed to Tanya's side and lightly touched her arm. 'Speak to her,' he said. 'She'll hear you.' Then he left the room and closed the door behind him.

Tanya swallowed past the lump in her throat and moved closer to the bed. She lowered herself to perch on the edge of the armchair and reached out to touch her mum's arm. Her skin was cool and dry, greyer in tone than it should be and it hung loose from an arm which had once been plump.

'Mum?' Tanya said.

The closed eyelids flickered.

'It's only me, Mum,' Tanya went on. With her free hand, she gripped a fistful of the pink, brushed-cotton sheet folded back over the layers of blankets, while keeping the pressure of her fingers gentle against her mum's skin. She wondered what else to say and eventually went with small talk. 'Sorry I'm a bit late home. It's raining outside, you know that always means the traffic's terrible.'

She saw the stringy tendons and withered muscles in her mum's neck and face move as though she was trying to speak. Tanya wanted nothing more than to hear her mum's voice, ideally to hear her say that everything was going to be OK. A foolish dream. She blinked back tears and went on.

'I gave Mary from next door a lift up to the airport first thing this morning. She was catching a flight to Malaga for a bit of Spanish sunshine.' Tanya's voice caught and she had to pause and sniff before she could speak again. 'Let's hope she brings us some home, could do with it.'

She reached up and swept a few short strands of thin hair back from her mum's forehead, saddened further by the memory of how luxuriantly thick it used to be in the days when it hung against her back in a thick plait which swung as it mirrored the vigorous movements of an active body. Her mum's lips moved and she breathed rather than spoke the word, 'Tanya.'

'Yes, Mum. I'm here.' Tears slid down Tanya's cheeks and she swiped them away before they could fall onto her mum's skin.

'Tanya,' her mum repeated, her voice a croaky whisper.

'It's OK. You don't have to talk.'

'Yes. I want to tell you. Here.'

Tanya leant closer desperate not to miss a single syllable.

'Your Dadda and Geena find this so hard. Geena's a child still, but he needs us too.'

Tanya nodded and sniffed.

Her mum's eyes opened and seemed to focus on Tanya's face. 'You are so clever, so brave,' she said. Then, after a pause, 'You know the right thing to do.'

Tanya sniffed but didn't bother to wipe the tears from her face again. She couldn't keep up with how quickly they fell. 'I do my best, Mum. I promise you I always will. And I'll look after Dadda and Geena. You mustn't worry about us.'

Her mum closed her eyes and moved her head so slightly it could have been an attempt at either a nod or a shake.

'My watch,' she said.

Tanya turned to where the tiny gold watch on its slim, black leather strap lay in the pool of light cast by the lamp on the bedside cabinet. The two halves of the watch strap arched away from the face in an echo of the curves of the wrist they once surrounded. She picked it up and held it close to her mum's face. 'Here it is.'

'I want you to wear it. My mother gave it to me.'

Tanya gulped. She hadn't known that. In all the times she'd admired the watch with its delicately decorated face, she'd never heard its story. Her grandmother had never been mentioned.

'Thank you,' she said, and then bit her lips together to hold in the sob which followed. When she had her voice under control again she said, 'I'll think of you every time I look at it. I'll think of you all the time.'

Her mum turned her head almost imperceptibly. 'Live your life well, Tanya,' she said. 'Be my daughter ...' She paused, her mouth still open.

Tanya longed both for her to finish what she was going to say, but also to stop working so hard to speak when it caused so much pain. 'It's OK, Mum. It's OK.'

The barest twitch of a cheek muscle. 'But most of all ...' Another pause. 'Most of all, be yourself.'

Tanya couldn't hold the sobs back any longer. She leant her face into the pillow beside her mum's head, careless of the tears soaking the pillow and how her shuddering shoulders shook the bed. She wasn't ready to lose her mum. None of them were.

Eventually, the ring of the doorbell and sound of Dadda letting the nurse in downstairs made Tanya sit up and wipe her eyes. She looked to her mum's face to find her eyes were open, the expression in them unreadable.

'Oh, Mum,' Tanya said. 'I love you.'

Dadda came into the room with the nurse and Tanya moved away from the bed, fastened the watch strap around her wrist, the buckle stiff as it slotted into a previously unused hole in the strap, and checked the time.

Even now, ten years later, Tanya still had to wipe her eyes as she recalled that day. They'd all moved on, of course. Tanya qualified as a radiographer and worked at the massive new hospital which had replaced the one her mother had worked in since she'd arrived in Birmingham in the 1980s. Geena scraped in to the college of art and design, gained a jewellery-making qualification and found a job in her chosen trade. And Dadda had survived the loss of his beloved wife, coped with redundancy from the company who'd employed him for over twenty years and now kept busy with a part-time job in a shoe repair shop.

Tanya blew her nose and scrabbled in her handbag for her mobile. The fact was that, while they'd all kept going, no member of the Gill family had actually achieved that much in ten years. While Dadda enjoyed his new job, he spent too much time in front of the television watching any programme the BBC screened, refusing to be more selective in his viewing than that if the Corporation had chosen it, he would watch it. Geena might be working in a jeweller's shop but she was more sales assistant than artisan and her salary came nowhere near supporting her dream of moving out of home. As for Tanya herself, she never had gone travelling and, while her job was good, she hadn't applied for any promotions recently and lagged behind the status of fellow students from her course in terms of seniority.

Her own stagnation was brought into focus recently when Anna, a college friend, invited a gang of the former fellow students to her wedding reception. Tanya had looked around the table at the other seven who'd been in her year, two of whom she couldn't recall names for, and ticked each off as higher ranked, post-graduate qualified, or having left the profession for something better paid. A list of accomplishments to which Anna had added "married".

While the leather case protecting her mobile phone remained closed, Tanya couldn't see if she'd missed any calls or messages. She thought back and guessed she probably hadn't checked it since just before she left the hospital late that afternoon. She looked at her mum's watch and calculated that four hours had elapsed in which she could have missed the ring tone or message alert should anyone have tried to get in touch. The lack of expectation that anyone would meant she didn't live with her phone as a constant companion.

She got up from the bed and sat on the chair at the desk in the corner of her bedroom, bought when she was studying for her A' levels and now home to her laptop. All she'd expected from this evening was the usual family chat, then an hour or so of vicarious air travel - browsing the internet for details of the destinations of planes leaving Birmingham while she imagined if she'd like to visit each place for herself.

Instead, Geena's careless sharing of personal details had made Tanya's phone an unexploded bomb. As soon as she opened the case and saw the screen the impact couldn't be changed. Will might have sent a message to which she'd have to respond. Or, worse perhaps, he might not.

She turned the case over and over on the desk and leant back in her chair. Geena was right: Will had seemed like a nice guy and yes, he was, as Geena put it, cute. And, technically, he was now just a man her sister knew rather than a patient.

Tanya sighed and looped her loose hair behind her ears. There was still at least one hour of the evening remaining in which it might be deemed socially acceptable to make a phone call. If he hadn't already rung.

While he was just a random man flirting with her it was fun, a bright moment in an ordinary day. Now he was exciting, and threatening; she was both flattered and disoriented. This kind of thing didn't happen to her.

The men she knew fell into two occasionally overlapping categories: unavailable and unattractive. Each category worked both ways; either she was too young/old/uninterested or they were. Will didn't fit the categories. Four years older than her was no kind of barrier. He appeared to be intelligent, amusing and single. Appearances could deceive though. She couldn't quite remember the detail of his features, only that they'd been pleasant to look at. He'd been well-dressed, his behaviour charming.

Even in the privacy of her own bedroom she covered her face with her hands to hide the blush. Geena's throwaway comment had caused her older sister to revert to a gauche teenager. Tanya wanted Will to get in touch while at the same time not wanting him to. She wanted him to like her while not wanting to acknowledge that because it meant she'd be upset if he didn't. She wanted him to do something while not wanting anything to actually happen.

The phone rang. Tanya jerked and nearly fell off her chair.

Chapter Four

Tanya took her usual seat on the sofa, settled her elbow into the dent she'd worn in the armrest and waited to speak. She knew better than to interrupt the theme music. She glanced at Dadda. His eyes were squinted to focus on the closing credits of the programme as they shrank down to a letterbox, while the announcer talked about other shows, pictures from which filled the rest of the screen.

It was one of his pet hates: that the BBC no longer respected the work of its own staff enough to display their names full screen after the viewers had enjoyed their programme. As though he understood what anyone other than the actors had actually contributed to the show. Or if it even mattered that everyone's contribution was acknowledged.

'I want to be witness to their accomplishment,' he'd said, when Geena challenged him about it once.

'Like their salary isn't enough,' she'd replied.

Tanya hadn't joined that argument and grimaced at the memory of it now. Her own opinion was that Dadda should spend more time engaging with the real world rather than the televised one, but his recent interaction with the real world was what she wanted to address now.

'I was thinking,' she said, once the programme had completely finished - trailers for forthcoming shows could be spoken over after Dadda had viewed them at least once - 'we should plan a holiday.'

'A holiday?' He began to fiddle with the remote control. He didn't look at her.

'Wouldn't it be nice to get away for a bit? A change of scene, a break from the routine?'

'I don't know. I mean, you should focus on your work.'

Tanya leant towards him. She was prepared for resistance. 'They let me take holidays, you know. And it's been over ten years since we went away properly. It was before Mum died. I know it'll be odd without her, which is why I thought we could do something different. We could go to India.'

He turned and stared at her. 'India?'

'I'd like us to go together, you could show me where you grew up. Maybe we could look up any family and friends of yours who still live there, or any of Mum's family.'

He shook his head. 'No. No family, there's no-one to look up.'

Tanya paused. Neither she nor Geena had ever questioned their parent's statement that they had no wider family, but she couldn't help thinking it unlikely. Even now there were surely some cousins or nephews and nieces still living. It was less than thirty years since the Gills emigrated to Birmingham. They must have left someone behind.

She tried again. 'OK, but you could show me your old home, where you went to school, things like that. I'd love to see it and it'd be nice for you to reminisce.'

He didn't reply but tapped his index finger fast against the side of the remote.

'I have some savings to pay for it,' Tanya went on, 'and I'd really like you and I to do this, Geena too if she'll come. When would be the best time to go?'

The remote slipped from his hand and landed with a clatter on the table beside his armchair. He looked down at it and frowned. 'No time. There's no good time to go back to the past. No need. This place is home. For now.'

Tanya sat back and turned her face to the TV screen where the news was starting. No point talking to him while this was on. She'd tried to sound bright but was still unsettled from the earlier phone call which, despite her immediate revealing reaction of hoping it would be Will, had turned out to be a saleswoman ringing from a call centre to offer an alternative, and pricier, phone contract. She'd mentally cursed the phone she already had for its capacity to both tease and disappoint, before adopting her usual tactic towards cold calls of responding to the scripted questions with questions of her own.

'Don't you find that you'd like a larger allocation of free minutes?' The woman's pronunciation was good, but the pacing of her speech was fast and she stressed words a native-English speaker might not have selected.

Tanya replied, 'I love your accent, you sound very much like my mum did. Are you in India?' She knew the call centre employees were trained to lie about personal details.

The woman paused, obviously considering how to work this interruption to her spiel to her advantage. 'Ah, Miss Gill, you have family in India? Perhaps you wish you could have more inclusive minutes for international calls?'

'My mum and dad came here from Delhi. Do you know Delhi?'

'Yes, um, we're near Delhi. Are you aware of the tariff for calls between the UK and India? I could look at ways to reduce the price for you.'

Tanya smiled. This woman was unflappable. 'I've never been,' she said. 'Would you recommend it?'

She wasn't interested in the answer and glanced at her watch to see how long she'd already strung the call out for. She smiled at the recollection that Will had admired the memento she always wore but then her smile faded. Her mum wouldn't have teased the saleswoman like this.

'Oh, Miss Gill, you must visit! The Gurdwara Bangla Sahib was home to the eighth guru and, well, um, talking about your phone contract I see you're due a handset upgrade in a couple of months ...'

'I know and I'm happy with my current contract so thank you for calling and I hope you have a good evening.' Tanya hung up quickly before her guilt at wasting the woman's time increased.

It was complex. She knew she should be annoyed at the waste of her own time, but her mum would have been right. There was no reason to be rude to a fellow human being who was just trying to make a living. Even one who turned out to not be the American man you'd hoped they might be.

Turning to her laptop, Tanya had run a search on 'Gurdwara Bangla Sahib' to find it was the most prominent Sikh place of worship in Delhi. She had little knowledge of the Sikh religion, but the call centre woman had made the usual assumption that Tanya was Sikh. Gill was a Sikh surname after all. Tanya had been happy to accept Dadda's statement that the family didn't follow a faith. She assumed her parents were secular either as a result of living in the UK, or because religion had never played a part in their lives.

She scrolled through images of the building's ornate white facade topped with golden domes and scanned the text about how the gurdwara welcomed people of all faiths to visit the shrine. Appalled by her ignorance, the idea had begun to grow.

All the time she'd been keen to travel out of Britain she'd never thought about a trip to India, but wasn't this the ideal opportunity? Dadda could do with a distraction and what better way than to get him to share his past with his eldest daughter who really ought to know more about her own origins? Perhaps it would also help address her own sense of being disconnected if she knew more about her history.

As she sat across the living room from him now though, Tanya realised he wasn't going to be easy to persuade. Not when he'd barely consider the concept. She frowned at the TV screen where a reporter spoke over a film which showed a protesting crowd. The people were all male, dark-skinned, extravagant in their gestures. Having paid no attention to the story, Tanya guessed something must have happened somewhere in the Middle East and turned to offer Dadda a cup of tea when she noticed how rigid his posture was, how he stared unblinking at the screen and his forehead gleamed with perspiration.

'Dadda? Are you OK?'

He fumbled to find the remote amid the clutter on his table and jabbed at the power button to switch off the television. Tanya crossed the room and knelt beside his chair with a hand on his arm.

'Dadda?'

His breathing was fast, his chin raised and he clutched at the armrests of the chair.

'Where was that?' Tanya asked. 'What was happening, do you know those people?'

He shook his head, closed his eyes and took deeper breaths as he regained his composure.

'No, that was Egypt. Nothing to us.'

'Then what is it? You're worrying me.'

He lifted a hand from the chair and patted her shoulder. 'No more talk of going to India, Tanya. If we go anywhere we'll go somewhere safer. But for now, we'll all stay at home.'

She frowned. She wasn't aware of any particular reason why India wouldn't be safe to visit; it was probably safer than Birmingham. She didn't want to argue with him or accuse him of paranoia though, not while he was clearly upset about something.

She made them a drink and took hers upstairs where she realised she'd left her phone unattended beside her laptop. She flipped the cover open and was surprised by how far her heart leapt when the screen revealed the envelope symbol of a new text message.

From an unknown mobile number the message read, 'Hey Supergirl. Any chance you'd like to switch off the X-ray vision and let me take you to see a movie instead in thanks for your introduction to the best watch repairer in Birmingham? Will x'

A grin spread across her face. Flattering superhero references in a text message, the rather forward inclusion of a kiss to someone still basically a stranger and the whole thing crackling with charm and positivity. Her anger with Geena evaporated.

This wasn't just tempting; it was irresistible.

*

As she queued at the till, Tanya spotted Deb, the military nurse, alone at a table across the staff canteen. She hoped it wasn't too cheeky to approach her. Although she was always friendly to all the other hospital staff, and would even have described a couple of colleagues on the radiology team as friends, Tanya usually took her breaks alone. Approaching Deb reminded her of knowing no-one on the first day at school.

She zig-zagged through the tables, squeezed past occupied chairs and asked, 'Mind if I join you?'

Deb looked up, smiled and pushed the remains of her lunch aside so the table was clear for Tanya to sit opposite. 'Please do.'

'Thanks. Having a busy day?'

Tanya tore back the cellophane from her sandwich and paused before she bit into it knowing its taste wouldn't match the anticipation built by the verbose description of the filling. She glanced across the table, noting from the screwed up cling film that Deb must bring her own food from home but had supplemented it with a coffee purchased from the canteen.

'Aren't they all?'

'Mmm.' Tanya chewed and swallowed before asking, 'How's that soldier doing? I'm sorry, I've forgotten his name.'

'Rob.' Deb was quick to supply it but paused before saying more. 'We see so many of them but I make a point of remembering the names. Sorry, I'm not criticising you for forgetting. I imagine you see even more patients on a daily basis, but ours tend to be memorable. Memorably injured, at any rate.'

'Of course. So, is he improving?'

'Physically, yes. Mentally, it's far too soon to say. He may never learn to live with the things he's seen. We're supposed to be prepared for horrors, aren't we, those of us in the medical profession as well as those in the military?'

Tanya looked at her half-eaten sandwich, put it down and pushed it away. It had been part of her training to stay calm, to act quickly but carefully, to remain alert to danger and respond when assistance was needed. Those requirements came easily to her. She could view mangled flesh and bone and assess what to do without any emotional impact because the flesh and bone belonged to patients, not people she cared about.

Rob had not only been horribly injured but also seen a friend killed in front of him. That emotional shock would leave terrible scars. Much worse than those from the everyday accidents and illnesses that made up the bulk of the problems for the patients Tanya saw. Even when the illness was terminal, even when it affected someone you loved, Tanya's own experience with her mum's cancer was that a calm acceptance of the situation made things easier to handle. Even if your own sister accused you of being cold-hearted as a result.

Rob's situation should have been avoidable though. It was the result of deliberate human action. That would be the hardest thing to accept.

'I'm sorry,' Deb said. 'I'm feeling a bit worn down by it today. I'm due a holiday. A bit of time at home with the hubby and kids will set me right.'

Tanya nodded and changed the subject. 'Do you live locally?'

'Yes, the postings at military hospital units are ideal for family life. Much easier on the kids then being out on ops. How about you, are you married?'

'No, I live with my dad and sister down in Selly Oak. Near the park, not in the studenty bit.'

Deb smiled. 'Chaos down there, isn't it?'

Tanya nodded, then said, 'Can I ask you something?' The mention of her home life had sparked a question in her mind. 'Those more emotional symptoms Rob had, the anxiety, hyper-awareness, tension ...'

Deb interrupted. 'Classic PTSD, post-traumatic stress disorder. Look at it from his point of view: he's twenty years old, joined up at seventeen. He's got no emotional maturity and has been thrust into this macho environment where his mates are the most important thing. Then he's exposed to such intense trauma, it's no wonder he's suffering.'

'Anyone would. But that anxiety and tension, is that a normal reaction?'

'Not always. Sometimes there's avoidance, you know, a refusal to think about let alone talk about what happened. Others constantly relive it as if they're trying to work out what they did wrong, how they could have prevented it. Survivors' guilt can be incredibly damaging.'

'I can imagine,' Tanya said. It didn't seem possible, but those symptoms Deb mentioned accurately described Dadda's behaviour in the last few days. Surely the stress of the incident on the bus hadn't triggered something so severe? But then his reaction to the conflict shown on the television news and his absolute refusal to even discuss going to India were odd. There was definitely something more going on.

'Anyway,' Deb said, 'let's talk about something more cheery. I'm glad you live with your family, you're too young to be married. But tell me, is there a man on the scene?'

Tanya looked down at the table but couldn't keep the smile from her face as she recalled the exchange of texts with Will. 'Well, I'm not that young, but I have got a date tomorrow night.'

Chapter Five

The pages of Geena's sketchbook seethed with the swirling lines, dots, curves and arabesques copied from the mehndi decoration she knew were traditionally painted in henna paste on a Hindu bride's hands. The designs inspired her concept for a range of jewellery replicating the grace and complexity of the patterns into something lasting and wearable. Not just for weddings or special occasions, but using a selection of materials from plastics to silver and gold so that the items ranged from affordable to desirable. She'd never seen anything similar and was convinced of the brilliance of the idea.

She flicked through the book until she found the page with her most recent drawings, then picked up a coil of copper jewellery wire from her workbench in the room behind the shop. Using the point of her tongs she curled the soft wire into loops which resembled petals, clipped the flower away from the coil and held it up. She smiled, able to imagine a chain of these made from a more rigid wire, perhaps in varied colours, soldered to a bar to form a brooch or drop earrings. The idea definitely had potential. Simplifying the designs into something which could be formed in three dimensions was the difficult bit.

'Very pretty,' Mr Davis said.

'Oh.' Geena jumped and quickly closed the sketchbook. 'I thought you were still out.'

She stood and moved away from the bench where she was meant to work on the jewellery repair jobs they took in. Rarely was she called on to do more than fix a broken chain, replace a clasp or resize a ring. Surely he couldn't mind that she'd been working on her own ideas; it wasn't as though she was busy.

'I've got everything we need,' he replied and held up a cardboard box from the supplier he'd been to visit in Hockley.

Geena took it from him. 'I'll unpack. Can I make you a cup of tea?'

'Yes, please. May I see this?' He gestured towards her sketchbook.

'Um, OK.' She handed it over and went to fill the kettle.

Usually he was eager to share the gossip he'd picked up from the colleagues and suppliers he'd met on his trip up to Birmingham's Jewellery Quarter, where lots of firms and suppliers clustered just outside the city centre. As well as the necessary trip to the wholesaler, he'd have popped in to a couple of other shops run by old friends, perhaps even the pub, and there were generally stories to tell.

But he remained silent as she brewed their tea in the kitchenette off the workroom and she didn't dare say anything either. Despite looking over her portfolio when he'd interviewed her for the job eighteen months ago, Mr Davis had never taken any further interest in her ideas. This was the first time he'd caught her working on them when she was meant to be working for him.

She sprinkled two spoons of sugar into his mug, stirred it and placed it by his elbow.

He looked up at her. 'Very interesting,' he said.

'It's just some ideas. I didn't have any urgent work and I thought ...'

'I understand, don't worry. I'm sure you're bored here, I suppose it'll soon be time for you to move on.' He handed the sketchbook back to her.

Geena frowned. 'No, I like it here. I'm learning a lot from you, but you know, I'd like to use my skills a bit more as well.'

'I'll keep my ears open,' he said. 'Something may come up. Although, Marcus at the suppliers was telling me two firms have closed in the past month. Rents and taxes, it's not the business it was.'

He continued to talk but Geena didn't really listen as she unpacked the box he'd brought back and entered details of the new stock into the spreadsheet she'd set up to track his accounts. Trouble in the trade was not good news. Her fellow graduates from the jewellery design course had mostly found work but only a couple were with big firms. She and three others were based in smaller companies in Birmingham or London, while only those from affluent backgrounds were living the dream and had set up as designer-makers in their own right. The recession meant none of them enjoyed much job security.

She sorted the materials into the relevant drawers in the supplies cabinet and fretted that Mr Davies was trying to break it to her that he was considering letting her go. Having him discover her under-employed was a disaster and worse if he now thought she wanted to leave. OK, so the job was a dead end and low paid, but it was a job, it was easy to commute there from home and he was a decent boss. Listening to her friends talk about their nightmare colleagues and brain-numbing careers made her grateful her own situation wasn't worse.

'Do you have the new watch glasses I brought?' he asked.

She slid out the drawer where she'd placed the new box of assorted glass faces and passed it over for him to select a piece to fit. He'd picked up Will's damaged watch to work on. It was just the kind of challenge he enjoyed.

She returned to the front of the shop to slot the slim cases containing new leather watch straps in varied widths and colours into the display carousel placed on the end of the glass counter. As she span the unit to find spaces for each box, she realised that her own wrists, adorned only with heirloom bangles, made her part of the problem. If she needed to know the time, she checked her phone.

*

Tanya dropped her handbag onto her bed and rummaged for her phone to make sure there were no new texts from Will. He might have needed to change the venue or time for them to meet. Or he might have decided to cancel at short notice. That had happened to her before. There were no new messages though, so she scrolled to the last one he'd sent instead. "7pm Odeon. I'll b 1 with wrist in sling x"

She dropped the phone and turned her attention to her outfit. Her usual evening ensemble of jeans and a casual jumper would have to be adjusted, but what to wear instead? The sparse contents of her wardrobe didn't inspire. As she slid hangers along the rail to view and then dismiss each skirt and pair of trousers, Geena came into the room.

'Knock knock?' Tanya said.

'If I'd knocked, you might not have let me in,' Geena replied.

Tanya raised her eyebrows and nodded.

'And I'm here to help,' Geena went on. 'I knew you wouldn't have been shopping for a date outfit like you should have. So, borrow these.' She slung a pair of glossy black trousers across the bottom of Tanya's bed and arranged a slinky red satin vest top above them to demonstrate how the outfit would look.

Tanya folded her arms, gripping the fabric of the sweatshirt she had on in tight fists. 'I'm going to the cinema. You know, that place where you sit in the dark and they have the air con on high. I am not wearing that top.'

'OK, OK. You have to try the trousers though. All yours are washed out and baggy. Let's look what tops you've got.'

Geena slammed the wardrobe door and went across to the chest of drawers while Tanya held the trousers against her and assessed herself in the mirror. She doubted they'd fit. Geena was slimmer. Slightly. Tanya pulled off her leggings and slipped into the trousers, delighted to find she could fasten them. 'They're a bit tight,' she admitted.

Geena turned to look. 'No, they're great on you. Shows off your curves.'

'Again - I'm going to the cinema. It's dark.'

'I don't know why you're going to a film. That's a rubbish first date. You don't get to talk much. Here, try this.'

Geena held out a jumper Tanya had forgotten she owned. The green wool was mixed with mohair making it soft and fluffy looking. She put it on and frowned at her reflection. 'You don't think it's a bit too ...'

'A bit too what?'

Tanya pursed her lips and Geena laughed.

'What?' she said. 'Too alluring, too tactile? These are good qualities in a date outfit.'

Tanya's skin prickled at the thought that Will might be tempted to touch the jumper. Worse, he might not. She remembered when she'd bought it: a couple of years before, in preparation for a first date with Nick, a registrar from the hospital. It hadn't gone well. He'd spent the entire evening staring at a point just above her left shoulder, as though neither her face nor her body could be safely observed. Conversation hadn't exactly flowed and Tanya developed a crick in her neck from leaning to the left in an attempt to make eye contact.

Geena had suggested that seeing her out of a work setting had confused him, either that or he was secretly gay. Tanya thought it more likely that there was a more interesting or attractive woman sitting just behind her. None of these options made her feel better about the disastrous date and, to compound things, no one else had asked her out since. Until now.

She slumped on to her bed and ran her hands into her hair, tugging it back from her face. 'What the hell am I doing? We don't even know who this bloke is.'

'We know more about him than if you'd met him online. My mates who've done Internet dating say the blokes never even turn out to look like the photos they put up. I mean, if they think they can lie about how they look, you've got to assume they're lying about everything.'

Tanya stared at her sister. 'None of this is making me feel better.'

'Boo hoo,' Geena said. 'Anyway, speaking of the Internet, you have Googled Will, haven't you?'

'What? No. Of course not. And don't you dare,' Tanya added as Geena stepped towards the laptop.

'We should make sure there aren't any international warrants out for his arrest or anything.' Geena tapped at the keyboard. 'Oh. Turns out there are a lot of people called Will O'Brien.'

Tanya shook her head and stood up. 'And how many of them are criminal masterminds?'

Geena swivelled on the desk chair and shrugged. 'My point is, we've both met him in person. You get a gut feeling about someone when you meet them and my instinct says he's all right.'

'All right can cover a multitude of sins,' Tanya replied and began to brush her hair.

One thing which concerned her was having met Will while he was away from all his friends and family, even his colleagues. Away from the context of people familiar with him, she'd been unable to read anyone else's responses to him. OK, so Geena liked him as well, but they could both be mistaken. The smooth strokes of the brush through her hair were less soothing than usual and, ignoring Geena's instruction to 'Wear it down', she fumbled to fasten the clip she used to hold it away from her face.

It would be rude to change her mind about the date now. She had to go and meet him, to get to know him a bit. She took a deep breath and picked up her handbag. She'd rely on her own judgement. If things weren't going well, she could always leave early.

Geena had flopped onto the bed and was watching with a critical glint in her eye. 'You are putting more make up on, aren't you?' she said.

Tanya took a final glance at the mirror. 'I might have had enough advice thanks, Gee.'

*

Tanya's watch confirmed it was a couple of minutes before seven as she entered the foyer of the multiplex. A few people were obviously waiting for friends but she couldn't see Will among them, so she selected a place to stand where she had a view of the door despite the fact that standing still and appearing relaxed seemed an impossible task.

She unbuttoned her coat, then fastened it again. She tucked her trembling hands into her pockets while she read the listings for the evening's films, scanned posters advertising forthcoming Christmas releases and deliberately didn't look at the door. Dating was many times worse than not dating.

She forced herself to read the listings twice more before she looked around the foyer to check if he'd arrived but not noticed her. Surely more than five minutes had passed, but she was loathe to be found checking the time as he arrived in case it looked like a criticism of his tardiness. Another glance around showed her that most of those who'd been waiting when she arrived had now met up with their friends and moved on.

Maybe it would be OK if he did stand her up. Dadda would be happy to see her home early after all; he'd been appalled when she'd put her head around the living room door to say she was going out. As a distraction from the guilt about that, she gave in to the temptation to check her phone and found it was ten past seven and she had a text from Will.

"R U being fashionably late or am I stood up?"

Tanya jerked her head up and scanned the foyer from side to side. Even allowing for the fact she couldn't remember exact details of what he looked like, he definitely wasn't there. She scrolled up through the chain of messages. His previous one clearly said "Odeon. 7pm" and she checked the sign above the film listings to be sure she was in the right place. It read "Odeon".

She stabbed at the phone to type, "Am at the Odeon. Been here ages. Where are you?"

The phone remained silent for an agonising length of time. Tanya paced across the foyer, the scent of popcorn combined with her anxiety making her nauseous. Eventually the phone vibrated and she swiped to answer before it had even rung.

'Funny story,' Will said. 'Turns out there are two Odeons in Birmingham. I guess you're at Broadway Plaza?'

'Yes, of course. Oh. You meant New Street. I didn't realise that was still a cinema. I'm so sorry. I should have known.'

He laughed. 'Still apologising. Don't worry. Listen I asked a guy here and he says Brindley Place is about halfway between us. How about we skip the film and go for a drink instead?'

Tanya paused. She hadn't agreed with Geena that seeing a film was a rubbish first date because she feared running out of conversation. A film meant they could sit in silence for the best part of two hours and then have something to talk about afterwards. Going for a drink had none of those advantages. No matter how dark the bar, she'd be fully exposed to the spotlight of his attention.

She took a breath to steady her voice. 'Yes, yes of course,' she said. 'I'll move my car and I can be there in ten minutes.'

She was already on her way down the concrete steps to the basement car park as they agreed where to meet. After dropping her keys then stalling the engine as she tried to pull out of her parking space, Tanya paused and instructed herself to calm down. It was just a date, even if it did feel like an exam she was already failing.

The Brindley Place multi-storey was busy and she had to drive up to the top level to find a parking space before running across to the canal side bar they'd chosen. Instead of appearing relaxed and punctual as she'd hoped at the start of the evening, she was breathless as she spotted Will waiting for her.

At least the rush excused her lack of composure; without that excuse she might have had to attribute her racing pulse to the effect of seeing him again. It was more than just nerves. He looked good: more handsome than she'd remembered with his cheeks dimpled by a smile. She smiled back.

'Tanya,' he said and reached out to touch her shoulder, 'I'm pleased we finally made it.'

'I really am sorry ...'

He interrupted her, 'Don't be. We're here now and this means we can talk properly.'

He held the door open for her and followed her into the bar. Already overheating, she shrugged off her coat and hooked it over her arm while he attracted the barman's attention.

'What can I get you?' he asked.

She paused. A glass of wine would be welcome but perhaps not helpful when she was already agitated, and driving. 'Orange juice and lemonade, please.'

'OK, and hey, is that Goose Island? I'll grab one of those,' Will said to the barman who bent to reach the bottled beer from the fridge behind the bar.

Once they'd taken seats on opposite sides of a table by a window overlooking lights reflected in the dark water of the canal, he clinked the bottle against her glass and said, 'Cheers.'

'Cheers,' Tanya replied. 'Is that an American beer?'

He glugged from the bottle then wiped the back of his hand across his mouth. 'All the way from Chicago, just like yours truly.'

His smile was infectious. She couldn't help grinning at him but also couldn't stop herself saying, 'You know you should probably still have your wrist supported.'

'You're right, doc. I just slipped the sling off so I could get my coat on. I appreciate your concern.'

She hadn't thought it possible but his smile widened and they stared at each other for a moment until she became too self-conscious and turned to look at the few other groups of people in the room, while he manoeuvred his arm back into the foam strap hanging around his neck. It rucked up his collar and made him appear vulnerable. She resisted the urge to straighten his shirt and tried to ignore her accelerated heartbeat.

'So, do you often date your patients?' he asked.

'Never,' she replied. 'Although, none of them have got my phone number out of my sister before now.'

'Who were you more mad at? Me or her?'

Tanya frowned. 'Her. I don't do this kind of thing.'

He laughed. 'You do now. And don't be too mad at her, I can be very persuasive. I've got a bunch of younger sisters of my own and can talk every one of them into anything. I convinced Paula we should pool our pocket money to buy bigger bags of pick and mix for years before she realised she didn't eat quick enough to get her fair share.'

Tanya pursed her lips and shook her head in mock admonishment. Having sisters explained his ease around women and ability to charm, although not why he wasn't in a relationship. If he really wasn't.

'How many is a bunch?' she asked.

'I'm the oldest of five kids. The rest are all girls, the youngest still in high school. While I'm out of town my dad's going nuts. Too many women in his life.'

Tanya nodded. Her own dad probably felt the same with only two daughters to contend with. 'Sounds like a close family. Is this the first time you've been away from them?'

'Well, hey, I'm a grown up. I flew the nest a coupla years ago. But, yeah, we're close. And this is the first time I've left the US. My mom thinks I'll probably catch some Dickensian disease from you Brits, raging consumption or something. Fortunately, I've been able to report that the hospitals over here are staffed by angels.'

The compliment was overdone, but she didn't react to it. His first comment stuck in her mind, that of course he'd left home, something she had no prospect of, not with Dadda needing so much looking after and property prices beyond the reach of her salary. Also, the fear of "raging consumption" wasn't far-fetched enough to be funny. Although he probably wasn't at risk, Tanya knew the numbers of tuberculosis cases in hospitals across the city were increasing. Losing control of a disease that could be so easily prevented troubled her.

The distraction of thinking about something else helped her nerves fade, but Tanya realised an awkward silence had fallen between them and was glad when he broke it.

'How about you, is it just you and Geena?'

She nodded. 'And our dad. Our mum died nearly ten years ago.'

His smile faded and he reached across the table to touch her hand. 'That's tough. You guys were still so young. I'm sorry.'

'Thank you,' she said, looking at his fingers against the back of her hand. His skin felt rough, as though he spent more of his life in physical labour than his career would suggest. The warmth and strength in that hand came from more than operating a computer. He stroked down towards her wrist, tapped gently, twice, then lifted and drained his beer bottle. She felt a chill as the warmth of his touch faded and wished he'd left his hand there longer.

Flustered by her reaction, Tanya went to fetch another round. She took a detour into the Ladies where she leant both hands on the edge of a sink and closed her eyes. She thought of her mum frequently, but rarely spoke of her. When she did, it usually led to an awkward moment when the other person would either realise they'd made an inappropriate comment or be unsure how to respond to Tanya's reminiscence if she'd mentioned someone they knew to be dead. People generally found it hard to deal with death. They never knew what to say despite Tanya mentally urging them, 'Say anything. Anything is better than silence.'

Will's quiet, sympathetic response was one of the best she'd experienced. He hadn't assumed she must be over it by now, hadn't felt an immediate need to change the subject. She'd done that, unwilling to expose more of her emotions in a public place.

Life was Tanya's problem at that moment though. The surge of both physical and emotional attraction she felt for Will unsettled her. She loosened her grip on the sink, opened her eyes, and looked at her reflection in the mirror. Harsh lighting accentuated the darkness under her eyes. Too many early shifts and not enough sleep. Hearing an echo of her mum's words she thought, I need to look after myself better, then smiled at the thought that Geena would tell her what she needed was to have more fun. She topped up her lipstick and went to the bar for their drinks.

Away from the subject of families they chatted easily, exchanging tales of school, university and jobs. Will told her that the placement with the Birmingham firm that was his company's most recent acquisition would be good for his career. 'It's got me noticed,' he said. 'All part of my five year plan to apply for promotions and take on increased responsibilities.'

Tanya shared less, although she kept up her end of the conversation in response to his enthusiasm and curiosity about Britain. His passion and intelligence impressed her, but she couldn't help feeling inadequate by comparison with his achievements and energy. Even his plan to visit the Irish village his ancestors had emigrated from sounded intriguing.

'What do you hope to find in Ireland?' she asked.

'I'm going in search of my roots, I guess,' he replied. 'If they exist.' He took a long sip of beer and considered before he carried on speaking. 'Thing is, I identify as Irish American, and that being American bit is really important to me, but I know next to nothing about that place in Ireland. I guess I'd just like to see it.' He paused before adding, 'How about you, do you consider yourself an Indian Brit, or something?'

She frowned. The usual term was "British Asian" but the Asian label held no recognition for her beyond a description of the colour of her skin. Even British or English didn't seem like clubs she belonged to. She envied his certainty about being American, the pride in his country that led him to have the stars and stripes tattoo inked into his skin, branding him for life. In chasing the Irish tag he was probably adding some romantic exoticism to the mix.

'I guess it's a tough question,' he said in response to her silence. 'In the US pretty much everyone came from somewhere else not so very long ago, especially in the big cities. I get the impression immigration is a bit more of a hot topic over here.'

'Yes. It is,' she said. But that didn't explain why she couldn't answer his question. At the hospital she found herself surrounded by colleagues whose accents represented countries from around the world, including a fair few Irish.

Most expressed a pride in their homeland and gave the impression that, despite the fact they'd had to leave it, their country of origin was better in many ways than this one. They had the certainty of knowing where home was. Even Dadda, who'd abandoned everything Indian, now took pride in calling the United Kingdom his home. The untethered sensation of not belonging gave Tanya a jolt. She couldn't understand how everyone else felt so sure.

'Am I boring you?' Will said.

'What? No. Sorry,' Tanya realised she'd yawned. It had been a long day.

He reached for her wrist and turned it so he could read the time from her watch. 'We should probably call it a night though. I don't want to miss my last train back to Bournville. Maybe we could reconvene this discussion some time?'

'I'd like that,' she said. 'And, um, I could give you a lift home if you like. Bournville's not too far out of my way.'

He tipped his head to one side and raised an eyebrow.

'Just a lift. I mean, you are injured after all.'

'If you're sure, that would be great.'

She waited, unsure whether or not to help, as he struggled with the sling and his jacket. Many of the patients she saw preferred to do everything they could for themselves, to preserve a sense of normality. Besides, helping him would have meant she'd have to stand close, touch him; temptations which would be hard to resist.

Perhaps Geena had been right to engineer this date. It had been too long since Tanya had been out with a man. Even longer since she'd met a man she liked quite this much.

They walked towards the car park and paused at the top of a path which fell in steps through the pools of a fountain in a square lined with sleek office blocks and the illuminated windows of restaurants. 'Now that's more like it,' Will said. 'That's what a city looks like.'

Tanya looked round. 'You don't think it's a bit plasticky, a little toy-townish?' She tensed. This was an echo of a conversation she'd had before.

He laughed. 'You Brits. Anything that's not hundreds of years old is bad, right?'

'No, of course not. I'm just not sure about this type of architecture.' She stepped aside to let a group of people pass them on the path, moving close enough to knock his good arm as she did. She flinched at the contact and turned away to point at the aquarium in one corner of the square whose roof was shaped like the curve of a wave or the wings of a manta ray. 'I like that.'

He placed his hand on her shoulder as he regarded the building. 'It's certainly different. As are you.' She could feel the warmth of his breath on her ear as he went on, 'I can't believe someone as smart and beautiful as you doesn't already have a devoted boyfriend.'

Tanya tensed. It was all too much. She hurried away from him, down the remaining steps, the rush of cascading water loud in her ears. Will called out and she stopped abruptly in the centre of the square, heart racing and gaze fixed on the paving. He caught up with her.

'Hey, I'm sorry. I guess I stupidly thought that was a compliment. Awkwardly put, I know.'

She forced herself to look at him. 'I'm sorry. It's just, you know, I did have a boyfriend ...'

'Of course,' he said and rubbed her arm with his uninjured hand. 'Look we don't have to talk about it. I could tell you again that you're smart and beautiful and leave it at that.'

Tanya took a breath. 'It's only that he was training to be an architect. Talking about the design made me think of him.'

'I see. Was that what he thought then: that this is toy town?' Will tilted his chin to indicate the buildings around them.

'No,' Tanya said. 'I think he said this was a practical solution to provide high quality office space in a part of the city crying out for renovation.'

Will squeezed her arm. 'Wow, he sounds like a whole bunch of laughs.' His eyebrows shot up and he put his hand to his mouth. 'Oh God. Please tell me he didn't die? I'm trying so hard to not say anything stupid and I go and say that.'

She smiled and shook her head. Recalling Jim's opinion had only made her realise that, since him, no man had mattered much to her, or she to them. There'd certainly been none who'd given any impression of devotion. And that hadn't mattered. Until she'd met Will.

For some reason, he mattered.

'No, he didn't die,' she said. 'We only split up. It wouldn't have worked. I'm sorry. Really, let me apologise this time. It's a while since I've done anything like this.'

He shook his head in obvious relief. 'OK. When you say it's been a while do you mean since you did anything like this?' he asked as he slipped his good arm round her back and pulled her close enough that she could feel the warmth of his body pressed against her. 'Or, maybe this?' He lifted the hand tethered by his sling to touch her chin and bending his face to hers pressed his lips firmly against her mouth.

For a moment all Tanya could hear was her own blood pumping. The crash of the fountain, the voices and footsteps of passers-by were all silenced as she focused on the kiss. The unfamiliar but enticing scent of him. The strangeness of being so close to him. Every sensation was heightened.

He pulled back and let her go abruptly to adjust the sling supporting his wrist. 'Sorry, that just got a little too painful.'

Tanya snapped straight back to professional mode. 'Are you OK? Does it hurt more than before?'

'No, I'm good. Just maybe next time I go to kiss you I'll get the sling out the way first.'

A smile spread across her face at the thought there'd be a "next time".

'Come on,' she said, 'the car's this way.'

Chapter Six

Tanya unlocked then, once she'd slipped inside, relocked and bolted the front door with as little noise as possible. She couldn't remember when she'd last been so late home, but Geena's keys were slung on the hall table so she knew even her younger sister was in before her. She bit back a smile, delighted for once to have had the more exciting evening. Dadda never went out at night.

She crept towards the kitchen for a glass of water to take up to bed, but the sound of the TV from the front room caught her attention in the otherwise silent house. Dadda must still be awake. Disappointed to find she wasn't the only family member to be acting out of character, Tanya pushed the door open to find him in the process of standing up.

'Where have you been?' he said.

She frowned. 'Out. With a friend. I told you.'

'Until this time?' He switched off the TV and stood in the middle of the rug with his arms folded.

'Yes,' she said, drawing the word out into a question. What was his problem?

'Geena said you were meeting a man.'

Tanya breathed out. Trust Geena to be indiscreet. There'd been no need to give Dadda any details. 'Yes, it was a date,' she said. 'I had a nice time, thank you.'

'You went to the cinema. The film must have finished hours ago.'

She nodded and sat down on the sofa in hope of diffusing the atmosphere. 'We went for a drink. We got chatting. Why does this matter? I'm a grown woman, Dadda. I don't have a curfew.'

'I was worried. Who is this man? Can he be trusted?'

Tanya closed her eyes. So this was her reward for being an obedient daughter: that the moment she had the slightest fun she'd be made to feel guilty about it. When Will kissed her again in the car before she dropped him off, she'd certainly wished he were a little less trustworthy and honourable. While his eyes held an invitation, he hadn't spoken it, only thanked her for the lift and asked for permission to call her to arrange another date, as though his manners were from a different century not just another country.

'He's normal,' she said. 'I like him. I'm going to be seeing him again.'

Dadda turned away and leant against his armchair. His fingers dented the cushion as he gripped the seat before speaking again.

'That's not a good idea,' he said.

'What do you mean?' Tanya raised her voice, not caring if Geena was asleep upstairs. 'You can't tell me what to do, Dadda.'

He lifted his head to stare at her. 'This is my house.'

'Where my salary pays all the bills,' she snapped back before regretting it. 'Look, I'm sorry, but I've had a good time and it's so long since I had a nice evening out that I don't understand why you're reacting like this. And I am an adult. I make my own choices.'

He sighed and shook his head. 'Even when it's not what your family want for you. You're so like your mother.'

Tanya stood and crossed the room to hug him. He remained rigid in her embrace, hunched in on himself. 'Isn't that a good thing?' she asked. 'We all loved her, Dadda. We all miss her.'

He nodded and patted her back. 'Your mother was so brave, but we came here so you didn't have to be. So we could be somewhere I could keep you all safe.'

Tanya stepped back. 'What are you on about? Geena and I don't need you to keep us safe. We have our own lives. We look after ourselves.' She didn't add that, just as she'd promised her mum, she also looked after him far more than he'd looked after them in recent years.

He looked away, towards the drawn curtains shielding the window. 'It's not safe out there,' he said.

'Oh.' She paused. 'I know what those boys did was frightening, but it was a one-off. And I know how to avoid trouble.'

He held up his hands as if the topic could not be discussed. 'I don't like the idea of you being with a man we know nothing of.'

Tanya frowned. 'You can't start acting like a strict Indian father now. Geena and I choose our own friends and you can trust us to choose sensibly. Well, you can trust me.'

He stepped away and slumped back into his armchair. 'This man you were with, he's a white man?'

Tanya blinked. Most of the men both she and Geena had ever dated were white, only a couple of Geena's boyfriends had been Asian or black. Dadda knew all about them, had met several of the boys. He'd never expressed any opinion about the fact most of their female friends were white either. The schools they'd attended had been. The neighbourhood they lived in was. It had never been an issue; but Dadda's recent experience with white men perhaps required some sensitivity.

'It's not a problem,' she said. 'Will's not racist. He's completely charming. He was interested in India, more interested than Geena and I have ever been. He wanted to know all kinds of details about where we're from, what it's like there. I couldn't answer his questions.'

Dadda was quiet for a moment. His fingers drummed on the arms of his chair and he took a quick, shallow breath and said, 'No, your mother and I came here for a new life, we agreed to talk only about the future. There's nothing in India for us now, no reason for us to be interested in it. But we have to look after each other so please, Tanya, promise you'll discuss your friends with me, that you'll take my advice.'

She knelt beside his chair and linked her hands in her lap. There'd been many sacrifices in the years since her mum died: staying in the family home to live with Dadda instead of moving into a shared flat as most of her peer group had, letting a relationship founder when Jim, who'd been her first serious boyfriend, left home to take his architecture qualifications elsewhere while she stayed in Birmingham, and using her salary to support her father and sister rather than saving for the deposit on a home of her own.

She didn't regret those actions, or resent them. Well, only occasionally, and only as part of wishing her mum was still alive so Tanya didn't need to act as her proxy.

But now Dadda was behaving as though they were no longer equals in the family.

'Look,' she said, 'I understand why you're upset by what happened on the bus, but it was a single nasty incident. You know that's not what most people are like. And you know I'm mature and sensible enough to make good decisions. I love you, Dadda, but I won't let you rule my life. I'll be seeing Will again.' She stood up, turned her back on him, and left the room.

No line of light showed under Geena's bedroom door as Tanya reached the top of the stairs. She placed her hand against the closed door, longing to turn the evening around by hearing her sister's response to what had happened on the date, to share her own excitement and anticipation, to feign offence at the salacious suggestions Geena was likely to make. Instead, she retreated into her own bedroom and lay, eyes open, on top of the duvet in the dark. Dadda's words ran through her mind: that he wanted to keep her safe, that she should take his advice. It made no sense.

She heard his footsteps on the stairs, the click of the bathroom light going on, then off again, and his bedroom door close. Everything was far from normal.

*

Geena woke to the hiss of water running through the pipes to the bathroom in the wall beside her bed and rolled over to check the time. Six am. Tanya must be on an early shift. Geena rubbed her eyes, yawned and hunched back under the duvet. There was no need for her to be awake at this time. Except, there was news to catch up on.

She waited until she heard the stairs creak under Tanya's tread, then got up, wrapped her dressing gown around her and followed her sister downstairs. 'Well?' she asked as Tanya put the kettle on to boil.

'What?'

'Will? The date? How did it go?'

Tanya turned to the cupboard for teabags and mugs. 'Fine,' she said without looking at Geena.

'Fine? Is that all you're going to give me? You were out late, I didn't hear you come in. It must have been more than "fine".'

Tanya stayed silent as she made their tea and poured out a bowl of cereal for herself. Geena took a seat at the kitchen table and waited. Tea slopped out of the mug Tanya slammed down in front of her and Geena raised her eyebrows. 'You know, if you're going to be in such a bad mood afterwards, perhaps you shouldn't stay out so late.'

'Shut up, Geena.'

Tanya scraped a chair out, leant her elbows on the table and propped her chin on her hands. It wasn't like her to be grumpy. Geena sipped the too hot tea.

'Didn't it go well?' she asked. 'I'm sorry, shouldn't I have bullied you into it?'

Tanya swallowed the mouthful of cereal she was chewing and took a gulp of tea, frowning at her watch as she did so. 'Honestly, Gee. It was fine. He's nice. But, well, I don't want to be late. Let's talk about it this evening.'

'Actually, there was something else I wanted to ask you.'

'I didn't think it was concern for my welfare that dragged you out of bed this early.' Tanya finished eating, stood and placed her bowl in the sink.

'It's about Dadda,' Geena said.

Tanya paused with her hand on the door handle. 'What about Dadda?'

'I came home early last night, talked to him and, well, have you noticed anything odd?'

'Odd like what?'

Geena lowered her voice. 'A couple of days ago he asked me to call his work and tell them he wasn't well. I mean, he seemed fine but I assumed he just fancied a day off after the whole bus thing.'

Tanya interrupted, 'Why didn't you tell me?'

'He was OK, you know. And I doubted you'd approve of him throwing a sickie.' Tanya's expression confirmed this. Geena went on, 'Then yesterday morning he asked me to get some stuff from the shops for him while I was out. Bit weird, you know he's always so self-sufficient. Normally he offers to do stuff for me. Anyway, I did what he asked, but, well the thing is, I guess I don't know when he actually last left the house.'

Tanya slumped against the door, eyes closed. 'How didn't I notice?'

'Hey, don't make this about you. You're out at work a lot. And you deserved your night out last night. But, you know, I'm just worried because he fobbed me off. Wouldn't actually admit he hadn't been out but said lots of weird stuff about how I should always come straight home from work, how he wished you weren't mixing with all sorts at the hospital. And then he made me tell him that you were out with Will. Boy, he did not like that.'

'Tell me about it,' Tanya replied. 'I had a great evening with Will then Dadda made me feel guilty about the entire thing.'

Geena nodded. 'Did he talk about Mum?'

'Yes.'

The sisters looked at each other. Geena knew she'd reacted badly when their mum died and now there was another problem she felt like a teenager again with no idea what to do and wanting to shirk any responsibility. She knew she shouldn't do that to Tanya, that she should share any response to Dadda's problems with her sister, but what she really, really wanted was her mum. She bit her lip, broke the eye contact with Tanya and stared hard into her mug, willing the tears to go away.

Tanya stepped away from the door. 'He's become so paranoid. Those idiots on the bus must have upset him more than we realised. I guess Mum's the one he wishes he could talk to about it.'

Geena nodded and sniffed. 'You better get to work. I'll suss out what he's doing today, maybe ask him to do something for me that would mean he needs to go out?'

'No. Don't put any pressure on him. But do find out what his plans for the day are and we'll talk about it this evening.' She turned and opened the kitchen door before stopping and saying, 'Oh, and Geena? Thanks for setting me up with Will. I lied. It wasn't just fine, it was fantastic.'

The tension dropped away as Geena grinned. 'You see? I'm not totally useless.'

She turned back to the table as Tanya left the room and put her head down on her folded arms. What she hadn't admitted to Tanya was the reason she'd been home early last night. Dadda wasn't the only one with problems.

Sami wasn't returning her calls so she'd decided to join her friends in town. But as she'd walked towards where the girls perched on high stools around a table in their usual city centre bar, their backs had seemed to turn towards her, their shoulders hunched in to exclude her. She'd pulled a stool up to the edge of the group and leant towards Jules.

'What's up?' she'd asked.

'Like you don't know,' Jules replied.

The others remained silent as Geena squirmed in her seat. 'I don't know what you mean,' she said, but a chill had settled in her stomach. Of course she knew. The question was how Jules had found out.

'Did you think Sami wouldn't tell me?' Jules said, her tone venomous. 'Oh, he was very keen to brag.'

'I didn't mean anything to happen,' Geena replied. 'We were talking about a business idea and ...'

'Spare me the details.'

Jules swivelled in her seat to turn her back on Geena. The two of them had argued before, of course, but Geena realised that for the first time she might have actually done something to betray her friend.

She'd picked up her bag, left the bar and gone straight home. No point staying to make her case about the fact Jules had been the one to end things with Sami and make him fair game, or that there was nothing serious going on, that they could laugh it off like any of Geena's other flings. Best to leave Jules to cool off for a while.

Geena had returned to spend the evening with Dadda in an attempt to salve her conscience. It had only made things worse.

Chapter Seven

'So, how was your date?'

Tanya flinched, distracted from brooding about Dadda as Deb pulled out the chair beside her in the canteen and sat down.

'Hi,' she said. 'How are you?'

'Fine, apart from needing information from you,' Deb replied. 'The date? Did he turn out to be the man of your dreams?'

Tanya paused, uncertain what qualities the man of her dreams might possess. Intelligent, obviously. Kind and considerate, of course. Tall, dark and handsome if she were to be completely honest. And actually, Will didn't score too badly against those criteria. Only his pale skin tone let him down.

Deb nudged her. 'I'll take the dreamy silence as a yes. So, come on, tell me everything. Leave no detail out. I'm an old, married woman, remember. I have to live vicariously on the drama of other people's lives.' She took a bite of her sandwich and raised an eyebrow at Tanya as she chewed.

Tanya stared down at her hands in her lap and tightened her fingers around each other. Despite the stabs of guilt because she knew she should prioritise Dadda's problem, she'd already relived the date several times in her head, recalled what Will had said, what she'd said in response, the warmth of his mouth when they'd kissed. The details were too precious to gossip about with Deb. She didn't want to share him, even in chit chat.

'We had a nice evening,' she said.

'And?'

'He said he wanted to see me again, that he'd call.'

Deb smiled and leant back in her chair. 'And so he should. Although I suspect you're keeping the most interesting details from me. I want a more comprehensive report next time, OK?'

Tanya sighed. What did it matter if Deb was a gossip? She'd get little material from Tanya's life. 'If there is a next time,' she said.

Deb immediately sat forward again. 'And why wouldn't there be?'

'My dad isn't exactly supportive of the idea.'

'How old are you?' Deb's voice was cool.

'Twenty-seven,' Tanya admitted.

'Even older than I'd guessed then. Maybe you'll tell me things are different in your family, but I'd say you're an adult quite able to make her own choices. What exactly does this have to do with your dad?'

Tanya twisted her fingers together again, aware Deb was right. 'It's not what you think. He isn't into arranged marriages or anything. He doesn't normally interfere with my decisions, he's just not himself at the moment and, well, I've always looked after him. Ever since my mum died.'

Like Will, Deb didn't reply with any of the common platitudes. Deb didn't say "Oh, I'm so sorry" or "You poor thing" or immediately change the subject. After a moment she did reach across and squeeze Tanya's arm.

'I understand how you might feel responsible for him, but you're young,' she said. 'You have to live your own life as well.'

Tanya picked up her drink carton and played with the straw. 'I have a responsibility to him and to my sister, same as you do for your husband and children. If Dadda doesn't want me to see Will again I can't just ignore that. I have to try to understand why.'

'But you want to see Will again?'

Tanya didn't hesitate. 'Yes.'

'Then do.' Deb screwed up the wrapper from her sandwich as though everything in life were so simple. 'You say your dad's not himself at the moment, what's up?'

Tanya finished her drink and wondered what to tell Deb. The racial abuse was unlikely to shock her with her own job exposing her to worse horrors, but equally Tanya feared Deb's responses would be hardened by her experience. It was fine to be cool and analytical when discussing a patient, but this was Dadda. Tanya couldn't hope to explain him.

'Am I asking too many personal questions?'

Tanya realised she'd been silent too long. 'No, I'm sorry. I'm not being very communicative, am I? There was an incident on the bus he was on the other day; people were really rude to him. Racist idiots, but he's taken it to heart and become even more security conscious. He keeps checking up on me and my sister and, well, she thinks he hasn't left the house for a few days now.'

Deb frowned. 'Sounds serious. Will he talk to you about it?'

'I didn't know about him not going out until this morning so I haven't tried. He was just so odd when I got in from the date last night.'

'And he hasn't been like that before?'

Tanya pursed her lips, then admitted, 'It's been a while since I went on a date.'

Deb nodded but didn't ask why. Her voice was almost expressionless as she continued to ask about Dadda. 'But in general he isn't a controlling personality?'

Tanya shook her head. 'No, I mean, he always wants to know what time we'll be back, that sort of thing. It was always more as if he was taking an interest though. He wasn't trying to control us. And most of his security stuff is reasonable, he just hammers it home. But last night he actually said he didn't want me to see Will again. It doesn't make sense.'

'And it's worse since whatever happened to him on the bus?'

'Yes. Oh, you're doing a diagnosis.' Tanya tensed and lifted her bag onto her lap as though ready to flee.

'Don't be offended. But you know I work with some severely traumatised patients. What you said about your dad being security conscious, wanting full control of his environment, sounds like some of the soldiers I've treated.'

Tanya thought about how Rob, the soldier she'd X-rayed had behaved. Of course Deb was right. 'But they've come from war zones, they've had terrible experiences.' She shrugged. 'Dadda got some verbal abuse. It's nasty but this feels like an over-reaction. He's never seemed so sensitive before.'

'Perhaps the abuse was a trigger. You say he's always been security conscious? Was that from before your mum died?

'I think so, yes.'

Deb nodded. 'If he hadn't finished grieving for your mum then I wouldn't be surprised that another emotionally intense event could trigger an anxiety response such as agoraphobia. But ...'

Tanya interrupted. 'I'm sorry, Deb. It's good of you to take an interest but I can't talk about him like this. I can't talk about him as though ...'

'As though he's got a problem?'

Tanya's shoulders slumped and she released her grip on her handbag. 'Good at this, aren't you?' she said.

'You should see me with the patients. Oh wait, you have.' Deb grinned and patted Tanya's arm. 'Look, you know him best and maybe he just wants some time out after what happened. Can't blame him - the world's a grim place.

But don't let him spoil what's going on with Will. He sounds way too delicious to be discouraged.'

'I barely described him,' Tanya said.

Deb winked. 'You didn't have to.'

Tanya smiled, but her guilt rushed back. 'I'll have to find out if Geena's right about Dadda not leaving the house. That would worry me.'

'Talk to him, that's usually the best solution.'

'I will.' She checked her mum's watch and realised she'd be late back to the clinic if she didn't leave now. 'Don't worry, I will be saying yes if Will calls to ask me out again. Got to go, but I'll see you around.'

'You can bet on it. There's nothing I like better than a romance. I'll be tracking you down for the latest instalment. Just one more thing, Tanya – you're not your mother. Remember that.'

Tanya nodded, then took her tray to the trolley by the canteen exit and walked down the long corridors to the radiology department with the memory of the promise she'd made to her mum on her mind. 'Be my daughter,' her mum had said. There was an implication there.

Tanya wished she could analyse an X-ray of Dadda's state of mind. Instead, she'd have to ask him directly if everything was all right. He'd be evasive if she only hinted. It was easy for Deb to suggest Tanya didn't have to take responsibility, but no-one else would. If there was a problem though, at least Deb might have useful advice.

She stopped, wondering if perhaps it would be useful for Deb to meet Dadda. She might be able to talk to him. Speaking to Deb was certainly helping her, almost as though she could ask her own mother for advice, even if Deb lacked some of her warmth. A porter bumped Tanya's arm as he steered a patient in a wheelchair past.

'Watch out, bab,' he said. 'Keep the traffic flowing.'

'Sorry,' she said and started walking again. She'd talk to Dadda herself first, but perhaps invite Deb to dinner as well. A second opinion couldn't hurt.

Geena's knife screeched across her plate as she put too much pressure into cutting her broccoli. She reached out with her fork to spear the stem which had flown onto the table and looked up to find both Tanya and Dadda staring at her.

'Well?' Dadda asked. 'Was everything OK at your work today?'

Geena held his gaze and nodded, unable to speak because she couldn't decide how to respond. He'd only asked how her day was to deflect Tanya's question to him. Tanya was obviously trying to be subtle about discovering if he'd been out today, but he hadn't really answered her query about how work had been, only murmured something about "the usual" before turning the question to his younger daughter: the one who knew he hadn't been there because she'd called in sick for him again. Obviously she'd tell Tanya that later, but not in front of him, not when he clearly expected her to cover for him.

When she'd made the call, Dadda's boss had pointed out that he was going to need a sick note to cover his absence if he was off much longer. Dadda hadn't responded when she'd passed that message on. Anyway, both she and Dadda knew that Tanya's style was to skirt around an issue for a while before finally getting to her point. She didn't appreciate being rushed into things. And Geena also knew neither Dadda nor Tanya were really interested in what she'd been up to at the shop.

'I had a lovely day,' she said. 'Thank you so much for asking.'

'There's no need to be sarcastic,' he replied. 'Thank you for dinner, Tanya. This chicken is delicious.'

Geena widened her eyes and attempted to pass on the telepathic message "You see? He's being weird" as she held Tanya's gaze.

Tanya nodded, then looked down at her plate and changed the subject to tell a complicated anecdote about something which had happened at the hospital. Geena tuned out, thinking instead about her jewellery designs. It was better than remembering the hurt in Jules's eyes last night.

The collection needed some more work, even if it didn't get into Sami's uncle's shop. He'd suggested it wouldn't be suitable for them unless the unit cost was higher. But she knew the cost of materials if she did produce the items in gold as he'd suggested would make each piece too expensive and not leave enough profit margin for her.

She wasn't convinced Sami was right, or actually that he had as much influence in the business as the impression he'd initially given. And, now she thought about it, he was an idiot, too fond of the sound of his own voice. No real surprise that he'd gone running straight back to Jules to tell her about his fling with her best friend. No wonder Jules had dumped him in the first place.

Geena suspected she was already more of an expert on the jewellery business than he ever would be as well. It might be a better option to use cheaper materials and target craft markets where she could go for volume of sales rather than larger profits.

'Gee, your plate?'

Geena looked up and realised she'd finished the rest of her meal without paying any attention to her family and Tanya was now clearing the table. Geena put her knife and fork down and passed the plate to her sister. 'Sorry,' she said.

'We need to talk,' Tanya muttered back.

Geena looked from her to their dad who was reading the television listings in the magazine she'd brought home.

'Look at this,' he said, jabbing at a page of photos of people whose fake tans, whitened teeth and surgically-enhanced bodies made them barely recognisable as human, especially viewed upside-down from Geena's viewpoint, 'more of this so-called reality television. I've never seen anything less real.'

Neither Geena nor Tanya bothered to respond.

'Yeah, um, I'll skip pudding, thanks,' Geena said. 'Something I need to be getting on with. Leave the drying up; I'll do it later.'

She pushed her chair back from the table and escaped into the garage where she'd set up a workstation in one corner. Her bench was the old student desk from her bedroom. It provided nowhere near enough work surface, but was at least equipped with two pedestals of drawers to store her tools and materials. The temporary hiatus in her social life would be a good opportunity to focus on the project.

She turned on the electric heater beside her chair and flicked the switches on the pair of lamps angled to shine onto the desk, also not an ideal arrangement as they cast conflicting shadows that made it hard to see detail. What she'd really like would be to work in the room behind Mr Davis' shop with its traditional horseshoe-shaped jeweller's workstations fitted with a gas supply for soldering, adjustable pegs to hold the piece you were working on and a leather pouch slung beneath to catch filings of precious metals. He'd never minded when she borrowed his tools with their worn-smooth wooden handles to work on her repair jobs, but now she wouldn't dare so much as sketch for her own project there. He had to believe she was indispensable to his business.

For now, she'd have to make do using what had previously been Dadda's workshop for his DIY projects. Since her mum died, he'd lost any interest in his woodworking or fixing things up. He'd made no protest when Geena packed his tools away and moved into the space.

She opened her sketchbook, turned to a blank page and began to list: earrings, pendants, rings. She paused, those were the obvious lines to include, but what about some items which might be more unusual or attract wider interest? Bookmarks, maybe mobile phone charms, hair clips? Engrossed in her business planning, she realised that working for Mr Davis was actually much better experience than she'd given it credit for.

Because of the tasks he gave her, she knew more about running a small business than when she'd left college. She felt equipped to plan costings, think about marketing and understand overheads. Boring though her job was, she resolved to be more appreciative. This first collection of her own work was just a beginning, but she was sure it was a beginning built on sound principles because of what she'd learnt from him.

'What are you doing?'

Geena hadn't heard Tanya come in and jerked her head up in annoyance at the interruption. 'Working.'

'Looks like playing to me.'

'Wow, thanks for your support. I'm only trying to make something of myself here, build something of my own.' Geena slumped in her chair. Trust Tanya to spoil her mood.

'What exactly?' Tanya's tone was conciliatory. 'Talk me through it.'

Geena narrowed her eyes as she looked up, but her sister's interest appeared to be genuine. 'A line of jewellery influenced by mehndi designs, probably made from these coloured wires,' she pointed to a spool, 'to sell at craft markets, online, that sort of thing.'

Tanya picked up the sketchbook and flipped the pages over. 'What do you know about mehndi? We never had it done.'

'I have.'

'With your white friends.'

Geena sighed and snatched the book back. 'Crossover appeal is not a bad thing. Didn't you ever hear that the future is multi-cultural?'

'Hmm,' Tanya replied. 'But they're trinkets. Gifts for girls to buy for their friends. Bit small scale, isn't it?'

'If you can't think of anything nice to say, just go away and leave me to it.'

Tanya sighed and leant against the wall. 'I'm sorry, Gee. It just seems a bit frivolous. You know, you've got a perfectly good job, wouldn't it be better to use that experience to move into a bigger firm, something with a bit more security?'

'My long term plan is to work for myself,' Geena said, her voice calm and confident, despite the fact that idea had only just occurred to her. 'One day I'll be a designer-maker with my own studio. I'll be commissioned to produce large pieces. My work will feature in magazines.'

'Sounds like a daydream. You'll have to get serious sometime.'

Geena bit back the retort which immediately came to mind. Accusing Tanya of lacking ambition and imagination, or pointing out how old-fashioned and boring she was wouldn't help. 'Yeah, thanks for your advice,' Geena said. 'Mum told me I should follow my dreams and do what I'm good at. Right now, I'm doing this.'

Tanya shivered, hugged her arms around herself and was silent while Geena turned back to her designs. Eventually she reached out to squeeze Geena's shoulder and said, 'OK, OK, I'm sorry. But listen, about Dadda, I take it he hasn't been out today then?'

'Not that I know of.'

'It's been five days then.'

Geena grimaced. When Tanya stated it like that it did sound bad. He'd only missed three days of work because of being part time, but she didn't think he'd been out on the other days either. 'Mary next door mentioned she'd picked up the paper for him the other day,' she said. 'She'd popped over to see if he was OK. Obviously didn't believe he was.'

'He isn't,' Tanya replied. 'The question is how bad it is. I just tried asking him about it and he won't talk to me at all. What's he said to you?'

'Only that he didn't feel up to going to work. He didn't go into detail.'

'And you didn't ask.'

Geena pushed her sketchbook aside and laid her hands flat on the surface of the desk. She took a breath before replying. 'No need to get your stroppy pants on. It's no wonder he prefers talking to me when all you do is give us both a hard time.' She shifted in her seat.

Tanya obviously thought twice about saying anything more and walked off without responding. Geena leant her elbows on the desk and rested her chin on her hands. Why did talking to Tanya leave her feeling inadequate? The situation with Dadda was worrying her too, but her role in the family had always been the baby. She didn't have to be the responsible one. That had never been her job.

Her bangles slid with their soft music up her arm as she moved and she bit her lip as she gazed at them. Maybe she really was better at communicating with Dadda than Tanya could ever be. He often seemed more willing to ask for her help. She decided that next time he asked her to do something which would mean he didn't have to leave the house, she'd speak to him about it.

She slipped the bangles off her wrist and laid them on top of her sketchbook where they overlapped to form a chain across the blank page. They'd entranced and inspired her right from when she'd watched them catch the light as a small child when they jangled on her mum's wrist as she worked, to being allowed to try them on when her interests turned to dressing up and adornment. The heavy, Indian gold wasn't hallmarked, was worth too much for everyday wear really, but her mum had worn them every day and now so did Geena.

Every time she touched the five golden bands, each one etched with a different pattern and each equally loved, her mum came to mind. She'd never worn much jewellery, didn't seem to own much. Except for the bangles, which she said she'd always owned, always worn. That couldn't be true though, and Geena wished now that she'd asked where they came from, who'd given them to her mum, what they symbolised to her.

The only time her mum hadn't worn them was at the very end. Her body drained by the disease which only grew a cancerous tumour in one place, but drew its nourishment and energy from the rest of her body and left Geena's mum's arm too weak to carry even one of the gold bangles she'd otherwise never have removed. Geena closed her eyes and swallowed hard in an attempt to shift the memory of how it had felt to sit by the bedside of a woman she'd known to be dying, but who she hadn't been able to imagine living without.

She sniffed. She preferred to remember the happy times, such as sitting on the grass in Selly Oak Park with her mum using the tip of an elegant finger nail to pierce long-stemmed daisies so Geena, whose childish bitten nails weren't up to the job, could lace them together into necklaces and flower crowns. Or the time she'd seen her mum's delighted face at a school open day when she realised Geena's painting had prime position in the art exhibition. For someone whose academic results failed to impress, it was good to have the validation that it wasn't only Tanya with her A grades who could make their mum proud. Geena's abilities lay in different, equally important areas.

After their mum died, Tanya had loosened Geena's clenched fist to slide the bangles onto her sister's arm, and shown her their mum's watch strapped onto her own wrist.

'She'll always be with us,' Tanya said.

Geena had looked at the bangles with their familiar weight adorning her arm and vowed to herself that she'd always try to make her mum proud. From that day she'd stopped biting her fingernails for one thing. She had to live up to the elegance of the bangles. She had to try to live up to what her mum would have wanted.

But a memory of her mother wasn't always enough. Sometimes what Geena really needed, the only thing which could actually help, was if her mum was there with them. That was what would solve Dadda's problems.

Geena gathered the bangles up from the page, put them back on, sighed and returned to her sketches.

Chapter Eight

Tanya kicked the mess of abandoned shoes away from the front door and let Deb in.

'Thanks for coming. I'm so pleased you could make it,' she said, unsure whether to greet Deb with a hug or kiss. They'd talked a lot at work, but not touched. Although Deb had immediately accepted Tanya's invitation to dinner, Tanya wasn't sure if this made them friends.

'No problem,' Deb said, as she handed over a bunch of flowers then squeezed Tanya in a warm hug. 'I'm looking forward to my dinner.'

Tanya gratefully returned the hug, but frowned. 'I hope you haven't assumed that because my family are Indian I'll cook you a fabulous curry? I'm afraid it's just a chicken casserole. Oh no, don't tell me you're vegetarian?' Tanya clapped a hand to her mouth but Deb smiled.

'No. I'd wondered if you were, to be honest. I guess I made some assumptions.'

Tanya led the way into the kitchen and invited Deb to take a seat at the kitchen table, which was already set for the meal. 'Don't worry. All our white friends do it. The problem is my parents were so keen to embrace everything English, that they abandoned pretty much all their Indian influences. I can make curries, but I use paste from a jar.'

Deb laughed. 'Me too. Although, I bet my husband is taking advantage of me being out to order an Indian take away.'

'Funny how the British are so keen on Indian food, while Dadda would be happy if he never saw it again,' Tanya said and opened a cupboard to find a vase for the flowers. 'Thanks for these, by the way. I don't know when we last had fresh flowers in the house.'

'That's OK. I would have brought wine, but I wasn't sure if ...'

Tanya interrupted. 'Oh we do drink. I mean, not a lot, but really, it's fine.'

She wondered if she'd ever develop social skills to handle the preconceived ideas people always had about her family. Probably not. She'd never enjoyed entertaining either; years of unsuccessful birthday parties when she and Geena were young had always started out like this: inaccurate cultural assumptions by all of the parents meant it was easier if they didn't invite school friends over at all.

She turned to the fridge and offered Deb a glass of white wine from the bottle she'd bought for the occasion.

'Hope you don't mind eating here in the kitchen?' she said. 'Can't remember when we last used the dining room.' She could remember, actually; in fact, she'd considered setting the table in there for Deb's visit, but it could have been a step too far for Dadda. A step too far for her as well.

'This is luxury,' Deb said. 'I struggle to persuade my husband and kids to move themselves off the sofa. Anyway, how's your dad today?' She'd lowered her voice and glanced towards the open kitchen door.

Tanya waved off Deb's compliment and moved to close the door. Their kitchen was not luxurious. It was functional. 'He's definitely not right. We don't think he's been out in a week now but he won't talk about it with me. Geena won't push it.'

The door opened and both women looked up. 'Guilty expressions,' Geena said as she closed the door behind her. 'What have I missed?'

Tanya shook her head. 'Deb, this is my sister, Geena.'

'Nice to meet you.' Geena smiled at Deb before glancing at their glasses. 'Is there one of those for me?' she asked.

Tanya poured another glass. 'Deb was just asking about Dadda. She's had some experience nursing people who've been through traumatic events. I thought we could see if he'll talk to her at all.'

'Unlikely,' Geena replied and raised her glass to Deb. 'No offence, but he's not great with new people.'

'I'm just happy to be here having my tea cooked for me. And I love meeting new people. I'm happy to chat about anything that comes up.'

Tanya caught Deb's eye and frowned. They'd already agreed that Deb would be on the lookout for clues about Dadda's mental state and Tanya didn't want her put off by Geena's reaction. Deb smiled back.

'Not going out tonight?' Tanya asked Geena as she joined them at the table.

Geena shook her head. 'Not tonight. No.'

A shrill ring from the cooker's timer caught Tanya's attention and she turned to lift the casserole out.

'Mmm, smells good,' Deb said.

'Thanks,' Tanya replied. 'I take it you'd like a bit of everything?'

'Of course.'

Geena joined Tanya at the counter to help. They worked together in silence, used to the routine of Geena placing a serving of potatoes and vegetables on each plate that Tanya passed her with its portion of meat.

Geena raised her voice to call, 'It's on the table, Dadda.'

'I'm sorry,' Tanya explained. 'I'd have introduced you to him sooner, but he hates it if we interrupt the news.'

He came into the room but paused as he noticed their visitor. Tanya introduced him to Deb and gestured for him to join them.

'We both work at the hospital,' she explained.

'Ah,' he said, 'are you another radiographer?'

Deb smiled. 'It's lovely to meet you, Mr Gill. And no, I'm a nurse.'

'Please, call me Jagtar if I may call you Deb?' He finally took his seat and lifted his knife and fork.

'Of course. It's easier to say than Sergeant Carson, after all.'

Instead of returning Deb's smile, Dadda paused with a forkful of food halfway to his mouth.

'Sergeant?' he asked. 'You're in the army?'

Deb nodded. 'Yes, I'm based at the Defence Medicine centre but most of our work overlaps with the general hospital, which is how I met Tanya.' She turned to Tanya and added, 'Thank you, this is delicious.'

'No problem,' Tanya replied, but she could see that there was a problem. Dadda put his untasted forkful of food back on his plate.

'I see,' he said. 'I didn't know that.'

'Deb does similar work to all the other nurses. All of us at the hospital are just focused on helping people get better,' Tanya said.

His voice was cold as he replied, 'Perhaps some of them shouldn't have been injured in the first place.'

Tanya looked to Geena who raised her eyebrows and shrugged.

'Well, no,' Tanya said. 'But that's hardly Deb's fault. Eat up, it's getting cold.'

They ate in silence while Tanya tried to think of a neutral topic they could discuss. She was about to mention the latest whinge going around the hospital about the price increase in the canteen, when Deb said, 'Are you opposed to some of the Army deployments, Jagtar? Tanya mentioned you follow the news.'

He stared at his plate as he replied, 'Yes, I watch the news. I see the troubles.'

'And you watch the soaps, and the cricket.' Tanya was keen to change the subject.

Unfortunately, Deb had different ideas. 'You aren't alone in disagreeing with the government's decisions. But most of us in the armed forces signed up because we want to serve our country.' She frowned. 'I don't claim to understand the situation in say, the Middle East, but I do believe in defending human rights. If we have to fight for that then I will pick up the pieces.'

Silence fell over the table, broken only by the sound of cutlery against crockery. Tanya gulped the rest of her wine and grabbed the bottle to top up Geena and Deb's glasses. Deb covered hers with a hand. 'I'm driving,' she said.

'Of course. Deb lives over the other side of the Bristol Road, Dadda,' she said, desperate to return to safe conversational territory.

He just nodded.

Fortunately Deb also seemed keen to step back from the tension and latched on to the new topic. 'Have you been in this house long, Jagtar?' she asked.

He paused for so long Tanya was about to answer for him. Eventually, he said, 'Since 1989. My wife and I moved here when Tanya was three, when Geena was a baby.'

Deb smiled at Tanya and Geena. 'So it's really the only home you guys ever had? That's lovely. I sometimes wish I could have given my kids that kind of stability.'

They both nodded. Tanya couldn't think of anything to say in response. It wasn't the only house she knew, it was the only street, the only suburb, the only city she had any familiarity with, and that made it more like a prison than a home. Another lull in conversation followed.

'I've had to move a lot in recent years,' Deb said eventually. 'Wherever I've been posted, you know.'

Tanya stiffened and put her knife and fork down on her plate, despite not having finished all her food. It seemed as though all three women held their breath while they waited to see how Dadda would respond.

'This is what army life does,' he said. 'You are sheep. You follow orders.'

Tanya stared at Geena who met her eye but didn't react. Obviously she didn't know what to do either. Dadda had never been so rude before, even to strangers. Perhaps especially not to strangers. For him to treat a friend of hers like this was not only odd, it was inexcusably bad manners.

'We choose to,' Deb said, her words slow and carefully pronounced.

Tanya jumped up from the table. 'Have you finished, Deb? Can I take your plate?' she said and placed a hand on her friend's shoulder using the opportunity of having her back to Dadda to mouth the word "sorry". Deb didn't react.

The clatter and activity of collecting up the used plates meant no conversation was required for a moment. The meal was going badly, but not for the reasons Tanya had expected. Everything Deb said rubbed Dadda up the wrong way and both of them were acting out of character. Tanya almost wished they'd obey the rules of social convention and make small talk. But she suspected Deb was trying to provoke him, to get him to react and reveal what was troubling him. It was possible, but a strange choice of tactic when she knew so little about him and things had very definitely gone off course.

Tanya winced as she realised it had been wrong to invite Deb into their home. She should have protected Dadda, not exposed him to extra stress. She leant against the worktop, squeezed her eyes tightly shut and swallowed hard before she turned back to the table.

'Can I interest anyone in pudding?' she asked, her voice tight and unfamiliar. 'Fruit salad, I'm afraid, but it is mostly mango.'

'Yes, please,' Geena and Deb said in unison.

Dadda pushed his chair away from the table. 'I'll take mine into the living room,' he said.

Tanya felt her mouth drop open, but she didn't dare challenge him. 'OK, I'll bring it through.'

After he'd closed the kitchen door behind him, she turned immediately to Deb and said, 'I don't know what to say. He's never been like this before. I didn't even know he felt so strongly about the army.'

'I did,' Geena said. 'I wanted to join the army cadets when a load of my friends did, and he completely forbade it. Totally put his foot down and said he'd never see his family in uniform. Which is odd because, you know, you do wear a uniform, Tan.'

'A medical one. Not a forces one. There is a difference.'

Deb frowned, then asked, 'Do you think it was a political reaction, or perhaps a response to a stranger in his house?'

Tanya paused to think but had no excuse to justify his actions. 'I don't know. We don't often have visitors, but he's not been so difficult with anyone before. I'm just sorry he's spoiled our dinner.'

'He hasn't. It's all delicious,' Deb assured her and picked up a spoon to dig into the bowl Tanya put down in front of her.

Tanya sank back into her chair. Despite the compliment, she wouldn't be surprised if Deb didn't want to develop their friendship any further, let alone help solve whatever the problem was with Dadda. She changed the subject to ask Deb about her family, encouraging her to tell stories about her children's achievements despite the glazed expression Geena's face took on.

Tanya at least had one positive to cling on to. Will had texted to suggest meeting up that weekend. She hadn't replied immediately for fear of appearing too keen, but she would. The thought of seeing him again, maybe sitting over a meal in which no-one would behave badly, would be enough to get her through the next few days.

*

Will had suggested spending the afternoon together before going out to dinner so, five minutes early as usual, Tanya sat on one of the wide wooden benches fixed to the external walls of the octagonal Rest House on Bournville Green, scuffing her feet against the fallen leaves collecting below it. The chill from the stone wall she leant back on seeped through her coat and she rubbed her hands together as she watched him walk past the parade of shops towards her.

She'd spotted him before he noticed her and she smiled as he waited to cross the road, looked the wrong way for cars, checked himself, and then looked both ways for a second time before stepping off the pavement. He glanced at the people and scenery around him in an interested manner as he approached, one hand in his jeans pocket, the other supported by the sling. Then he saw her and stopped abruptly, staring at her, his expression unreadable. Worried something was wrong she almost stood up and rushed to his side. But then he grinned and jogged the remaining distance to drop onto the bench beside her and kiss her cheek.

'You're in the right place this time, then?' he said.

She faked offence. 'I think you'll find I wasn't in entirely the wrong place before.'

'You were definitely in the right place when I needed my X-ray. No-one I'd rather have had look inside me.'

His suggestive tone brought warmth to her cheeks and she couldn't think how to reply.

'Hey, I brought you a present,' Will said and handed her a paper bag he'd stuffed in his jacket.

'Oh. Thank you.' She peeped inside to see a cellophane packet full of wrapped chocolates: the kind normally packed in boxes. She lifted it out and asked, 'Did this fall off the production line?'

'Why, are they damaged?' His eyebrows lifted in concern and he reached out as though to take the packet back.

She clutched it to her. 'No, it's just a phrase, you know, to imply something wasn't bought legitimately, as in "it fell off the back of a lorry". What I mean is, even if you stole it from work, thank you.' She put the bag down on the bench beside her handbag and clasped her hands in her lap. It was great to see him again, and even nicer to be given a present. She shouldn't risk messing things up by teasing him with sarcasm and jokes he wouldn't understand.

'I guess that's a British phrase,' he said. 'But I can assure you there was no five finger discount on those chocolates. I legally acquired them, though I admit they came from the factory shop. Um, you do like chocolate, right?'

She nodded. 'Yes, I love chocolate. And I am not at all envious that your job has perks like daily access to the factory shop.'

'You mean you don't help yourself to bandages from the hospital?'

She shook her head.

'Prescription medication?'

She smiled and shook her head even more emphatically.

'Those wooden sticks doctors use to hold your tongue down when they ask you to say "ahh"?'

Tanya laughed. 'Nope. Call me incorruptible, but I steal nothing from the NHS.'

'OK. Good to know.' He leant back and stretched his legs out in front of him but nudged her so that she turned to catch his wink. 'If I could have stolen chocolate from the line, I would have, but they watch me like hawks in there,' he whispered.

She returned the pressure of his nudge then took a deep breath and held it a moment before exhaling and forcing herself to relax. When she'd imagined the date she'd become anxious: what if they had nothing to say to each other, what if he'd gone off her? But now he was here, beside her and the fact that they had an afternoon with no particular schedule ahead of them was bliss.

She also stretched her legs out and focused on the nearest tree to them. It was a copper beech with deep purple leaves, one of the many large trees scattered across Bournville Green. The leaves on most of them had turned orange or brown while they'd already fallen from others, but the autumn sunshine was bright and the puffs of white cloud in the sky didn't threaten rain.

'I guess this place hasn't changed much in a hundred years,' Will said.

'Why would it have to? They didn't put a picture of it on the front of chocolate boxes for nothing. It's a particular kind of British dream made real.' She glanced at him. 'Do you hate it?'

'Of course not. It's just not my dream, I suppose. American dreams are built a bit bigger, you know. Everything's bigger Stateside.'

Tanya frowned. 'Bigger doesn't necessarily mean better.'

He sighed. 'No, but old ways aren't always the best either.'

She pulled her legs in and twisted on the bench to face him. 'Are they giving you a very hard time at work?'

'Well, I wasn't joking when I said they watch me like hawks. But it's not because I'm likely to steal the products. None of the existing management team were pleased to see us Americans and I completely understand why.' He shrugged. 'But the company's been sold. Things have to change, and all of this,' he gestured at the Rest House, which had been built a century earlier to celebrate a wedding anniversary of one of the chocolate company's founders, 'hasn't been to do with the company for years. Beautiful though it is, it's irrelevant to the business of selling chocolate.'

'So they're not listening to your ideas?'

He looked directly at her and Tanya froze as their eyes met. Neither blinked and she didn't breathe or even register any details of his expression or body language. All she knew was her heart was racing and she didn't want to look away.

He reached across, lifted her left hand from her lap and ran his thumb across the pads of her fingertips. 'You're the person who's listened to me most since I've been here. And I couldn't have hoped for better company.'

She took a deep breath and forced herself to look down and get her heart rate under control. Perhaps Americans were more direct than Brits, maybe their relationships moved faster, but this was only the third time she'd met Will, only their second date. Flattered though she was, things were moving far too quickly. The excitement was undeniable though.

He squeezed her hand. 'Sorry, too much?'

'No.' She risked meeting his gaze again. 'I'm flattered. But perhaps we should stop sitting here like a pair of pensioners and get on our way.'

'Of course,' he said and stood up.

She followed more slowly, disturbed by how her words had triggered a memory of her mum giving her advice about boyfriends many years earlier. They'd been in the kitchen talking about Ian, a boy who hadn't called Tanya after their only date, and they'd looked out into the garden where Dadda was snoozing in a deckchair on the patio. Tanya had wondered how she'd ever be able to spot a decent man when her own parents with the sixteen year age gap between them were proof that finding your match was unpredictable.

'Keep looking,' her mum had said. 'If you can imagine sitting in the sun with him when you're old, then he's the right man.'

She'd laughed at the time and promised, 'OK, Mum. I'll apply the old folks bench test to all the men I meet from now on.'

The poignant memory unsettled her now, though. She missed her mum's advice, wished she could chat to her about Will and how he made her feel.

Tanya couldn't have imagined growing old with Ian, not least because he didn't call when he said he would. She had been able to imagine Jim in the role during their relationship through their A' levels. But he'd changed of course, once he'd left Birmingham. So had she, she supposed, what with having to put her family first while he was making the most of university life.

She didn't yet know Will well enough to be able to judge and actually, couldn't quite believe he was single when she found him so attractive.

'So is this your dream then?' he asked as they walked across the grass. 'A cottage on a village green?'

'No way,' she replied. 'Fond though I am of Birmingham, my dreams tend to involve leaving it, I'm afraid.'

'So where would you go, if you could go anywhere in the world?'

She paused. It was too big a question. There was so much she wanted to see. From art treasures in Europe to wildlife safari in Africa, there was no travel experience Tanya hadn't indulged in online. There was no destination she'd say no to; well, maybe she wouldn't risk the countries listed as too dangerous by the Foreign Office. Other than those though, she hadn't put a top ten list of destinations in order and couldn't answer such a simple question.

'No, let me guess,' Will said when she remained silent. 'India?'

She frowned. Dadda's reluctance to return there had made her curious about where he came from. 'Maybe,' she said, and shrugged. 'I'm just keen to travel really.'

'Well, you'd be very welcome in Chicago. Any time,' he said.

'Thanks. I'm only sorry we're not making you more welcome in Birmingham.'

'You for one are. And Geena.' He tipped his head towards Mr Davis's shop across the road. 'Has she worked there long?'

'No, only a year or so. It's her first proper job since college, but isn't quite what she's after.'

'I see that. She seems like someone with big dreams.'

Tanya frowned. 'What makes you say that?'

'She gives that impression, that she's on her way somewhere.'

'Oh. Don't I seem as though I'm on my way?'

Will stopped walking and put his good hand on her arm. 'When I first saw you at the hospital you struck me as someone who was in the right place. You seem a good fit with your career. But, outside of work, maybe there's scope for changes.'

'Changes?' Tanya's voice croaked as a bolt of anxiety dried her throat. What was she doing that he didn't like? She realised she was staring at him and blinked to avoid getting lost in his gaze again.

'Yeah, I mean you could do worse than spend more of your time hanging out with an American.' He squeezed her shoulder. 'And these ideas about leaving Birmingham, maybe we could come up with a plan.'

She smiled in relief. Perhaps she wasn't doing anything wrong and at least if she felt things were moving quickly, it seemed to be what he wanted as well.

'For now, maybe we should stick to the within Birmingham plan,' she said. 'Come on. If you think you're stuck in the past already let me take you even further back in time.'

Chapter Nine

Tanya pushed Selly Manor's heavy wooden door open and stepped into the dimly-lit room. The aromas of wood, smoke from the fireplace and dust rising from woven matting covering the stone floor evoked the building's history. Will's expression when he'd first seen the ancient, timber-framed building on a corner plot surrounded by ordinary suburban houses showed his confusion. Now he ducked his head to avoid cracking it on the lintel as he followed her inside.

'How old is this place?' he whispered.

'Thirteen hundreds I think. We did projects on it at school. Believe me you don't need to whisper. They're used to hordes of screaming kids.'

She smiled as he looked around in amazement. If he'd thought the factory was stuck in the past, then their visit to an authentically-furnished medieval house must be really blowing his mind.

'I've seen this kind of stuff in films. I can't believe this is for real though. And look at you, little miss "I've never been anywhere", travelling through time as though you're born to it.'

'Hardly.' Tanya pointed out of the small window whose leaded glass panes had settled at odd angles, distorting their view of an ambulance with sirens blaring as it zoomed past. 'We're well within the twenty-first century, but one of the founders of the chocolate firm thought this worth saving, so he brought it here for the workers to enjoy.'

Will shook his head. 'Course he did. Why would you spend your profits on anything practical?'

Tanya led the way into the next room where the dining table was laid for a meal. 'They were Quakers; philanthropy was a big deal. The workers loved them for it.'

'I know. All very worthy, for sure.' He rapped his knuckles against a plastic loaf of bread on a steel platter. 'Not so hot on catering though.'

She folded her arms. 'Don't you dare criticise the chocolate.'

'Hmm, I did wonder about that. I mean, it's not very ...'

Tanya held up a hand to silence him. 'Whatever you're going to say, you're wrong. This,' she pulled the packet he'd given her from her bag, opened it and offered him one, 'is exactly how chocolate should taste.'

He took one and popped it in his mouth before reaching out to hold her hand. 'OK, OK. I get the message and will keep my counter-arguments to myself. Come on, let's look around.'

He didn't let her hand go as he climbed the narrow staircase and she bumped into his back as he came to a sudden stop in the room at the top. 'That bed's tiny,' he said. 'They must have liked cuddling up.' She flushed as he took advantage of their physical proximity to slip the arm not tethered by his sling around her waist and squeeze her.

'Look at the mattress though, just a layer of straw on top of that mesh of ropes. I wouldn't guess it's very comfortable,' she replied.

He smirked and took a step closer to the bed. 'I'm not sure. We could always try it out.'

Laughing, she pulled away. 'Behave.'

He wandered to the window and looked out at the garden below. 'Was this where normal folk would have lived? You see palaces on TV dramas; I guess I'd never thought about the people who weren't aristocrats or their servants.'

'I think even this house was for fairly rich people.' Tanya searched her memory for what a teacher might once have told her. 'Merchants, maybe?'

'Of course. Peasants would have been in hovels, right?'

She raised her eyebrows. 'Where did you get your vocabulary from?'

'TV. Best education there is. Although, we did read some Shakespeare in high school: Macbeth. And my friend Emma totally loves Jane Austen. Made me watch all the films. That counts as Understanding the British 101, right?'

'Things have moved on a little.'

Tanya smiled at him, but felt a wrench at his casual mention of Emma, obviously a female friend he spent a lot of time with. Still, right now he was in Birmingham with her. They wandered through the other upstairs rooms, where Tanya also had to duck her head to get through the doorways.

'I think one reason I like it here is it feels like the size of a home. You can imagine living here,' she said.

He screwed up his nose. 'Hmm. American houses are a bit bigger than this.'

'Like I said, bigger isn't necessarily better.'

'Whatever you say, ma'am. What's your place like?'

It was her turn to frown. 'Very ordinary three bed semi-detached on a street of identical houses. Crazy-paved driveway out the front, strip of scrubby grass out the back. Pretty standard for Birmingham's suburbs. Bournville isn't standard, the buildings here are posh, really. And anyway, the house isn't mine.'

'So what would you choose?'

They'd seen all Selly Manor's upstairs rooms and she thought about her answer as they walked back out to the garden. She'd visited friends in every type of home from studio flat to country cottage, but had never given much thought to property ownership. It seemed a more distant dream than her hopes to travel. And how could she leave Dadda?

'I guess I'm not fussy,' she said. 'Maybe the location matters more than the house. Or the people, probably the people matter more.'

'Good answer.' He stretched his free arm above his head. 'Ceiling height also matters though. I've turned into a hunchback from stooping in there.'

She surprised herself by reaching out to rub his neck. He leaned back against her hand and turned his face up to the sky.

'Do you own a property in Chicago?' she asked.

'No, I rent a condo. Not too far from my folks' place so I can visit with them though.'

'I suppose you need to be flexible about where you live so you can grab any job opportunities.'

He nodded and smiled. 'Sure am glad I grabbed this one.'

She returned his smile, swallowed hard and overcame her shyness to say, 'So am I.'

'Any chance you fancy coming to see the place I'm staying in here?'

Tanya bit her lip. She liked him. She liked him a lot. They had definitely been flirting and she had very much enjoyed it when he kissed her. But this was only their second date. She wasn't at all sure she was ready to sleep with him. Was that what he was suggesting?

'I don't know. I ...'

'Sorry,' he said, interrupting her, 'is that inappropriate? I just meant to see the house, have a drink - I have proper English tea.' He frowned. 'Is it a religious thing; should we not be alone together or something?'

His contrite expression made her laugh despite the fact he'd made all the usual assumptions. 'I think that if it were a religious thing, we may have already crossed several lines.'

His smile returned. 'You mean the kissing by the fountain thing? I did wonder if I was going to be struck down for that one.'

'Struck down? By what?'

He looked up and scanned the sky at the same time as he stepped forward and put his arm around her waist. 'A thunderbolt from God, obviously.'

'That didn't happen though,' she said and slipped her arms around his waist also looking up to where the vapour trail from a plane stretched across the sky above them.

'No. Can't beat a bit of Catholic fear and guilt to make me mind my manners, though.'

'This is you minding your manners?' she asked as he bent his head and rubbed his nose against hers.

He kissed her before replying. 'Yes. My pops always said if I found a good woman, I should be good to her. This is the good stuff.' He kissed her again.

When she finally pulled away, she pointed out, 'I'm not Catholic though so I don't suppose your God would ever send his thunderbolts on my behalf.'

He ran his hand down her arm then linked his fingers into hers. 'I'll be honest with you, I'm lapsed myself. But if I do or say anything that's inappropriate you should tell me, you know.'

'Believe me, I would have told you. Me and my family aren't religious at all though, so you haven't caused any offence on those grounds.'

He raised his eyebrows. 'But I've offended you in other ways?'

'No, that's not what I meant. It's just, well maybe things are moving a little quickly.'

He squeezed her hand then let go. 'OK, point taken. So, with the reassurance that all I'm offering is a tour of some slightly more modern real estate and a cup of tea, would you like to come back to mine?'

She grinned. 'Yes, I very much would.'

Tanya smiled to herself as she locked the front door behind her. The whole afternoon and evening with Will qualified as the best date she'd ever been on. At no point had he seemed bored by her company and, apart from that mention of Emma, she'd been continually delighted by him. His positive attitude and gentle teasing kept her constantly entertained and as for the kissing ...

Her smile faded as she became aware of the canned laughter, audible even in the hall, which told her that Dadda was waiting up for her again. Guilt at having enjoyed herself all day and barely spared him a thought soured her memories. Before she went into the living room to speak to him, she brushed the fingers of her right hand across her lips. The lipstick she'd applied earlier was gone and her skin still tingled with the memory of the goodnight kiss Will had sent her home with. She took a breath, then pushed the door open.

Dadda looked round as she entered. 'Did you have a nice time with your new friend?' he asked.

Tanya nodded and replied, 'Yes, thanks. Bournville Green's looking lovely at the moment, isn't it, Gee?' She'd noticed that Geena was also there, uncharacteristically home on a Saturday night and curled into the armchair at the far end of the room, the one which had been their mum's favourite place to sit. Geena didn't shift her gaze from the television.

'That's nice,' Dadda said.

'You should go up there and take a look,' Tanya said and sat down on the sofa which filled the space between the two armchairs. 'You used to walk there and back every day for work. The fresh air and exercise would be good for you.' She watched his face carefully to see how he'd react, but he changed the subject instead.

'Geena tells me your friend's working at the factory.'

'Hmm, she says a lot of things when I'm not in the room, doesn't she?'

Geena turned her head to glare at Tanya. 'I was just making conversation.'

'Did I miss anything interesting?' Tanya replied. 'Either of you been up to anything special today?' She kept looking at Geena but raised a questioning eyebrow and tilted her head at Dadda.

Geena gave an almost imperceptible shake of her head. He hadn't been out then.

'Nothing special,' Geena said. 'I'll make us a cuppa, shall I?'

Tanya moved her legs to let her sister pass before she said, 'Will, my friend, was talking about religion, Dadda. He was asking about our background and seemed surprised when I said we're not religious at all.'

He tutted. 'It's not unusual. How many of your friends are religious? Very few.'

'No, but things were different for your generation, weren't they?' She paused before asking, 'What about your parents? I mean Gill's a Sikh surname so someone must have been.'

'Yes,' he said, but didn't elaborate.

Tanya shifted in her seat to face him. His lips were clamped together and, while he was looking towards the television screen, she didn't get the impression he was watching the action any more. 'So were you brought up as a Sikh then?'

He remained silent but a muscle twitched in his cheek. Tanya didn't break the silence and eventually he said, 'Why do you want to know this? It has never been important to you.'

'It's only that I've never thought much about it before. Doesn't mean it's not important.'

He closed his eyes and pressed the remote control to mute the TV. Tanya frowned. She could hear Geena's voice in the kitchen, obviously on the phone, although it sounded more like an argument than a chat. There'd be a long wait for that cup of tea.

When Dadda spoke again, the tone of his voice had changed. Like Geena, he sounded angry. 'Do people make ignorant assumptions about you?' he asked.

She shook her head. 'You mean like the people on the bus who assumed you were Muslim and therefore a terrorist? No, of course not. Sometimes other Asian women ask which gurdwara we go to, but they never say anything when I tell them we don't.'

'Of course, you mostly mix with white people. I suppose we seem exotic to your new friend.'

'I doubt it; he comes from a huge city. It's probably more racially mixed than Birmingham is.'

There was tension in Dadda's voice as he asked, 'And what religion is he?'

'His family are Catholic. Will's not.'

Dadda shook his head. 'Your generation give things up so easily.'

'I guess we have less need to believe in a religion. We know so many things these days.' Tanya shrugged and smoothed a palm down the fabric of her trousers.

He gave a short, harsh laugh. 'You think you know things. Your X-rays look inside people and see their physical problems, but your pictures don't tell you what's really happening.'

Tanya bit her bottom lip. They'd never talked like this before. The anger may have faded from his voice after she'd told him no-one was threatening her, but his philosophical comments were out of character. Dadda was not given to introspection or rhetoric. 'And what is really happening?' she asked carefully.

He glanced over his shoulder. 'Is Geena making tea for us, or not?'

'I'm sure she'll get round to it. But why won't you talk to me about our family?'

'This is our family,' he said. 'Me, you, and Geena if she ever comes back. You know all you need to.'

Tanya leant forward. 'I don't. I'd like to know about my grandparents, about your time growing up in India. You've never told us anything.'

'There's nothing to talk about. Nothing to tell.'

'I don't believe that.'

He reached for the remote control, changed channels and put the sound back on then folded his arms across his chest. Keen to diffuse the tension, Tanya sat back, but watched him from the corner of her eye. His jaw moved as though there were words he swallowed rather than spoke and his focus was obviously not on the screen. Loathe to push him when he was clearly upset and while she was already worried about his mental state, she let the subject drop and feigned an interest in the programme.

Geena delivered their drinks without breaking off her phone call. When the programme finished, Dadda stood up to go to bed then paused and said, 'Your mother and I put many things behind us when we came to this country. Birmingham welcomed us, but I no longer feel that. Will you trust me when I tell you it's time to move on?'

Tanya looked at him. He seemed older, more fragile, but she had to stand her ground. 'I don't understand why, Dadda. This is my home.'

The words surprised her. That wasn't what she felt. She was desperate to leave, but not for his reasons. She had her own life to live. She was no longer a child who he could rule. And anyway, how could he expect her to understand him when he refused to explain?

'I would never be able to forgive myself if something happened to you or Geena.' His voice was quiet, tortured. It stabbed guilt into her heart. 'I need to make plans to protect us all.'

Tanya blinked and swallowed. His pain was obvious and the need to ease it became imperative. 'We're fine, Dadda,' she said. 'You do look after me and Geena. There's nothing to worry about.'

'There's everything to worry about. You girls may be sensible, but other people are the problem. Other people can't be trusted.'

'Oh, Dadda,' she said, but he interrupted.

'You must promise me,' he held her gaze with a ferocious stare, 'you must promise that you, me and Geena will always know where each other are. That you'll always put safety first.'

'Of course, Dadda. Of course I will. I do.' Tanya responded immediately and said the words without considering them. All that mattered was to comfort him. He bent down to pat her shoulder as he left the room and went upstairs.

She rubbed her eyes then picked up their used mugs and carried them through to the kitchen. Geena was sitting at the kitchen table, spinning her phone on its surface.

'What?' she said in response to Tanya's questioning look.

'Dadda,' Tanya replied.

'Oh.'

'This is serious, Gee. He's being so weird.'

Geena didn't respond. Tanya prodded her in the arm.

'What?' Geena snapped.

Tanya frowned. 'Who were you arguing with?'

Geena span the phone some more before she replied. 'Jude,' she said eventually.

Tanya waited, knowing the story would come out. Geena wouldn't be able to resist telling it.

'She and Sami had split up.' Geena's voice was plaintive. 'There was nothing wrong with me seeing him.'

So that was why Geena had stayed home for the past few evenings. She'd fallen out with her best friend, and over a man as usual. 'Hmm, but did you maybe fail to mention it to Jude?' Tanya rubbed her eyes. Fixing her sister's problems came pretty low down her list of priorities at the moment.

'There was nothing to mention. And it's over before it began anyway. She's got no reason to be stroppy with me.'

Tanya sighed. It would have been nice if she could have shared her excitement about Will with Geena rather than have to listen to her sister's self-inflicted dramas. 'You could have mentioned to her that you liked him, maybe? Friendship should come first you know.'

'Oh, take her side why don't you? Everyone else has. Turns out they're all at Steph's for a party this evening, didn't even invite me. Just because I had a bit of a fling with a man who was single at the time.'

'At the time?'

'Also turns out he and Jude have got back together.'

Tanya nodded. That was exactly the way things would have happened in the overly dramatic soap opera of Geena's social life.

'So you're getting the cold shoulder?'

Geena nodded and sniffed.

'Worse things have happened, Gee. Worse things are happening.'

'Yeah, thanks for the sympathy,' Geena said and stomped out of the kitchen.

Tanya stood up and caught sight of her reflection in the dark window pane behind the sink. It could have been her mother's face looking back at her. Except for the fact that her mother would have known what to do.

Chapter Ten

For the first time since the incident on the bus, Tanya's shift pattern meant she was at home on a day Dadda should have gone to work. Knowing that she hadn't paid him enough attention while she'd been distracted by Will, she decided to stay in to monitor his activities and, when she went down for breakfast, found him sitting at the kitchen table using Geena's laptop.

'Morning,' she said. 'Not working today?'

He clicked the mouse a few times before looking up at her and replying, 'I've reduced my hours.'

'Oh. You didn't mention it.' She didn't add that, if what he said was true, it hardly fitted his new regime of knowing where all family members were at all times. She really hoped that wasn't going to be strictly enforced.

She crossed to the sink and filled the kettle but when she turned round to ask if he wanted another drink, he'd gone. The laptop was still open on the table and she swivelled it towards her. As she'd suspected, those quick mouse clicks must have been him closing the Internet browser. She navigated to the web history and could tell that the most recently visited page had been one Dadda had chosen. It stood out among the fashion, gossip and social media sites that represented Geena's recent activity.

Tanya clicked on the link and was taken into a search on a property website which had returned a list of three-bedroomed houses for sale in Wiltshire. She scrolled past the photos of a few. It seemed you didn't get much for your money in that part of the country. Hopefully the prices would have made him reconsider any ideas about leaving Birmingham.

The kettle came to the boil and she closed the browser again and went to make her drink.

'Morning,' Geena said as she came into the room and slumped into a chair. 'I'd love one if you're making.'

'You're talking to me today, then?' Tanya said as she reached for a second mug. 'You barely said a word yesterday. I thought the bad mood might never lift.'

'What? I'm not in a mood. I'm in the right.'

'You always are,' Tanya said which earned her a scowl from Geena. 'Dadda was just using your laptop,' she added.

'Yeah, he asked me to show him how to look stuff up the other day. More baldy browser than silver surfer. He got the hang of it though.'

'Of course he did. He's not daft, he's just ...' She paused, unsure what she wanted to express. At the moment he was being illogical, frustrating, a source of worry. None of which was quite what Geena was talking about. 'Well, anyway, I asked if he was going to work and he lied to me.'

Geena didn't reply and when Tanya turned to pass her drink over she could see Geena had been distracted by something on the computer screen. She put the mug down and prodded her sister in the arm.

'Gee? What's the last thing he's said to you about his job?'

'Hmm? Oh, nothing really. Speaking of which, I better get a move on towards mine. Lover boy's watch should be finished today. Want me to pass any messages on when I call to let him know?'

'Ha ha, no thank you.'

Geena closed the lid on the laptop and stood up. 'Things going OK with him, though?'

'Yes.' Tanya smiled. 'I like him.'

'Well, cheers to that.' Geena's bracelets jangled as she lifted her mug and took a gulp before carrying it and the computer to the door. She paused then turned back to Tanya and said, 'You know those jewellery designs I'm working on?'

Tanya nodded.

'I need to get some more materials, enough so I can build up a decent collection.'

'And?' Tanya said, although she could guess what was coming.

Geena fluttered her eyelashes at her sister. 'Any chance of a loan, pretty, pretty, please?'

Tanya sipped at her own drink. 'How much?'

'Well.' Geena's posture straightened, all trace of sleepiness shaken off. 'The full costs of my business plan come in at around a thousand pounds for everything from materials, display shelves, web design, marketing ...'

Tanya sat down at the table and cut her off. 'But you don't have a business at the moment so what are you actually asking me for?'

'Couple of hundred, maybe five?' Geena smiled widely, her head tipped to the left.

'Five hundred pounds? I'm not made of money.'

'But you do have some. And it would only be a loan. Promise.'

Tanya crossed her arms. 'Let me think about it,' she said.

'Best sister ever,' Geena said and blew a kiss from the doorway.

Tanya sipped her tea and listened to the creak of floorboards and slam of doors overhead that accompanied Geena's urgent preparation to leave the house. There was no point suggesting there'd be less panic if Geena only got up a few minutes earlier. This was how she'd always been. Tanya could remember their mum's frustration at Geena's inability to focus on or set the same priorities to tasks as her parents or teachers might like. She also remembered their mum's delight at Geena's creativity and passion.

Tanya fetched herself a bowl and opened the cereal box to find only a few crumbs left inside. As usual she'd have to be the one to pick up the pieces. She turned over an empty envelope left on the table and began to make a shopping list.

'Going to the shops?' Dadda said as he came back into the room.

'Yes. I could do with some help if you're free?' Tanya replied. If he wouldn't talk to her directly then trying to trick him was one option. Not one she was comfortable with though.

'No, um, you know I don't like the supermarket.' He stuck his hands in his pockets. 'Could you get me a couple of things?'

'OK. Or, maybe you and I can go out to lunch? It's a nice day, I could drive us out to a country pub or something?' She wondered if the unnaturally bright tone in her voice sounded as fake to him as it did to her. She wished she'd been able to get more advice from Deb about Dadda's mental state. Pushing him like this was probably not at all recommended.

'No. Thank you but I don't feel like going out.'

Tanya sighed and pushed the envelope away. She didn't have the energy to be anything but direct. 'Listen, Dadda,' she said. 'I'm worried about you. Geena told me you haven't been to work recently and I'm wondering if you've been out at all since those people were so cruel to you.' She paused but he didn't react. 'Have you?'

He dropped his chin to his chest and his shoulders rose as he took a deep breath in. 'I don't feel well enough to work, Tanya. I've had no need to go out.'

She turned towards him in her chair. This was progress. 'It's been well over a week, Dadda. Perhaps you should see the doctor about how you're feeling. How about I make an appointment? If we get one today I can drive you down there.'

'I don't need a doctor.'

She spoke gently. 'You can't carry on as you are.'

He shook his head. 'I am making plans for us.'

'You can't still be talking about moving away from Birmingham? You must be able to see that wouldn't be right for Geena, or for me?' She bit back any other comments, not wanting to admit she'd snooped at what he'd been looking at online.

'It is what's right for our family.' He finally looked up at her and nodded. 'I know best.'

Tanya stared back at him but didn't speak. She didn't doubt that her mum would have found a way to support him, a way to turn his ideas into a workable plan, but she was struggling to see what she could do without her mum's help, without Geena's. 'Dadda,' she said eventually, 'I know what happened was scary and upsetting, but we've lived here for nearly thirty years and this is the only really bad thing that's happened. I think you might be overreacting.'

'Bad things have happened before now,' he said. 'I will always take the right action to protect my family.' He turned and left the room, his departure shortly followed by the sound of the TV being switched on.

Tanya dropped her head into her hands. Yes, she wanted to leave Birmingham, but not like this.

*

Dadda's behaviour was still troubling Tanya when she went out that evening. He'd avoided her as much as he could while they both remained inside the house and she hadn't known what to say to him. She glanced at Will and realised there'd been a gap in the conversation long enough to seem uncomfortable. She should have left her problems at home.

Will continued to eat his starter as though everything was fine, but Tanya needed to say something, needed the conversation to flow as it had on their previous dates. She was sure he'd been more talkative before. The silence between them gave her the sense that he wasn't quite at ease and she wondered if his wrist was troubling him.

'How's it feeling?' she asked and indicated Will's plaster cast where his arm rested on the restaurant table.

He smiled and replied, 'A bit too light.'

She put her cutlery down and widened her eyes in concern. 'What do you mean? Is it tingling or aching?'

'Chill out, doc. I only meant I'm looking forward to getting my watch back. Geena said it's done but I didn't manage to get there before they closed this evening. Too busy grilling my colleagues for suggestions of where'd be a good place to bring you.'

'Oh, OK.' She smiled but couldn't shake off the sense that she was misjudging everything. 'Good choice, by the way,' she added, although the fancy, city centre restaurant he'd selected wouldn't have been her own preference. She didn't think she fitted their target demographic who were more likely the suited businessmen at nearby tables. The starched tablecloth and ironwork centrepiece suggested a self-conscious attempt to make the formerly industrial building suitable for fine dining, while the food seemed designed to impress rather than nourish.

Will had made positive comments on the menu though, even while selecting food which would be easy to eat one-handed, and was eagerly devouring his duck terrine so she returned to her own starter, keen to give the impression that the evening was going well.

'My Gramps would have been mad at me if he'd seen the state of that watch,' Will said. 'It was his most treasured possession.'

Tanya smiled and nodded. 'My mum loved hers too.' She finished her food and pushed her sleeve back to look at the oval clock face inlaid with mother of pearl. The numerals for each hour were etched in fine gold paint onto pale pink enamel dots and the central pin holding the minute, hour and second hands in place was tipped with a tiny chip of diamond.

'Nice way to remember them, isn't it?' Will said. 'Makes me think of Gramps whenever I check the time.'

Glad the conversational gap was bridged, Tanya asked, 'Did you know him well?'

'Sure, he looked after us kids while mom and pop were out at work. He was a big personality. Just the thought of what he'd have to say about it kept me out of trouble.' He grinned and Tanya caught a glimpse in his expression of the cheeky little boy he must once have been.

'I wish I'd known my grandparents,' she said. She dropped her hands into her lap and looked down. Will's last minute dinner invitation had surprised her, but she'd grabbed it after spending the day lurking around the house. Even investigating the destinations of planes hadn't been any kind of distraction that afternoon. The first one she looked at was going to India and, after Dadda's weird reaction to talk of his homeland, it wasn't a location she wanted to dwell on.

'I wish I could have introduced you to Gramps,' Will said and winked across the table. 'He'd have loved you.'

She smiled and wished she could return a similar compliment. If things ever came to the point where she needed to introduce Will to Dadda, it would only be something else to worry about. His rudeness to Deb, erratic recent behaviour and rules about security meant she couldn't guess how he'd react to Will's confident, flippant manner.

Their waiter cleared away from their first course before returning with plates almost too big for the size of the table, definitely over-sized for the amount of food on them.

'Looks amazing,' Will said and used his fork to scoop a mouthful of sea bass. 'Oh, you have to try this. Here.' He loaded his fork again and held it out to her.

She hadn't even tasted her own meal, but leant forward and opened her mouth. Their eye contact held while he fed her and she had that sense of being mesmerised by him again. She smiled and nodded her approval of his choice then turned her attention to her own plate.

Before she was even half way through, she noticed that he'd put his fork down and glanced at his plate to see he'd already finished.

'Hey,' he said, 'I'm from a big family. You gotta be quick if you want seconds.'

'Um, do you? I mean, would you like to try mine?'

'Of course. As long as you're happy to share.'

She sliced off a piece of her steak, loaded her fork with the meat and sauce and reversed the feeding process across the table. Tanya flushed at the sensuality of the repeated action. She sensed that the business men had all turned to watch as Will placed his fingers on her outstretched wrist and their eyes locked. Aware that he was now waiting for her though, she looked down and hurried to finish her meal.

'Do you have a favourite restaurant at home?' she asked, in the hope it would give him a topic to talk about while she ate.

'Oh yeah, there's an awesome Italian downstairs at my building. Me and Emma go there all the time, but I love the diner near my folks' place too. We used to go there for pancakes every weekend. I'd love to take you there.'

'I'd love to go.' Those four words didn't come anywhere near expressing how much she'd enjoy that. She had looked up Will's home town online and found images of Chicago with skyscrapers looming over Lake Michigan. The tourism website assured her that the city boasted all the fine dining and cultural attractions any major destination should have, with the addition of parades and festivals almost every month. Admitting her knowledge to Will could seem too much like stalkerish behaviour, but Chicago had definitely elbowed its way up the list of places she most wanted to visit that she'd been mentally compiling since Will had asked her what her choices would be. He was frowning at her response though.

'This is going to sound crazy, but don't get pissy with me, OK?'

She raised her eyebrows. 'Pissy?'

'Uh, mad, angry?'

'OK, I won't.'

'Good,' he said, 'because I know this is only our third date, I mean, I guess we don't count the whole X-ray thing as a date despite how intimate it was?'

She laughed. 'No, we don't count the X-ray as a date.'

'Anyway, I know this is only our third date, but I want to say I'd like it if you would come over to Chicago sometime. Meet my folks, let me show you the town, see how we do things in the Mid-West. It's a little different to the West Midlands.'

'Are you serious?' She froze with her fork halfway to her mouth. 'I can't tell you how much I'd like that. But ...' She paused, put the food in her mouth and chewed carefully. Regardless of any of her own concerns about the journey, how would Dadda react to her leaving the country to visit a virtual stranger? He'd been alarmed when she told him she'd accepted Will's last minute invitation tonight. She'd smoothed over his ridiculous concerns that a lack of planning meant the situation might be dangerous. Even considering a trip to Chicago wasn't an action likely to pass his current stringent security reviews.

She'd need to manage how she told him very carefully, if she could actually go at all. It might not be wise to leave him with only Geena's slapdash attention until she was sure he was back to normal. Still, any potential trip was probably months away.

'But what?' Will asked.

Tanya finished her meal as she considered. What she really wanted to do was run away to Chicago right that moment. It would have been disloyal to her family to admit that to Will though, so what she actually said was, 'We have only been on three dates. We should probably get to know each other a little better before we start planning a holiday.'

It was the truth. She'd have to introduce him to Dadda if she did agree to travel so far. Everything was suddenly moving far too quickly. He nodded and something about how his mouth was pursed gave her the impression she'd said the wrong thing.

'I'm sorry,' she said. 'I'm not being "pissy", I promise. Just, um, cautious.'

'I know, and I totally understand, it's just … OK, look, I'll come right out with it.' He pressed his hands flat against the tablecloth and Tanya realised she'd been right. There was something bothering him. 'I had a call from my boss in the US today and the thing is,' Will said, 'he wants me back in Chicago to input to a project there.'

A jolt of nausea made Tanya fear she might lose the meal she'd just finished. Will represented the one positive thing in her life at that point. The dream, the potential of Chicago was being snatched away because, whatever Dadda might have to say about it, realistically, how could she go anywhere with Will when she still knew so little of him? She pressed a hand against her mouth and mumbled, 'You mean you're leaving?'

He grimaced. 'Looks that way. In a couple of days.'

Chapter Eleven

The following day, Geena got home from work and went straight to the garage. With Tanya on a late shift, she was on cooking duty for the evening, but she had some new ideas she wanted to try for her design project first. She needed the distraction. Otherwise she might have to admit to herself how much it had hurt to find that ten of her supposed friends had unfriended her on Facebook the previous morning.

She'd thought the news feed seemed quiet and hadn't dared look online since for fear that more would have followed. Her one night stand with Sami definitely hadn't been worth it.

The fluorescent light flickered into life as she pressed the switch by the door and immediately she could tell something was wrong. She always left her workspace tidy, with materials and tools in their allocated places and sketches stored in drawers where they'd stay clean. As she approached the desk along the offcut of carpet she'd salvaged from a skip, she could see things weren't quite right.

While everything was tidy, it wasn't how she'd have done it. The lamps pointed out to the corners of the garage rather than being angled in to illuminate her main working area, and the toolboxes and drawers were pushed aside rather than being within arm's reach of her seat.

She backed away, switched off the light and returned to the house.

'Dadda?' she said from the door to the living room.

He glanced up from his newspaper. 'How was work?' he asked.

'Fine. Did you go out for that?' She pointed at the paper.

There was a pause before he replied. 'Mary popped in to ask if I wanted anything when she went to the supermarket earlier.'

It wasn't actually an answer. 'I see,' she said, trying not to sound judgemental. 'Um, have you been in the garage? Some of my things have moved.'

There was a longer pause.

'Yes, sorry. I wanted to borrow a small screwdriver to tighten the hinge on my glasses.'

He hadn't looked up from the paper as he spoke, had in fact lifted it closer to his face. Although what he'd said was plausible, Geena didn't believe it. While considering how to respond, after all, she couldn't be angry with him - there was no damage, she just didn't like anyone else touching her stuff, she glanced around the living room.

Things seemed different here as well. The pile of newspapers under the coffee table had gone, a peace lily in a ceramic pot had been moved from the end of the sideboard and placed on the bookcase near the window. Dadda never did housework and Tanya couldn't have had time. It had been past midnight when she'd got back from her date with Will and she hadn't been up when Geena went out to work that morning.

'Did you find one?' she asked.

'Hmm, find what?'

She frowned; something was definitely up. 'You've moved things in here as well. What's going on?'

'Nothing is going on. I did a little clearing up.'

This was so far out of character she couldn't keep the accusation out of her voice. 'Why?'

He finally folded the newspaper and looked at her. 'You've lived all your life in this house, I think it's time for a change.'

Her eyebrows shot up. 'A change? Do you want to redecorate?'

Geena looked around: the patterned carpet and floral wallpaper definitely provided plenty of scope for updating. The decor had all been chosen by her mum twenty years earlier. Pointless to be sentimental about it though. Even her mum would have been ready for the room to be refreshed by now. She looked back at Dadda to offer her support, but he was no longer looking at her. He shifted awkwardly in his seat.

'I've put the house up for sale,' he said. 'The estate agent came to take photographs today, that's why I tidied up.' He shook his newspaper and lifted it to his face again.

Geena was silent for a moment then, realising she hadn't even been breathing since he'd spoken, gasped a lungful of air. 'For sale? But, but this is my home.' Decorating was one thing, leaving completely another.

Dadda nodded. 'I want us to live somewhere safer. I worry now every time you and Tanya are out of the house. We'll move to a different area, out of the city.'

Geena's arms hung limp at her sides. 'But, we're adults, Dadda. Tanya and I don't have to live with you but we do because we like living here.'

'Don't be silly. You can't afford to live on your own, Geena. You'll stay with the family and I say we should move.'

Her mouth dropped open and she blinked as tears immediately filled her eyes. Of course her financial situation wasn't stable, but to hear how he really saw her position, learning that he still believed her dependent, that her career was irrelevant, stunned her.

Her voice was weak when she managed to speak again. 'You've always been so supportive. You said it was OK for me to work towards my dream of being in the jewellery business.'

'Of course I support you. But dreams come second to safety.'

Geena rubbed her hands over her eyes. She wasn't dependent on him. She wasn't a child. She had skills, a job, a life of her own. He couldn't make her go. Could he? She wasn't just going to let him tell her what to do. There had to be a discussion, surely.

'You're overreacting, Dadda,' she said. 'A couple of people said stupid things to you on the bus and your reaction is to run away? That's not what you taught me and Tanya to do. You always said we should be brave, stand up for ourselves. Why can't you do that?'

He put down his newspaper and stood up. 'This is no time to be brave. This is the time to leave.'

He pushed past her and left the room.

*

Geena was still sitting on the sofa replaying what had happened when Tanya got back from work.

'He's put the house up for sale,' she said in response to Tanya's concerned look. The fact that Tanya's mouth also dropped open made her feel a little better. 'No discussion with you then?'

'No. I knew he'd considered moving, but, I mean, what? He can't have just done it without telling us.' Tanya sat down next to Geena.

Geena nodded. 'He has. It's his house and he's going to sell it to move god knows where and he expects us to go with him. He even pointed out that I have no other options because I'm broke.'

'Oh, Gee. Don't worry, we'll sort this out.'

They both turned to look at the door as they heard Dadda's footsteps on the stairs.

'I'm glad you're home safely, Tanya,' he said as he came into the living room.

'Of course I'm home safely,' she replied. 'But I didn't expect to get here and find my home's being sold from under me.'

'Not from under you. You'll still have a home, somewhere new.'

Tanya's voice was conciliatory. 'I can't leave Birmingham, Dadda. I have my job.'

He shrugged. 'You can find another job. You have skills, you'll be welcome at any hospital.'

Geena interrupted, 'While I suppose my career isn't important enough to take into account?' She shook off the hand Tanya placed on her arm and stood up. 'You can't just do this, expect to drag us around after you as though we belong to you. You always encouraged us to be independent - you can't start behaving like some kind of old-fashioned Asian father who keeps his womenfolk locked up. You want to be British? Start acting like it.'

She'd stepped closer to him as she spoke and it was only when she finished that she noticed how he'd flinched at her raised voice, cowering away from her with his head bowed. Tanya's hand was on her arm again.

'Geena? Maybe we can discuss this less aggressively?' she said and pulled Geena to sit down while saying, 'Geena didn't mean to upset you, Dadda. You've taken a big step and it's come as a shock to us both, that's all.'

'I never thought I would hear words like this from my own daughter,' he mumbled.

'I'm sure Geena didn't mean to upset you,' Tanya said, standing and guiding him into his armchair. She glared at her sister.

Geena cringed with remorse. Perhaps Tanya hadn't been overreacting by thinking the incident on the bus really had triggered something serious.

'I'm sorry, Dadda,' she said. 'It's just, I'm young, I'm only just starting out on my career and this is a great location for me to be near my friends.' She gulped at the sudden lump in her throat. Those friends had disappeared. Anger at the way they'd treated her fuelled her reaction. 'Anyway, this is our home. Of course I'm attached to it.'

He drew in a long breath before he spoke again. His voice was quiet but steady. 'You are both older than your mother was when she left her home and family and came here with me. She made a more difficult choice than either of you will ever have to. I cannot allow her wish for us to live in safety to be undermined.'

Geena exchanged a confused glance with Tanya. She'd never heard their mum talk about safety or difficult choices and it seemed Tanya hadn't either.

'What do you mean by live in safety?' Tanya asked. 'Was there a particular reason why you and mum decided to live here?'

He shook his head. 'It's the past. It's all in the past. Now I have to decide how to protect my family today. We will be moving.'

'Dadda, please ...' Geena started to speak but stopped when she saw Tanya's grim expression and shaking head indicating she shouldn't. She got up and went to the kitchen to start on dinner instead.

Tanya joined her a few minutes later. 'I have no idea what's going on,' she said.

'You and me both,' Geena replied. 'But what are we going to do?'

Tanya pulled out a chair to sit at the kitchen table and put her hands over her face. Geena started slicing an onion. It made her eyes sting but wasn't the only reason for the tears she wiped from her cheeks. A black smear across the back of her hand showed that her mascara had run and most likely left blotches below her eyes. Men. It was always something to do with men and their attempts to control her. She shook her head and pointed to her face.

'Hey, remember Taj, that boy from school I went out with and how he refused to be seen with me unless my make-up was perfect?'

Tanya looked up and smiled. 'He was marginally better than the one who insisted you wore the perfume he bought you so you smelt like his ex.'

'Mick. Yeah, he wasn't my finest choice, was he?'

'Who was the one you went out with for six months before he mentioned that he didn't believe in monogamy?'

Geena pulverised the remains of the onion and scraped it into the pan she'd been heating on the hob. 'Pete. That was Pete.' The onion hit the oil with a fierce sizzle. Her recent experience with Sami had been worse than pointless as well and she was almost glad Tanya seemed too distracted to give her a hard time about what had happened as a result of her fling with him.

Her friends giving her the cold shoulder was more than enough punishment. Utterly unfair though. She sighed. Maybe Jules just needed to throw a strop to get over it. With any luck the whole thing would blow over. She hoped.

'At least you're having better luck with men at the moment. Things seem to be going well with Will,' she said.

Tanya didn't answer immediately and, once she'd finished deseeding a green pepper and given the onion a stir, Geena glanced over her shoulder to look at her sister. When she saw her face, she put down the knife and took the pan off the heat.

'Oh, Tan, what is it?' she said as she bent and draped an arm around Tanya's shoulders. 'Don't say he's turned out to be a bad one too.'

Tanya sniffed and shook her head. 'No. But it's all pointless because he's going back to Chicago next week and that will be the end of that.'

*

At work the next day, Tanya saw her friend further down the corridor and hurried to catch up. 'Deb? I'm so sorry about the other evening. Dadda really isn't usually like that.'

Deb turned at the sound of Tanya's voice, but kept walking. 'I'm in a hurry, can you walk with me?'

Tanya nodded and fell into step with her, weaving around patients and porters headed in the opposite direction. 'I've been hoping to bump into you,' Tanya said. 'I was wondering how Rob was getting on, that soldier whose lungs I X-rayed.'

'Not good news,' Deb replied. 'Long way to go yet.'

Tanya nodded and looked down. "Not good news" would be the type of understatement used in the medical profession as an emotional buffer against the pain of the truth. Sometimes you had to care a little less to be able to cope.

Deb stopped by the doors to the lift and pressed the call button to go up. 'How's your dad been in the past few days?' she asked.

Tanya grimaced. 'Worse,' she said. 'He's decided to sell the house, says we need to move out of Birmingham.'

Deb frowned up at the illuminated number which indicated the lift was failing to move in their direction. 'When he says "we", I take it he expects you to go with him?'

'I'd have to. How could I not?'

'Can't you afford your own place?'

Tanya shrugged. 'Maybe. But I have to look after him. No-one else will.'

Deb jabbed the button several more times. 'There's only so much you can do for other people. I see soldiers like Rob all the time. Horrifically wounded and we patch them up and support their recovery, but ultimately they have to want to get better. They have to find some motivation to work with us.'

'I've come across a few of them doing sports or amazing physical feats to raise funds for charities.'

'Yep, motivation,' Deb said.

Tanya thought about this for a moment. 'Are you suggesting Dadda needs to motivate himself to get over the abuse, that maybe I'm being overprotective?'

A ping indicated the lift had arrived and Deb stepped forward as the doors slid open. 'Possibly,' she said. 'I really need to ...'

'I'll come with you.' Tanya joined her in the lift. 'I'm on a break. So, maybe moving house would be good for Dadda?'

Deb frowned. 'I doubt it, but look, I don't really know. I'm just working on the fact that you say he hasn't been himself since the incident so it's obviously affected him.'

'But why do you doubt it?' Tanya gazed at her friend, eager for information.

Deb took a deep breath. 'Tanya,' she said. Her voice was calm, measured.

Tanya put a hand to her mouth. 'I'm sorry. I'm being needy, aren't I?'

'You strike me as someone who's more than capable of making her own decisions, that's all. It seems like you're asking me to tell you what to do, but you don't really need me. You know something's wrong with your dad. You think he's overreacting to what's happened and you already know that moving house won't fix it. If you bury a traumatic experience, it'll only come back to haunt you.'

Tanya nodded. 'You're right.' She took a step backwards as the lift doors opened and more people joined them for the trip up through the floors of the hospital. A tense silence fell in which Tanya was certain everyone would be eavesdropping, so she lowered her voice and said, 'I guess I'm just used to being able to rely on his opinions.'

Deb nodded and glanced at her watch. 'I can't give you the answers instead,' she said. 'And, like I said, sometimes there is only so much you can do for other people. Put yourself first for once. How are things going with that man you were seeing?'

It wasn't only the lift coming to a halt which caused Tanya's stomach to lurch. She followed Deb out onto the fourth floor of the hospital, grateful that at least she didn't have to discuss this in front of a crowd. 'Things have been going really well. But that's bad, because he's leaving Birmingham. Tomorrow.

Deb stopped walking and placed a hand on Tanya's arm. 'I'm sorry to hear that. Look, I've got to run. But listen, maybe what happened on the bus wasn't the problem. Maybe it reminded your dad of something, or was the final straw in a chain of events.' She shrugged. 'We sometimes see with some of the patients we treat that their trauma is delayed. Soldiers come to us acting calm despite horrible experiences and then, weeks, months, perhaps even years later, something can trigger the emotional reaction you might have expected at the time. Maybe that isn't the case for your dad, and you can't force it, but if he will talk about things that's usually the best option. I'll see you around, OK?'

Tanya nodded and watched Deb hurry down the corridor. It looked exactly the same as the corridor they'd just left on the ground floor. The entire hospital was a functional box within which time of day, season and weather were meaningless. All that mattered was what role you played and hers was to look carefully and then diagnose. Deb was right, she should be applying those skills to her own life.

She turned and pressed the button to summon the lift, registering as she did so the thudding of a helicopter coming in to land outside. It explained why Deb had been in such a rush, she'd have been alerted to an incoming patient. Summoned to do her duty.

As Tanya waited she thought about the other thing Deb had said, that sometimes you have to put yourself first. Her priorities weren't in doubt: her desire to go to Chicago was not just to spend more time with Will, but also for the excitement of travelling to another country, another city, to meet new and different people. She blinked hard to dispel the tears self-pity brought to her eyes.

Dadda and Geena had to be her first priority. That was her duty. She'd have to force Dadda to talk to her.

Chapter Twelve

The only illumination in the room came from the screen of Tanya's laptop. She sat in bed and followed the airplane symbol for the flight which, on its repeat journey the following day, would carry Will back to New York where he'd pick up a connection to Chicago. BHX to JFK. JFK to ORD. Total journey time just under fourteen hours.

The icons on the screen had previously represented freedom and adventure, but that plane blinking on its way across her screen towards the Atlantic was now her enemy. As were both of Will's bosses: the one in America summoning him back, and the temporary manager here in Birmingham who'd insisted he work late on his last night in the city.

He'd called Tanya earlier to complain about this woman who'd demanded he complete some work before he left. He said it was nothing he couldn't do remotely once he was back in the US, but she'd insisted he finish it before leaving the country. The necessity for a good reference from her was the only thing which had persuaded him to do what she said rather than spending his final evening with Tanya. Only the fact that she was on call meant Tanya didn't push it.

Neither had wanted to say the word goodbye on the last evening they'd spent together. At the restaurant, after he broke the news he was leaving, she'd lost her appetite for any more food. They sat in silence while the waiter cleared their plates and turned down his suggestion they look at the dessert menu.

'Just the check, thanks,' Will said.

He'd paid, helped Tanya with her coat and held the door for her as they left. When they reached her car she asked, 'What now?' The only plan they'd made had been to go for the meal and with the atmosphere soured by disappointment she didn't know what to suggest.

He squeezed her hand. It had felt so natural to be holding hands with him that she hadn't even registered he'd taken it as they walked.

'Let's go somewhere we can talk,' he said.

Without any hesitation, she drove back to the house the company had rented for him, but the presence in the hall of his packed suitcase brought tears to her eyes.

He turned to her and saw her expression. 'I know,' he said and put his arm around her. 'I love my job, but right now I also hate it.'

'We've only just met,' she said, aware of the whine in her voice and not bothering to suppress it. 'I thought we had time.'

He didn't reply, but the increased pressure from his arm assured her he'd thought the same.

They stood like that for a moment then he let go and led her through to the kitchen. 'Come on, let me make you a proper English cup of tea.'

She sniffed and leant against the kitchen worktop while he filled the kettle. 'Indian, actually,' she said and pointed at the box of teabags. 'Darjeeling's in India.'

'Even more appropriate then.' He flicked the power switch then used his good arm to pull her towards him, lifting her hand and lacing his fingers through hers. 'Tonight I'll make you English tea and, one day, I'll take you to India to see the tea grown. I'm picturing blue skies, lush vegetation, bright saris and elephants, definitely elephants.'

'I can see it,' she said, caught up in his enthusiastic daydream. 'One day.'

'First though, I really would like you to come over to Chicago.'

She didn't reply but her mind raced over the idea. The logistics were feasible, the desire was there, but in reality, could she actually do it? Travel nearly four thousand miles to spend time with a man she knew so little? She closed her eyes and wished she were more impulsive, more like Geena. What if things didn't work out when she was there? What if, when surrounded by friends and family on his home turf, he behaved differently? What if this Emma woman he kept mentioning was more than just a friend of his?

She'd never left Britain. To travel so far for a relationship as yet so new would be a massive risk, not something she could commit to.

Risk-taking just wasn't in her nature. In every aspect of life she paused, checked, double-checked. But that night there wasn't time. It might be the last time she saw Will.

Tanya didn't need inspiration from her more dynamic sister to know there was one thing she needed to do. She extracted her fingers from his and stepped closer to embrace him instead. He returned her kiss and they both ignored the kettle coming to the boil.

When she had left his house just after midnight, too conscious of work the next day to stay any longer, neither stated the fact that they might not see each other again. Neither had mentioned it on the phone earlier either. The word "goodbye" was unnecessary and neither wanted to puncture their intimacy. But as she watched the plane move in incremental flickers across her screen, Tanya knew Will would be on it the next day while she might never make the trip.

It was too painful to keep watching the plane in the silence of her bedroom. She closed the browser window and instead opened a document containing an application to attend a training course in MRI scanning. She'd started filling in the form ages ago and needed to finish it this week. With the additional qualification from the specialist course, she'd be able to apply for other jobs, on higher grades, with larger salaries. With more money coming in, perhaps she'd be able to help Geena even more.

There'd be competition to get funding for the course though, so she needed to get this application right. She scrolled down and positioned the cursor in the next box she needed to complete. She paused.

If she'd mentioned this to him, she had no doubt Will would have been supportive. Career was his first priority and opportunities were not to be ignored. That was the attitude which had brought him to Birmingham.

She hadn't mentioned the course though. In all their conversations she'd said very little about herself, about her plans for the future and now realised it was because her ideas just weren't as concrete as his. Regardless of her dreams, family had to be her first priority. That was the promise she'd made her mother.

She could tell Will had tried to hide his disappointment that she wouldn't commit to visiting him in America. He'd frowned but stopped pushing her for a response, hesitated when she changed the subject, but allowed her to do it. If this was where their relationship ended, it had been her choice, not his. She wasn't happy with that realisation, but couldn't afford the risk of any other option.

She typed half-hearted answers to the remaining questions on the application form. The easy bit was summarising her experience so far, after that, her fingers hovered above the keyboard as she tried to compose a suitable response about why the course would benefit her, what she'd bring back to the job. She entered a couple of bullet points, clicked save, and gave it up for the evening.

On her way to the bathroom she heard Dadda switch off the television downstairs. He'd been watching a film when she got in from the late shift at work and she hadn't tried to speak to him beyond letting him know she was home. He'd nodded and turned straight back to the screen despite the fact he never normally had time for romantic comedies. He'd seemed engrossed in that one.

Now, she paused on the landing and waited for him to climb the stairs. Thinking of Deb's suggestion that she should get him to talk, Tanya asked, 'How are you feeling?'

'Fine,' he replied and paused with one foot on the final tread.

Aware that her position above him on the landing could appear threatening, Tanya slouched against the wall to make herself look shorter. He stayed where he was.

'You didn't go out with your new friend tonight then?' he asked.

Tanya frowned. 'No.'

'You were out so late with him last night I assumed things had become serious between you.'

She felt her cheeks flush hot with the embarrassment of talking about a boyfriend with him. It wasn't a situation she was used to.

'Serious?' she said. 'I've been on three dates with him. I like him a lot, but ...'

Dadda interrupted. 'You're not like Geena. I know you wouldn't have seen him so often if you didn't find him interesting, but it worries me.'

Her mouth dropped open. The pain of letting Will go was a raw wound she didn't want to probe, and here was Dadda suddenly taking an interest in her love life, pointing out how much more successful with men her sister was, and then trying to intervene. She leapt to Will's defence. 'He's a great guy, not that it matters, because ....'

'Appearances can deceive,' Dadda said, interrupting again and finally taking the last step up to the landing. 'People are not what they seem and your gentle nature means you always want to find the good in them. Believe me, you must be careful.'

Tanya shook her head at the madness of having to talk about Will when she was trying to avoid thinking about him, when he was really not the biggest issue she had to discuss with Dadda. 'Will's going back to America,' she said. She couldn't look at Dadda's face, but she didn't need to see his reaction to this news because he spoke immediately.

'Ah, good. That's good. Things were moving too quickly, I felt. You were with him too much, too soon.'

Tanya gaped. 'Good?' she said. Her attempt to keep from shouting made her voice hard, her words clipped. 'It happened too quickly?' Was Dadda actually referring to whether or not she'd slept with Will? It was none of his business. Her shoulders slumped even lower and she choked back tears. Wasn't as if it was likely to happen again.

'You have always been the sensible one, Tanya. I know I can rely on you.' Dadda passed her and pushed open the bathroom door.

'No,' Tanya said, and stood up straight. 'I am sensible, but that doesn't mean you can assume I'll always do what you think is the appropriate thing. I have to think about my career. And I have to think about my life.'

She turned away, grabbed her handbag from her room and raced down the stairs and out to her car dialling Will's number from her mobile as she moved. He'd be back at the rented house by now. He hadn't left the country yet.

*

'It's definitely not that I want to leave,' Geena said to Mr Davis as she delivered his first mug of tea of the morning. 'But you've been so good about giving me opportunities that I wanted to warn you I might have to go. If we do move house, I probably won't be able to afford to commute here, if it's even possible to.'

While her instinct had been to ignore what Dadda was doing, she knew that she owed Mr Davis more than that. He'd given her a chance when no-one else had. She'd only suffer from guilt if she didn't let him know the situation, and the truth might also delay any ideas he had about making her redundant as well. She'd worked conscientiously in the past few days, charming the customers and giving the entire store a thorough clean, but still kicked herself for that one slip where he'd caught her working on her own ideas.

Mr Davis didn't look up from the inner workings of the faulty carriage clock in front of him, although he hadn't touched it in several minutes. With his cheek scrunched up to hold his eyeglass in place, she couldn't even read a reaction from his expression.

'And I can't afford to rent anywhere,' she continued. 'I promise I'm not complaining, just being realistic. You know.'

Finally, he rocked the clock backwards onto the soft cloth padding he'd prepared, removed the eyeglass and looked at her. 'I would be sorry to lose you,' he said. 'I suppose I'm fortunate you've stayed so long. I know you have ambitions rather bigger than this.' His gesture took in not only the limitations of the shop, but also the mug steaming beside him.

Geena pursed her lips. She'd tried to conceal her boredom with the work he gave her, tried not to reveal her frustration. He was a nice bloke, after all and the customers were generally a sweet bunch; but apparently he'd seen through her.

'I do like it here,' she said. 'I've learnt a lot from you.'

He nodded and she turned away as the ding of the street door opening caught her attention.

'Hey, Geena,' Will said. He wiped his feet on the doormat and propped his dripping umbrella into the stand placed by the door for that purpose before crossing the shop towards her. 'Sorry I couldn't come in sooner.'

She smiled; the anguish he was causing Tanya wasn't his fault, after all and he looked tired. 'No problem,' she said and went to the safe to retrieve his watch. She spread a leather pad on the glass surface of the counter and laid the watch on top. 'Good as new,' she said.

'Wow.' He reached out with his index finger to stroke the gleaming glass face. 'I barely recognise it.'

'We didn't fit a new strap.' Geena tilted the watch and showed him the leather which had been scuffed by his fall. 'But I can do it right now if you'd prefer?'

He shook his head. 'No, leave it. Then I won't just have a reminder of Gramps when I check the time; I'll think of Birmingham as well.'

'Anything in particular about Birmingham?'

He wrinkled his forehead and clenched the hand resting on the counter into a fist. 'You know I mean Tanya. I wish I'd had longer to get to know her. For her to get to know me. Feels like a massive missed opportunity. The last two weeks, well, meeting her has been ...' His words trailed off.

Geena stared at the second hand counting its way around the watch face. She didn't know what to say. Tanya's tears when she'd revealed that Will was leaving had shocked Geena. Tanya always remained calm and in control. Tanya was the one who picked up the pieces, who found the solutions, who fixed things. Now Tanya was not only desperately sad about Will leaving, but also lost for what to do about Dadda.

Geena had no words of comfort to offer her sister, let alone Will. She could only wish things were different. Tanya deserved better.

They both silently regarded his watch on the counter while the ticking from the clocks around the shop marked the time passing.

'Anyway,' he said, breaking the silence, 'I should go. Few things to finish up at the office then I'm off to the airport. What do I owe you?'

Geena took his credit card and processed the payment with no words other than those required for the transaction. As he still couldn't wear the watch on his injured wrist, she packed it into a box and slipped that into a small carrier bag. 'I usually ask customers to keep us in mind for anything else they might need,' she said, 'but ...'

He finished her sentence, 'I guess I might not be coming back.'

'She's going to miss you.'

He had to clear his throat before he could reply. 'I'm going to miss her.'

Geena nodded. 'We might not be around here much longer ourselves.'

He raised a questioning eyebrow and she gave him an outline of Dadda's decision and how it would affect her and Tanya.

'That sucks,' he said and frowned. 'She didn't mention it last night.'

'You got to see each other last night?' Geena smiled. At least Tanya had made the most of the remaining time they'd had, and it meant she needn't apologise for hiding out in her bedroom all evening either. They'd both needed some time away from Dadda and Geena hadn't had anywhere better to go.

She'd really begun to miss the constant chatter of her friends and had put a DVD on with the volume turned up through her headphones to drown out the silence left by a lack of message alerts. 'Everything about the house escalated into a row,' she told Will. 'Probably the last thing Tanya needed really.'

'She told me before that she was concerned about your dad. Maybe ...' He reached for the carrier, folded it around the box and slipped it into the messenger bag he wore slung over his shoulder. 'Well, maybe I don't know enough about it.'

He sounded frustrated, as though he'd like to help but was powerless to do anything.

'It's OK,' Geena said, 'our problem, not yours.'

'Hmm, well, listen, would you do me one favour?'

'Of course.' She flicked her hair back and put on her best sales voice. 'How may I be of service?'

He took an envelope from his bag. 'This is for Tanya. Can I trouble you to play postie?'

Geena took it from him. Despite being a brown A4 envelope which he'd most likely picked up at work, the package bulged. It obviously contained a present.

'Any message with it?' she asked.

'There's a letter inside. I didn't know what to say, but I hope I said something right.'

Chapter Thirteen

Tanya was trying to not think about the fact Will would be checking in for his flight at that moment. She needed all her attention for the patient in front of her, a white man in his fifties with a knee injury she needed to X-ray. The task would be easier if he were capable of listening to her instructions.

'It's this side,' he said and pointed to the right of the swollen joint. 'That's where the pain is.'

'Yes, but I need a complete review of your knee. That pain may be masking other problems. Please lie back and keep your leg at this angle.'

He tutted and she turned her back on him to head to the control room. Once there she double-checked he had done as she asked before firing the image. She took a deep breath in and exhaled it all through pursed lips as she reviewed the picture. Irritating patients appeared at a rate of several a day. Judging them or letting them annoy her wouldn't help.

'OK,' she said as she went back to him. 'Now the other side.'

He folded his arms. 'Just like I said, eh?' There was a sneer on his face and she fought to keep her expression neutral.

'No, as I said, a full review of the joint, meaning all sides.'

'Huh, are you sure you know what you're doing? Bet you didn't even do your training here. Did you buy the certificate online?'

Preserving her neutral expression became more difficult. 'Just turn your leg this way, please. And hold very still.' There was no need to justify herself to this idiot.

'You come over here,' he went on, 'taking jobs from Brits and you don't even know what you're doing.'

She walked away. It was far from the first time she'd heard this kind of nonsense. No point talking to him. Her only motivation was to get the job done.

'Hold still,' she said and took the final image. The diagnosis was straightforward and she quickly typed up a couple of lines to support the pictures.

Medical staff had been known, in the past, to add acronyms to patient notes to summarise sensitive details of the patient's history, or to warn each other about difficult people. The code UBI signified 'Unexplained Beer Injury' and advised colleagues that there was no point questioning further. Tanya had never been tempted to indulge, especially knowing it would be a disciplinary offence these days if the acronyms were found, but her fingers paused over the keyboard this time. Now she had first-hand experience of the effect the hurtful comments made by ignorant wastes of space like this man had on hard-working and sensitive people like Dadda.

In her own experience, adults behaved far worse than children. There'd been a mix of races, genders and nationalities at the school she and Geena attended and it had never been an issue; all the kids played nicely together. During her radiology training it had been the same. But, since starting work at the hospital, the amount of casual racism and sexism she and her colleagues experienced meant the comments, taunts and outright insults had to become a laughing matter. The hospital couldn't continue to function if only the white British staff turned up for work or if the racially diverse employees took offence at every incident.

She paused with her fingers hovering over the keys of her computer. It must surely have been like that for Dadda as well, he must have heard jibes about race or religion in the past. The incident on the bus had been deliberately cruel rather than casual, thoughtless comments, but it wasn't on the scale of the racist violence which had made local news headlines over the years. Dadda's response really was disproportionate. She'd have to get to the bottom of it.

She finished her notes, resisting the temptation to mark the man down as an OPD - Obnoxious Personality Disorder - and sent him back to the clinic. Her shift was nearly over.

*

She was back home lying on her bed, trying not to think about Will, when Geena put her head round the door.

'Got something for you,' Geena said.

'Oh?' Tanya replied, hoping it wasn't another problem.

Geena came in to the room, pushed Tanya's feet out of the way and sat down on the end of the bed before she handed over a brown envelope.

'What's this?' Tanya asked. It was addressed to her in blue ink, but she didn't recognise the handwriting.

'It's from Will.'

Tanya sat up and turned the envelope around in her hands. Its softness and weight suggested it contained a wad of papers.

'Open it then,' Geena said.

'I will. When you've gone.'

Geena sighed and left. Tanya ran a fingertip over her name, tracing the strokes of Will's pen along the letters. He'd be in the air now, although she'd deliberately not looked at the computer to check on the flight. She couldn't bear to see the symbol of the plane carrying him away, or worse, to potentially hear news that his flight was the one in a million, the plane she feared, the one which didn't reach its destination.

She hadn't expected to hear from him, not until he'd had time to land and catch up with friends, family, work and whatever else might distract him from emailing her, if he even remembered to contact her at all. But now there was this.

She slid her finger under the flap and opened the envelope. Inside was a sheaf of papers, with a letter clipped to the front. She pulled herself backwards on the bed and propped her pillows behind her to read. He'd written:

Dear Tanya,

It's years since I wrote an actual letter so consider yourself privileged. Though, actually that's how I feel. Privileged to have met you. I was looking forward to being in Birmingham because I thought it would be good for my career. Well, maybe that hasn't worked out so well but I got something better - my time with you.

I totally understand why you were hesitant when I hassled you about coming over to Chicago. How do you know you can trust me, right? We've known each other all of five minutes. But the invitation is there and I'm going to be repeating it.

I thought about getting you flowers to say thank you for showing me some of your city and for just being you. But, well, it wasn't enough. It wasn't right for you. I hope the enclosed is better.

The one thing I really wanted to say was - even if it seems we've only known each other for five minutes, I want to know more. I'll be in touch.

With love,

Will x

Tanya rested the letter on her legs and tried to swallow to soothe the burning sensation in her throat. Reading his words had been like having Will there, speaking to her; she could practically hear his deep-toned voice and the unfamiliar stresses in pronunciation that were part of his accent. The ache in her throat was evidence of how much she already missed him.

She pulled the letter out from the paper clip to reveal what he'd attached it to. The remaining papers were a set of A3 pages, each folded in half and stapled into a sheet which wrapped around them like the cover of a book. On this front page Will had written in a green pen the words "For Tanya: The World" above an image of the globe, tilted on its axis to show Europe facing out. Next to it was a picture of a plane which he'd obviously cut and pasted from a different set of stock imagery and struggled to scale alongside the planet. It looked as though it was blasting off into space rather than carrying passengers to a different country. Tanya pressed the tip of her index finger to the plane and smiled.

She opened to the first folded sheet and discovered he'd printed an outline map of Australasia onto the page and decorated it with lots of images including koalas and crocodiles. He'd placed pictures of the Sydney Harbour Bridge and Uluru in roughly the correct locations and added signposts such as "This way to the Great Barrier Reef" and labels like "Outback". The map was titled "G'day from Down Under" and Will had attached a sticky note to the page which read: "An Atlas for Tanya to plot her travels. I look forward to hearing from her how bad my map-making skills are. W x".

She laughed out loud. He must have spent hours in the office making the atlas when he should have been finishing his work that morning. The proof that he'd had as much trouble keeping her off his mind as she'd had trying not to think about him put a grin on her face. She turned the other pages and found maps for Asia, South America and Africa, all annotated like the first one with pictures and signposts. Another page had outlines of both the Arctic and Antarctic with a penguin stood by a signpost which read: "Not so much worth looking at here. Also, very cold".

The penultimate map was of Europe and in addition to photos such as the Eiffel Tower, the Acropolis and a sun lounger pasted over southern Spain, Will had marked the approximate location of Birmingham with a large cross and a label stating: "Rare treasure found here".

Tanya gulped and turned to the final page which featured an outline of North America. Pictures also adorned this, but they were smaller than on the other maps so that the Statue of Liberty, Grand Canyon and Golden Gate Bridge were dwarfed by a giant heart centred over where Chicago should have been. Within the heart, Will had handwritten the words, "Tanya needed here".

She closed the pages and pushed the atlas away, afraid that her falling tears would spoil it. He'd been right, his hand-made present was far better than flowers could ever be. It was the best, the most personal present she'd received since her mum had patted the watch newly fastened around Tanya's wrist. She wiped her eyes and traced a fingertip around the watch face.

'Oh, Mum,' she murmured, 'what should I do?'

She'd been unable to relax in Will's bed the previous night, both in fear that she'd be called to attend an emergency at work and upset about the argument with Dadda. Now Will was gone, but he'd changed her.

He'd given her more reason to travel, good reason. Reason enough to overcome her anxiety about flying and leap on the next plane to Chicago. But she couldn't abandon Dadda. She had to speak to him and apologise. She had to make him speak to her.

Geena yelled, 'Dinner's ready,' up the stairs and Tanya blew her nose and went to join them.

She helped Geena with the plates and took her usual seat to Dadda's right at the table. He nodded to her without actually catching her eye. They hadn't spoken since she'd stormed out when he'd said he was glad Will was leaving.

'Dadda,' she said, 'I'm sorry if I was rude to you last night.'

Geena looked between the two of them, obviously intrigued by what she'd missed.

'It's all right,' Dadda replied. 'I think I understand how you felt. But you must also understand that I know best for you, that I want what's best for you both.'

Tanya swallowed hard. How could someone who hadn't even left the house in nearly a fortnight possibly know what was for the best? Before she'd decided how to respond, Geena said, 'You are brilliant at looking after us, Dadda, but we both know Tanya's the brains of this operation, don't we?'

Tanya raised her eyebrows as she caught her sister's eye. It wasn't like Geena to be the peacemaker. But Geena had flattered Dadda into a position where he had to agree with her.

'Of course,' he said, 'just like your mother.' He glanced at Tanya with a quick smile and continued eating in silence.

'Anyway, Tan,' Geena said, 'you know that loan we talked about?'

So that was what Geena was up to with the flattery. She was still on about her jewellery project. Tanya didn't make it easy for her. 'Loan?' she said.

'Just a small one, only for materials. You can see the business plan if you like.'

Tanya sighed. She probably did owe Geena a favour. Without her, Will would have flitted through her life as just another patient, albeit one of the more pleasant ones. 'Tell me again how much,' she said.

Geena grinned. 'Best sister in the world,' she said. 'I think we agreed on five hundred.'

Chapter Fourteen

Exhausted by her day of emotional extremes, Tanya joined Dadda in the living room and flopped onto the sofa with her legs outstretched. Geena had sloped off to her bedroom. Again. Tanya wanted nothing more than to collapse into bed and sleep rather than worry about Geena's personality transplant and Dadda's problems, but knew they had to discuss it sometime so she brought up the subject of the house.

'Have you heard anything from the estate agent?' she asked.

Dadda shifted in his seat but didn't look at her. 'Not yet. He said it would be on the website by the end of the week, in time for people to see it if they look this weekend.'

'Did he think there'd be a lot of interest?'

'Hmm. He's a sales man, of course he sold it to me that there would be, though maybe not as much as if I'd waited until the spring. We'll see.'

Tanya nodded and stared unseeing at the TV for a moment. 'And what about looking for a new place, what are you thinking about that?'

'I've been considering some options, no decisions so far.'

The calm discussion couldn't have been more different from the strong opinions aired last time the topic had been raised. Tanya was already wrung out. She didn't want to start another argument with her dad. She wanted something to go smoothly.

'You need to talk to us about it, Dadda. This affects me and Geena too. I'm really settled here with my job and everything. Mum always said it was a great hospital to work at.' She paused, wondering if mentioning her mum was wise in the circumstances. The family usually skirted around references to her, made each other aware she was on their minds, while never actually starting a conversation about her. Deciding it was too late, Tanya went on, 'Isn't the hospital the reason you came to Birmingham in the first place?'

'One reason. And I've been thinking about that,' he replied. 'You really are so like your mother, her job was almost everything to her, after us of course. Geena is right that you make intelligent decisions. I have to accept that you may not come with us wherever we move but obviously I would like you to. It would be better for the family to stay together.'

'Us? You mean you think Geena will go with you?'

He shrugged. 'What else can she do?'

It was a good point. Geena contributed almost nothing to the household expenses yet was still always broke. Unless Tanya took her sister in, she'd be forced to stay with Dadda. And while Tanya earned a decent salary, enough to have savings which would fund the loan for Geena to start making her jewellery designs, entirely supporting her sister wasn't something she could budget for. And why should she?

She'd need to think it all through. Being left alone in Birmingham didn't feel as though she was being granted her freedom. It felt more like being abandoned. And that wasn't the only problem.

'But Dadda, Mum asked me to look after you. You're right that the family were her first priority and she wanted us to stick together. She'd want me to stay near you. Is it really so important to move away?'

He nodded and turned to look at her. 'Geena was still a child when your mum died. So were you, really. But you're an adult now and your mum would be proud of you. You should not feel you have to look after me. She would have said that you have to make your own way, find your own place.'

Tanya blinked. That wasn't what her mum had actually said. She'd left Tanya with very specific instructions. She sighed. 'I don't know what my own way or my own place would look like,' she said. It was true and the realisation appalled her. 'I don't know where I want to be. I don't even know where I come from.' Her voice cracked and she blinked quickly to hold back her tears as she said, 'I don't feel British, or Indian. I know I was born here but I don't know where you're from, or Mum, or any other family. You never talk about the past.'

He chewed on his bottom lip as he watched her. Finally, he said, 'Delhi,' then paused. 'Both families from Delhi but we left there in 1984 and have not been back. You're from here, Tanya. The past has no influence on you.'

Tanya nodded. She really didn't feel at all Indian the majority of the time. Until an idiot like the patient she'd X-rayed earlier brought it up. Then she felt that disconnect, that she wasn't entirely British but couldn't lay claim to anything else. She envied Will his certainty that Chicago was the place to be and felt choked by a confusing mix of emotions, chief among which was the fact that she really missed her mum. She sniffed.

'Why did Mum choose to come here for hospital work? It's not the only big hospital. You could have gone anywhere in the world, or stayed in India,' she said. She realised how strange it was that she'd never asked for details before, that Dadda had never spoken about it, always

147

changed the subject if she or Geena had made any reference to their parents' life before they'd married and come to Britain.

His tone of voice had always indicated that the subject was closed, their presence in Birmingham accepted, a given, a fact not to be queried. Family conversations were always about the present or the future, never the past. Even since their mum died. Especially since then. But her mum's career had brought them, of all the cities in the world, to Birmingham.

The fact he didn't answer immediately only increased her curiosity.

'Dadda?' she prompted. He sat facing the TV but with his eyes closed. She noticed he'd clenched the hand he'd rested on the arm of his chair into a fist. 'Are you OK?'

His mouth opened and closed a couple of times as though he couldn't commit to actually speaking. Then he opened his eyes, leant forward and hit the power button on the remote. The chatter of voices from the TV died.

'Your mother and I,' he said, his voice slow as though each word had to be chosen with care, 'we came to Birmingham to put so many things behind us, things which I thought should be forgotten. She and I agreed on that.'

He paused and Tanya found she was holding her breath, anxious not to break his concentration. She sat up and faced him.

He dipped his head in a sharp nod. 'Perhaps you should hear though,' he said. 'Perhaps you need to understand your history to be able to see your way forward. Maybe you won't understand why I cannot tolerate what is happening here until you know why we came.'

It wasn't as though he was addressing her directly, more like he was debating things with himself. Tanya was reminded of the months after her mum died when she'd hear Dadda's voice in their bedroom late at night, talking as though his wife were still there to reply.

She swallowed down the lump which had formed in her throat and prompted, 'Tell me, Dadda. I'd like to know.'

His posture altered as he straightened his back, lifted his chin and glanced at the silver-framed wedding photograph on the mantelpiece. The picture had a grainy blurriness which neither disguised the couple's dated hairstyles, nor concealed the seriousness of their expressions. Geena had always laughed at the formality of it.

'I served in the Indian Army, Punjab Regiment,' he said. 'For fourteen years it was my job and I questioned nothing. I was born into an independent India, but things were never peaceful. Always there was some fighting somewhere over land, government, religion. I only ever believed that we should serve the best interests of India herself; not fight among ourselves or with our neighbours.' He drew in a deep breath and glanced briefly at Tanya. 'But my family were Sikh; I was Sikh and we are a proud people. Some felt we should have our own homeland in the Punjab, as the Muslims had in Pakistan after Partition. The government was led by Hindus and they had different ideas.'

Tanya bit her lip to keep silent as he paused again. She was increasingly appalled that she'd never taken any interest in Indian history. Words such as independence and partition meant little to her. They were words from history, they resonated with a story she didn't know.

Dadda nodded again, as though he'd come to a decision about something. 'There is a Sikh holy shrine, the Golden Temple at Amritsar. In 1984 the Indian Army attacked it, to capture Sikhs they believed were plotting a separatist revolt. Rumours spread, news was patchy. All I heard was that many people were killed, innocent people only there for worship.'

Tanya gasped. 'That's awful. Why would they hurt innocent people?'

Dadda was silent for a long moment and Tanya feared he wouldn't tell her any more. She wanted to prompt him

149

again, but didn't want to distract him. Eventually, he spoke again, his voice unnaturally calm.

'Lies are still told. The truth of that decision may never be known but afterwards, everything changed. I did know Sikhs who wanted our own homeland, but many more like me who wanted only to be Indian, until we were attacked like that. Tensions grew, many Sikhs I knew deserted the army and the prime minister was assassinated, killed by her Sikh bodyguards.'

He fell silent again and Tanya leant forward to touch his arm. 'What about you, Dadda? What did you do?'

He didn't look at her as he shook his head. 'What could I do? I knew nothing but army life but how could I continue to follow orders? And then ...'

Tanya couldn't bear his hesitation. Her fingers closed around his wrist. 'What?'

'Then I heard what was happening back in Delhi. What they were doing to the place where I grew up, where my parents and siblings still lived.' He nodded. 'At that I left the army. I went to Delhi to see these things for myself.'

The silence buzzed in Tanya's ears as he paused for another intolerable moment. 'What, Dadda?' she asked. 'Who was doing what?'

He squeezed his eyes even tighter shut as though that would block out the images in his mind. 'Hindus were killing Sikhs: riots in which thousands died in retribution for the assassination. Sanctioned by the government. Nothing done to stop them and the police turned a blind eye.'

Tanya's mouth dropped open. 'Surely not?' she said, but knew her reaction was inadequate. She could tell from Dadda's expression and blank tone of voice that he was telling the truth. There was no hyperbole, only the facts as he had seen them. She shivered with a premonition that the story would only get worse.

'I arrived in Delhi and went to the street of my father's house. There was nothing there. Everything was burned.' His voice had become constricted with emotion.

'Oh, Dadda,' Tanya said and dropped to the floor to kneel by his chair from where she could reach to cup his clenched fist in her hands.

'I asked people what they knew, if there was any chance ... They told me to leave, to go while I could. These were neighbours, people I had known and they would not help me. I went towards the hospital thinking perhaps I would find my people there, perhaps they were only injured, but I didn't make it. A mob grabbed me, beat me, left me bleeding in the street.'

Tanya gripped his knee. The agony of seeing his face wet with tears made her nauseous with impotence. How could he have kept this from her? And the way he talked about it - so measured and direct - as though he'd rehearsed the words but never spoken them, preferring to bear the truth alone. He should have trusted her. She mumbled his name again.

Dadda unclenched his fists and lifted her hand in his. 'Your mother saved me. She found me and took me back to her family's home. They hid me and she nursed me. They were a Hindu family but the violence appalled them. They were not anti-Sikh; not at first.'

Tanya laced her fingers into his. 'What happened?'

A fleeting smile brightened his face. 'I fell in love with your mother, their kind, bright, beautiful daughter. You know I was sixteen years older than her, well, the age difference would have been no trouble to them had I been suitable in other ways. Marriage in India is not only about love. But I was an army deserter, I had no family now, no work, no money and anyway, I was Sikh. All that was not acceptable to them. They didn't understand that I would do anything for her as she had done for me.'

'So you came here?'

He nodded. 'We both came. I had lost everything but your mother gave everything up to come with me. It was her vocation which brought us together, which brought us here. She came for me, not for the hospital. Birmingham was just a place I hoped we'd be safe. She was the bravest woman, the bravest.'

Tanya gulped shallow breaths through the tears she couldn't hold back any longer. 'I know,' she said. 'She was.'

Dadda sniffed, sat back and patted Tanya's hands. 'Now you know why we have no past, why I always told you there is nothing to go back to. Our little family is the only thing which matters. I promised your mother I would keep you girls safe.'

'And I promised her I'd look after you,' Tanya said.

He shook his head and placed a hand on her cheek. 'Ah, Tanya, you are truly her daughter. But that's why I see that I have to let you choose. I don't wish to stay where there is hatred or violence. I cannot live with these things but you have to make your own choice.'

Tanya nodded. 'I see that, Dadda. I understand,' she said.

But there was no choice. It was obvious she'd have to continue down the path her mother had started.

Chapter Fifteen

Geena scuffed her feet through the piles of fallen leaves as she crossed Bournville Green from the bus stop down towards the parade of shops. She hadn't lied to Mr Davis, she really would miss working there. The entire suburb had a quaint, calm atmosphere. It gave her a sense of being grounded, as though she had a place in history and that her work, with its values of beauty and quality, was worth something.

The sense of perspective was what she needed. Bored of waiting for her friend to back down, Geena had given in to what had become an overwhelming sense of shame and texted an apology to Jude the night before. There'd been no reply.

As she reached the shop, she could see Mr Davis had already arrived, but not yet drawn up the security shutters and the display cabinets in the windows remained empty. It was her daily task to make an enticing display and she loved to trick passers-by with changes and unexpected items.

More than once someone had knocked on the window to get her attention and given a thumbs up in response to a joke or comment on current affairs she'd included. Like the time she'd cut out a headline from the local paper about the opening of the new Library of Birmingham and displayed it alongside a set of silver bangles placed to echo the design of the loops of steel which adorned the building.

As she opened the door she gulped down the disappointment she felt at the realisation that she might not be there to complete some of the ideas she'd already dreamt up for Christmas. Dadda was right: she had no alternative but to follow him to wherever he made their new home.

'Ah, Geena.'

She forced a smile onto her face. 'Morning, Mr Davis.'

'If you can bear to break from our routine, I'd like to suggest something different for today,' he said.

Geena tried not to let her surprise show on her face. 'Of course, what's up?' she said.

'I thought we'd delay opening for a couple of hours and take a trip up to Hockley. I have something I'd like to run by you.'

She frowned. Changes to their routine were unheard of. Mr Davis's life ran with the same reliable predictability as the workings of his clocks. But he'd written a note to stick in the window explaining that the shop would be opening later today because of "staff training". There weren't any staff, only Geena, and she wouldn't be there much longer.

'Whatever you say,' she replied.

He locked the door behind them and led the way to his car. While the rush hour and school-run traffic had cleared, the roads were still busy and he didn't speak as he drove, obviously concentrating on the task in hand. Geena's mind wandered. She'd loitered in her room for most of the previous evening and seen neither Dadda nor Tanya.

She admitted to herself that she'd acted cheerful when she was with them and avoided them afterwards. She had almost been able to hear Tanya's voice telling her sister to make the apology to Jude a good one. Dadda really didn't need to know the details of what his youngest daughter had done.

Tanya must have been on an early shift as she'd gone by the time Geena got up that morning. It was probably for the best. Of course she was worried about Dadda with the whole not-going-out thing and now wanting to move, and of course she felt bad for Tanya with Will leaving, but her own plans were being messed with as well.

While it was great Tanya had agreed to the loan so she could get her collection off the ground, moving to a new place meant she'd have to find different suppliers and think of alternative places where she could sell her work. It was a big setback.

She paid more attention to their surroundings as they arrived in Hockley, the centre of Birmingham's jewellery trade. They drove past the new buildings of the School of Jewellery where Geena had studied. She gazed into the large windows of the extension linking the Victorian buildings to the more modern annexe and felt envious of the freedom enjoyed by the students working inside. They could try anything. They hadn't failed yet.

Mr Davis slowed down and pulled into a parking space in a side street.

'Are we picking up supplies?' Geena asked. She'd checked their stock the previous day and hadn't thought there was anything they needed.

'No, picking up ideas,' he replied.

She fell into step beside him as they walked onto the main road where many of the small jewellers' premises clustered. Each of the shop fronts lining the street had a showcase window featuring their particular specialism, from diamond rings to watches. Others carried a more general stock but aimed at different sectors of the market by offering traditional products or a more artisan experience.

'Ideas for what?' Geena asked.

'These people,' he gestured to indicate the shops they were passing, 'are our competition.'

'Not entirely,' she interrupted.

'No?'

'No. I mean, we don't compete for the same customers. People travel here for a particular experience, don't they?

Like going to Antwerp for diamonds. Most people come here for the destination as much as the product. It's like we're not competing with the big name high street jewellers, either. We're offering a local service.'

'Yes, you're right. Our customers are mostly local. But the reason I've brought you here is to ask this: why does a customer go into one of these shops rather than the one next door?'

Geena smiled. 'OK, well, imagine a man looking to buy a present for his wife. Maybe he's bought her jewellery before. In which case, as long as he thinks she liked what he chose, he'll probably go back to the same shop. Repeat custom, we get a lot of that. You can't buy loyal customers, you can only build them.'

Mr Davis nodded. 'What about a woman though, maybe someone who wants to treat herself?'

'Then it's about what the look of the shop says and whether that ties in with how she sees herself. Is it as stylish, individual, as classy as her, or maybe she wants something kooky or gothic, then she'll be looking for a different type of specialist.'

'I see, and what does my shop say?'

Geena pressed her lips together and arranged a thoughtful expression on her face. The first words which came to mind weren't entirely complimentary and she didn't want to offend him by suggesting old-fashioned, staid or dusty. The shop wasn't actually dusty, she made sure of that. It did have an air of decay though.

The shops here were at least freshly painted even if most of them were also painfully traditional. Finally she had to speak. 'Well, it does say quality. People know they can trust us.'

'Yes, which breeds these loyal customers you mentioned. But we have very few new customers. What I want to know is how we could tempt more people in. What they've got which we haven't.' As he spoke, a couple who'd been studying the window display of the shop to their right had decided to go inside. 'If that couple leave without spending money, then there's something wrong. But they got the couple through the door in the first place.'

'There's less passing trade in Bournville,' Geena said.

He pursed his lips and nodded. 'So how do we make ourselves a destination?'

Geena felt she was back at school and faced with a test she hadn't revised for. She shook her head, flattered that he'd asked her opinion but with no immediate response to his question.

'I apologise,' he said, 'I'm putting you on the spot. Come on, let me buy us some coffee and I'll explain what I'm after.'

There was a small café on the street corner, its windows littered with handwritten signs on neon star-shaped cards which advertised a range of breakfast deals. Geena took a seat while he went to the counter to order. By the time he came back, she'd worked out how to answer his question.

'Bournville already is a destination,' she said, 'but not because of us. People come from outside to visit the chocolate factory or Selly Manor, they even travel for the garden centre. What we need to do is tap into that traffic. Stand out somehow and give people a reason to come through the door.'

He smiled and placed a cup in front of her. 'Such as?'

'Well, there's already a café and newsagent on the parade so those types of impulse visits are covered. We need to be intriguing enough to stop people in their tracks.' She lifted her drink and sipped the coffee as she thought.

He waited in silence.

'The local angle,' she said eventually. 'Stock locally-made products, not only jewellery perhaps. You know how people are into farmers' markets, craft markets, that sort of thing? Well, we find the best local craftspeople, the very best, and stock their work. A few paintings or ceramics - there's loads of people doing that sort of thing locally - and a selection of high quality designer-made jewellery.

'We take commission on each product, act as a hub for other local businesses and give customers a constant place to shop so they don't have to wait for the third Sunday or whenever the market comes round. They can buy whenever they want to and our stock is all great quality.' She remembered Tanya's dismissive attitude to craft markets. 'And it's not useless tat, but desirable items. We'll source the very best Birmingham has to offer.'

'Would that really work? I'm not sure I like the idea of having such diverse stock in the shop. Clock and watch repairs have to remain a key part of the business.'

'Of course.' Geena nodded and didn't remind him that the amount of income generated by his favourite part of the job was dwindling. 'But here's the clever bit. We only run very short contracts with each person. We stock their products for maybe three to six months so they get exposure and tell everyone they know that we exist. We run loads of social media advertising all the new stuff, and then, next month: all change. All new promotional material and a new audience of customers to tap in to.'

He put his cup down and raised his eyebrows. 'Social media?'

'Don't worry, I could do all that, I mean ...' She stopped and looked into the cold dregs at the bottom of her cup. She couldn't do that. Not if she wasn't there anymore. The idea had run away with her imagination and the realisation that she was supplying ideas for him rather than them was a chill disappointment.

'Yes,' he said, 'you could.'

Her shoulders drooped. 'I really wish I could. But it's very unlikely I'll be able to stay.'

'Which is what I wanted to discuss with you. I'd like to offer you a promotion, Geena, with consequent increase in salary of course and an option to rent the flat above the premises for a nominal fee as I'd expect you to increase your hours, take on a business development project, administer our, um, social media, and, perhaps, if you'd like to, supply some of your own designs to sell in the shop.'

Geena blinked several times and her mouth dropped open. 'Really?' she managed to say. 'You really want to do that for me?'

He smiled. 'Yes. I believe the time is right.'

*

Tanya slumped into a seat in the staff canteen and rubbed her eyes. After talking late into the night with Dadda and finally persuading him to go to bed in the early hours, she'd been unable to sleep herself. She couldn't stop thinking about his story of what had happened all those years ago in Delhi.

It was horrific to think about, but compelling as well as unnerving that the people involved weren't strangers. They were people she loved and an extended family she ought to have had the opportunity to meet. She conjured violent images, pictured the horror of the bloodshed, and could completely understand how recent events had brought those terrible days back to torment Dadda. The desire to hide or to run away was the instinctive response.

She wished she hadn't had to leave him alone at home today, but he'd assured her she shouldn't take time off work and convinced her they shouldn't tell Geena. He wanted to protect his younger daughter. He always had. It was up to Tanya to decide what to do with the knowledge and she'd carried her worries through what had been a busy morning.

'Hey,' Deb said as she pulled up a chair on the other side of the table. 'What's up?'

Tanya tried to smile but it didn't prevent tears filling her eyes. 'Thanks for meeting me. You were right,' she said, 'about Dadda. It is all about something else, something worse.'

Deb pressed her lips together and nodded. 'I'm sorry to hear that. Anything I can do?'

Tanya closed her eyes. Deb had said a lot of other things when they last spoke, chief among which was that ignoring a problem was rarely the solution; finding a way forward worked better.

'Thanks, but probably not directly. Family stuff, you know. I guess I just wanted to see a sympathetic face.'

'I hear you.' Deb reached across and squeezed Tanya's forearm. 'You know, accepting that something bad happened is often the hardest bit. If your dad's talking about his problem with you, that's a huge step forward.'

'I know.' Tanya sniffed and sat up straight. 'And he's been so brave already. I just need to make sure he gets the right help now. I'm not sure talking to me is enough.'

Deb nodded and prised the plastic lid off her coffee cup to empty two sachets of sugar inside. 'I won't pry; you don't have to tell me what happened, I'll just offer you two bits of advice you probably already know.' She held up a finger and thumb to count them off. 'First: medication might help, but not if it only covers up the problem. Second: going through counselling to come to terms with whatever happened isn't easy. Things might get worse before they get better.' She stirred the coffee and took a sip, grimacing at the heat of it.

'Right.' Tanya nodded. 'Those are good points, not entirely encouraging, but useful to know.'

'Sorry. I'm sure you'd rather be prepared. Oh, and third thing: it can be tough on the family as well. Make sure you have enough support, plan something to look forward to.'

Tanya bit her tongue and squinted in an attempt to hold the tears back. It wasn't Deb's fault that Geena was unlikely to be any use, even if Dadda would share what had happened with her, or that Will, the one bright spark in Tanya's life, had left the country.

'Yes,' she said and looked down at the table where she began to push the crumbs from the pastry she'd eaten into a line. Except, her mum and dad travelled to escape their problems. The idea that she could do the same, even temporarily, was very tempting.

'Um, Will asked me to go and visit him in America. Maybe I should arrange to do that. Perhaps in a few months Dadda might be well enough for me to go away for a bit.'

'Sounds ideal. What's stopping you?'

Tanya froze, then swept the crumbs aside. She couldn't think about leaving Dadda. Not now.

'I don't even have a passport,' she said. 'When I think of my parents, being brave enough to come all the way here where they knew no-one, it just amazes me. And I'm nervous about even thinking I might cross the Atlantic. I've never been in a plane. I'm,' she gulped, 'well, I guess I'm afraid of it.'

She felt ridiculous admitting that out loud. How many hours had she spent looking at planes crossing the skies online? Observing from a safe distance while the people on board actually went somewhere. Completely idiotic.

'Really?' Deb wiped milk froth from her top lip and winked. 'It'd be worth it though, right?'

Tanya flushed. Anything would be worth it for more of Will's company. But the guilt of allowing herself to be distracted by him when Dadda should be her first priority wormed into her stomach. She pushed against the table and cleared her throat.

'I need to be around for Dadda. And I need to be here. You know what it's like trying to get leave booked.'

She wondered what her mum would have done in Tanya's place. She'd given up everything to be with the man she loved - left her family, her home, everything she knew to move to a strange new country and make her home with him. Tanya wondered if her mum had thought Dadda was over the things he'd seen and the violent loss of his family, or if there had always been things they'd talked about. Things which Dadda had no-one to talk about with in recent years so that the city centre riots and abuse he'd received on the bus had built on top of worries he'd been keeping to himself. The role her mum had played in first rescuing and treating an injured man, then loving him enough to step into the unknown with him was astounding. For Tanya to be so nervous about the thought of even visiting Will was pathetic.

She sighed. 'I'll get Dadda to see our GP and hope we can get a referral for counselling sorted. That's what I need to focus on for now.'

Deb screwed up the empty sugar sachets and drained her drink. 'And you really should get yourself a passport.'

'Yes, I know. I do want to. It's just a big step.'

'No. It's admin, forms and bureaucracy. It's what you do with it that counts,' Deb said. 'You understand that fear of flying is irrational, don't you?'

'Yes,' Tanya said, without conviction.

'And you've never actually tried it.'

'No.'

'So what you have is a feeling of apprehension. Don't let it become a phobia, don't let it stop you doing something wonderful.' She stared hard at Tanya. 'Don't let it taint your life.'

Tanya broke the eye contact and frowned. This really wasn't her biggest problem. 'OK. I get it. Thank you.'

'You know where I am for now if you do need to talk about your Dad.'

'For now?' The words triggered alarm bells.

Deb gathered her things together. 'Yeah, I got the paperwork through for my next posting, down to the military hospital in Surrey. Not far away, but, you know, I won't be on the premises anymore.'

'I'll miss you,' Tanya said although the words went nowhere near expressing her sense of abandonment. 'Can we keep in touch, maybe by email?'

'Of course.' Deb scribbled her email address on the back of the till receipt for her coffee and passed it over.

'Thank you,' Tanya said. 'I know why Dadda was rude to you by the way, about the army - it's all linked, he used to be in the military himself.'

Deb smiled. 'I guessed it might be something like that. It's never the simplest of career choices. Shame it often looks like an easy one.' She shrugged her bag onto her shoulder and glanced at her watch. 'And they say nursing's a vocation. I'll see you around.'

As she watched Deb leave, Tanya frowned. Being a nurse certainly hadn't made her mum's life easy. She'd been proud to hear her eldest daughter was following her into healthcare though, even if it had been a change from Tanya's original plan to do something more intellectual.

They'd been caring for her at home by the time Tanya decided on radiology as a career. She'd been to all the appointments with her mum, seen the X-rays which revealed the terrifying, expanding mass of the tumour which should not have been there.

Dadda couldn't cope with it, not after the diagnosis. The news that his beloved nurse could not be cured was too much to bear. Tanya cancelled her travel plans, deferred the university offer she held for one year, before giving it up to study instead the science of reading what human bodies hid below the skin. All too late for her mum, hopefully in time for others.

Her mum had squeezed her hand and smiled. 'Yes, that's a good choice,' she'd said. 'And you must always speak clearly about what you see. I know you'll always do the right thing.'

Only with the knowledge she now had could Tanya understand the full meaning of her mum's words back then: that if something looked wrong, she had to act. And now she wouldn't even have Deb to discuss her decisions with.

Supporting Dadda was the obvious first reaction, but would her mum really have thought the best thing for her daughter to do would be to give up her life for him, even if that had been what she'd done herself so many years before? It seemed unlikely. Her mum had given up the life she'd known, but made a new one with her own family.

If Tanya was going to stay in Birmingham while Dadda and Geena left, then what she was staying for needed to be enough. The job she currently had didn't deliver. The increased responsibility of additional training and a promotion where she could apply new skills might. And visiting Will in Chicago wasn't a scary thing to do. Deb's reaction proved that. It was the kind of thing people did all the time. Normal people.

She realised she'd be late back from her break and tripped on a chair leg in her haste to leave. The nurses at the next table looked up.

'Oops,' Tanya said as she stumbled and regained her balance. 'That was clumsy of me. I wasn't looking where I was going.'

Chapter Sixteen

Tanya had expected the city centre Post Office to be quiet. Compared to the crush of people streaming in and out of the high street stores further up New Street, the side road leading down to it was deserted. Confident that the process couldn't take long and she'd have time to look around the shops to start some Christmas shopping herself, she pushed open the door and was confronted by a crowd of people inside.

She'd been afraid that if she didn't act immediately to apply for her passport, she'd lose her nerve, so she'd got the form straight away and, although Deb had warned her about bureaucracy, couldn't believe the queue was so long. It was almost worse than clinics at the hospital. She jabbed at a touch screen check-in counter, selected the purpose of her visit from a list of options and took the slip of paper it printed out which numbered her position in the queue.

The passport application with its straightforward early questions had appeared simple. She'd used the correct colour ink, written in block capitals, collected all the supporting documentation she'd require. But then the form veered into incomprehensibility as it described the requirements for the photos she should supply. Alarmed by how long the process could take, especially if she made a mistake, she'd decided to seek advice and get the photos taken by the Post Office themselves.

Now she'd committed to the concept of being able to travel, if not to the journey to Chicago itself, the idea her application might be refused because of a simple admin error was unthinkable. A point on which she agreed with Dadda was that unnecessary risks were to be avoided and the price of the official checking service to buy the guarantee that things would go right first time was well worth it.

She squeezed into a gap on a red vinyl-upholstered bench and checked the documentation she'd brought with her. She had her own birth certificate and both her mum's birth and naturalisation certificates to prove she'd been a British citizen. The decision not to ask Dadda for his documentation had been easy - why trouble him with the idea that she was planning to travel when she didn't yet know if she'd go through with it, especially when the thought of any journey was likely to alarm him.

Tanya frowned as she read her grandparents' unfamiliar names on her mum's birth certificate, uncertain how to pronounce them. These were people she'd always assumed were dead; and they most likely were dead by now. These were the people who hadn't wanted her parents to be together, people her mum had turned her back on to be with Dadda. Alive or dead though, Tanya could never know them. The link had been severed.

She felt more bereft than she had when she only believed her grandparents had died before she was born. Then they'd been an abstract concept. Now their names signified real people, people who'd made difficult choices in frightening circumstances. The uncertainty of the situation confused her. She flinched as the man next to her on the bench stood and walked over to the counter after the automated voice of the queue management system announced his number.

Around her people were addressing parcels, paying bills, renewing car tax or collecting foreign currency. The diversity of the crowd was similar to that she saw at the hospital with all ages and skin colours represented, as well as a variety of accents and languages. But the languages highlighted the key difference from the people who found their way into the radiology clinic.

The people here were lively and chatty, almost everyone but her was there with friends or family, treating this as part of a shopping trip or a day out. She was the only one on her own and probably the oldest one applying for her very first passport. Almost definitely the only one nervous about doing so.

She slipped the papers back into the envelope she'd brought them in and mentally reviewed the other paperwork she needed to complete. The deadline to apply for the MRI training course was approaching and her form only needed a check over before it was ready to submit. No photos required for that, thank goodness. Almost as much trepidation involved though.

If she wasn't accepted for the course, she couldn't justify staying in Birmingham, not without Dadda and Geena to give her presence there meaning. She'd have to look for other opportunities, alternative jobs elsewhere and, if she was going to move, she ought to go with them. She chewed on the inside of her cheek. Regardless of what was the right thing to do, she had to make sure her application form was the best it could be. To do anything less would be wasteful.

The screen above the counter refreshed and the computer-generated voice announced Tanya's number. She grabbed her bag and envelope and stepped forward.

'How may I help you?' the post office cashier asked in a strong Birmingham accent.

Tanya slid her papers through the slot in the perspex screen protecting the man from his customers. 'Check and send my passport application, please.'

She waited in silence as the cashier looked through the pages. She shifted her weight from one foot to the other and wondered why she felt queasy until she realised she'd been holding her breath and took a lungful of air.

'Do you need me to take the photos?' the man asked.

Tanya nodded and noticed his name badge. His name was Sean and he was not someone to be scared of.

'Just step into the booth,' Sean said and pointed to a partitioned area at the end of the counter. Inside Tanya found she was facing a camera lens mounted above a screen. Sean's voice cracked though an intercom. 'Look at the screen and keep your face expressionless. That's right.'

Tanya didn't recognise herself in the image the camera was capturing. She wasn't just expressionless, she looked gormless.

'Perfect,' Sean said.

Tanya glanced across and saw that he was studying his computer monitor, so she went back to stand at the counter. After five minutes of silence while Sean typed, clicked and cross-checked details on forms, Tanya slumped to lean her arms on the counter and began to wonder if there was a problem.

It was probably suspicious to not hold a passport; anyone she'd ever admitted her lack of travel experience to was always surprised. They assumed she'd be familiar with exotic destinations having travelled to visit family back in India. While Dadda's obsession with Britain provided justification for not travelling while she was a child, now the only thing stopping her was herself.

'Right,' Sean said, 'that's almost everything. If you can sign here and here.' He slid the form back through to Tanya's side of the counter and indicated where the signatures were needed.

Tanya picked up a pen and paused. 'Is it all OK?' she asked.

'Everything's fine. I'll send it all off and you should hear from the passport office within four to six weeks. But it all looks in order.'

'OK.' Tanya hesitated with the pen poised over the page. This was it. Two signatures would take her closer to holding proof of her British citizenship but, more importantly, to being able to leave Britain. Just two signatures. She bit her lip and signed.

*

'Finally,' Geena said as Dadda left the kitchen, 'I didn't think I'd ever get a chance to tell you.'

She hadn't wanted to mention her news in front of him. Not while he was being over-sensitive and both he and Tanya were acting weirder than ever that evening. Dadda kept looking at Tanya as though he was afraid of her, while Tanya behaved as though she was from another planet, a planet where they did difficult mental arithmetic for fun rather than chat to their families.

The dinner-time conversation had been practically non-existent, almost as though there was something the pair of them didn't want to say in front of her. Well, she had secrets of her own, but couldn't keep this one to herself any longer.

'Tell me what?' Tanya replied.

Geena turned off the hot tap and dipped the first of the glasses they'd used that evening into the soapy water. 'I've been offered a promotion!' She lifted the glass now coated in bubbles and raised it in the air as though toasting her news.

Tanya took the glass from her and held it above the draining board while the suds slid down it. 'Promotion? Mr Davis's shop isn't exactly a career ladder. What do you mean?'

'He's offering me the chance to develop the business, implement all my ideas and, best of all, make and sell my own range of jewellery.'

Geena grinned at her sister. In the absence of a network of friends to share the news with, she'd been hugging the excitement to herself all afternoon and was desperate for some positive feedback. It was obviously not the right time to tell Dadda about this, she understood that, but she'd expected Tanya to be more supportive.

Instead, Tanya frowned. 'I thought you'd be going with Dadda to wherever he decides to move? I know it's probably not ideal for your work, but staying in Birmingham's too expensive. How could you afford to rent anywhere?'

'I won't need to, the job comes with the flat above the shop. And I'll get a raise as well.' Geena shook her head. This was unbelievable. She shouldn't have to justify herself. She glared at Tanya. 'It's a great opportunity, I thought you'd be pleased for me.'

Tanya looked away. Geena washed the rest of the glasses and moved on to the plates. When the draining board was becoming full she flicked some foam at her sister. 'Hey, a little help here? What's up with you? This is great news for me.'

'Is it? It's still a local jeweller's shop in Bournville. I thought your plans were for something bigger, something more, I don't know, stylish?'

'Which could still happen. This is a great next step. He'll let me have control of all sorts of things - from ordering to our Internet presence. I can really put my stamp on the business.'

Tanya pursed her lips as though considering what else she could criticise. 'And live there too? Is that a good idea?'

Geena sunk her hands back into the water to retrieve the cutlery. 'Bournville's great. Why shouldn't I live there?'

'Bournville's a time capsule. And who'll look after Dadda?'

Geena rubbed at the food residue caught in the tines of a fork. She hadn't considered Dadda, but surely he wasn't her responsibility? Tanya had always taken the lead in that sort of thing.

She spoke carefully. 'Does one of us have to look after him? Is that really what he wants for us?'

Tanya was quiet for a moment, before replying, 'No, he wants us to live our lives, but he wants us to do that in safety and thinks we'll only be safe if we're with him. I'm really worried about him and we both know he won't like the thought of you doing this.' She wiped a few more plates before adding, 'How about if I rented a flat big enough for both of us once the sale of this place goes through? Then you can still be in the city, look for a different job, a better opportunity. I know you like Mr Davis, but I'm not sure this job offer isn't just his way of tying you in because he knows you're really too good for him.'

Tanya's voice held no conviction. It didn't sound like a genuine offer, more a patronising sweetener to attempt to persuade her sister. Geena really wished she was still on speaking terms with Jude and the girls. Her friends would have understood how big a deal this was.

She frowned at Tanya. 'You want me to stay in my place. Both you and Dadda have always tried to control my life. Now I've got a chance to actually achieve something, and you want me to turn it down. Well, I don't think so. I'm twenty-five years old - an adult. I get to make my own decisions.' She hurried through the rest of the washing up then ripped off the rubber gloves, turning them inside out in the process. 'This is my opportunity. They don't come along that often and I'm taking it. Say what you like, and do what you like about Dadda. I'm taking this job and you'll see what a success I make of it.'

She left the room, slamming the kitchen door behind her. In the hallway she paused and glanced into the living room. She could make out Dadda's head in profile, turned away from the television towards the sound of the slammed door. Neither of them spoke and he eventually turned back to the images on the screen. Geena stomped up the stairs.

As she reached into the cupboard above the kettle to replace the mugs she'd just dried, Tanya wondered whether her mum would have handled the situation any better. True enough that Geena was an adult, but she rarely behaved like one. She'd been spoiled since their mum had died, probably since long before then, if Tanya was honest.

In many ways, Geena still behaved like a sixteen-year-old who'd lost her mum, operating as though the safety net of Dadda's home and Tanya's back up would always be there. She'd become used to constant encouragement and support. Tanya could remember overhearing their mum talking to Geena after a stressful parents' evening at school.

'Listen, my darling,' their mum had said, 'your grades aren't the most important thing. Your happiness means so much more to me.'

Was that good advice for a girl about to embark on her GCSEs? It certainly didn't match the way Tanya herself had been guided by her parents. Academic achievements were presented as the target she should aim for. She couldn't recall happiness being mentioned. And she was the one who'd been asked to look after Dadda.

She closed the cupboard door, turned to lean against the counter and covered her eyes with her hands. The memory of sitting by her mum's bedside, both of them aware that she was close to death and both aware that Dadda and Geena were not as accepting of what was happening, were not coping well, came back to her. Instead of releasing the sobs building inside and wailing at the world's unfairness, Tanya had sat quietly, held her mum's hand and taken on the burdens she could no longer carry.

Tanya pressed her palms against her eyelids so a kaleidoscope of colours appeared behind them. How was that fair? Did she now have to sacrifice her entire life to the tasks her mum was no longer there to accomplish for herself? She longed for the other women who should have been there to help her: the grandmothers, aunts and cousins who, even if they'd been overseas, could have advised her, could have given support. Instead they were dead, or lost.

She felt a stab of anger at her situation, anger at religion, at tradition, at everything that had led to the violence, ultimatums and heartbreak which meant she, Dadda and Geena had only each other to rely on. Tears leaked from under her palms and she dragged her hands down her cheeks to dry them. She could see her face reflected in the glass of the kitchen window opposite and shook her head.

Stupid to be so self-indulgent when it wasn't as though she had a big plan that responsibilities at home were preventing her achieving. She didn't feel the vocation that Deb had mentioned about military service, or her mum had felt for nursing. Tanya knew she was neither hero nor angel. She might be doing what her mum had asked, but she doubted she'd have made her proud.

Geena on the other hand, Geena wanted to follow her desires, be impulsive, not plan too far ahead. She was the one who was really like their mum, whatever Dadda said. She was the one with the pioneer spirit, the one who would be brave enough to drop everything and follow a dream as their mum had done for Dadda. Tanya couldn't even apply for a passport without making a meal of it. Well, there was one thing she could do.

She went into the sitting room and lifted the remote control from the table beside Dadda's armchair to mute the sound. He looked up at her with a frown.

'You need to talk to a doctor about how you're reacting,' she said. 'I can't give you the support you need.'

He shook his head. 'These so-called specialists know nothing. What can they do? They can't change what's happened.'

'No, but they can, I don't know, maybe change the way you think about things, how you allow yourself to respond.' She shrugged. What she did know was that she couldn't be the solution. She wasn't her mother.

He didn't reply, only looked at her through narrowed eyes.

'I'll call the surgery first thing tomorrow,' she said, 'get you an appointment as soon as I can. The GP probably can't help but you need her to refer you to counselling, or therapy, or something which will help in the way Geena and I can't. You can't expect us to solve this for you, Dadda.'

He mumbled his response of, 'I don't. I expect to solve things for you. You never listen.'

'No,' she said, and handed the remote control back to him, 'you never listen.'

She turned away and climbed the stairs to her bedroom where the thump of bass from Geena's room penetrated the walls. Tanya only paused briefly to acknowledge the fact that Geena was in for the night again, then shoved on her headphones to block out the noise.

She picked up her laptop and sat on the bed, opening the flight radar website to see which planes were in the skies overhead. She needed the escapism more than ever.

Flights from Stockholm, Barcelona and Brussels had recently landed at Birmingham airport, but instead of wondering about the travellers who'd made those journeys, or surfing the web to discover where other planes might be journeying to overseas, Tanya closed the website. The fact that there was no plane from Chicago, no proof that a connection between the two cities existed, was too agonising.

If it was the American dream that anything was possible, she wondered what the Birmingham dream could be expressed as. That everything would change, even if not for the better?

With her fingers resting on the keyboard, Tanya made herself a promise. All the changes she faced could be viewed as opportunities if she herself decided to frame them that way. Dadda telling her about his past meant she could ensure he got the professional help he needed: she'd book that appointment first thing. She'd filled in two applications which could open doors for her: the chance to progress at work and to follow a long-held idea that she might travel beyond Britain's borders. And if the family home was sold, well that just meant she had the chance to set up in her own place, something friends of her own age had done years before. As long as she could get things with Dadda settled first. Perhaps that would have to be a longer term plan.

She sighed. While everything could appear positive if she viewed things that way, her underlying motivation was suspect. Where Geena and Will had ambition for their careers, where Dadda had conviction that he should protect his family, where her mum had love to guide everything she did, Tanya herself was lacking. There needed to be a better reason for her to act. She craved her own vocation. Without it, supporting other people was so much the easier option.

She looked back at the screen and logged in to check her emails. Will's name leapt out at her from the list of unopened messages and her finger trembled on the touchpad as she moved the cursor to open his mail. He filled his messages with news about what he was up to back in Chicago and the mad things his family had done, all of which painted an intriguing portrait of his life in America. But then there were the mentions of this woman Emma, casual, frequent mentions. Things she'd done to make him laugh. Times she'd been with him at some kind of social event. But he signed off each messages with love and kisses to Tanya.

She wished she'd asked him straight out who Emma was. To ask now felt idiotic, she'd sound clingy and possessive when Tanya knew she had no reason to cling. Will had gone home.

She clicked to open his email.

'Hey you - big news,' he'd written. 'I'll be flying back to Birmingham in a coupla weeks to implement some new software. Very much hoping you'll be free for dinners, conversation and everything else. Will confirm dates as soon

as I can, but until then, sending kisses across the ocean, Will
x'

Tanya grinned. At last something was going her way.

Chapter Seventeen

The telephone ringing downstairs woke Geena for the second time that morning and, also for the second time, she left it for Dadda to answer. Anyone who wanted her would be more likely to call her mobile. Not that they had recently.

She pulled the duvet up to her chin but knew she was too awake now and should just get up, so she sighed, threw the covers back and stumbled as she tried to stand. Too much sleep, that's what the problem would be. Her body was used to late nights and partying, not long hours of inactivity.

As she opened her bedroom door, she heard Dadda end the telephone call with the words, 'Yes, of course. We'll see them shortly. Good bye.'

'Not having visitors, are we?' she called down to him.

'Not visitors, no,' he replied. 'A viewing. People coming to see if they want to buy the house.'

Geena stopped half way through the stretch she'd been enjoying and peered over the banisters at him. 'A viewing? When?'

Dadda consulted his watch. 'Half an hour.'

She looked down at the T-shirt she'd slept in. 'Better get dressed, then.'

Back in her room, she pulled on a pair of skinny jeans and dragged her hair up into a ponytail before running down to the kitchen where Dadda presented her with a mug of tea.

'Didn't realise you knew where the kettle was,' she said.

'I wondered,' he replied, not meeting her eye, 'would you speak to the people about the house? I'd rather not talk to them, really.'

She sipped the drink and tried not to grimace. How would he know she no longer took sugar, after all? 'Yeah, sure, um, maybe you could just hang out in the garage or the garden while they're here?'

'Thank you. And, are you free for the rest of this morning? Tanya's made a doctor's appointment for me and I hoped you'd come with me to that as well.' His voice was hesitant.

Geena put the mug of tea down. In the three weeks since the incident on the bus he hadn't left the house, hadn't seen anyone besides her, Tanya and Mary from next door, had behaved like an invalid or a recluse. And now two events in one morning were going to force him out of the bubble. Of course she had to help.

'I'll be right by your side, Dadda,' she said. 'But first we better get this place fit for inspection.'

She left him working to tidy up his papers in the living room while she zoomed about upstairs to pick up the clothes dropped on her bedroom floor and give the bathroom its fastest clean ever. Tanya's room required no attention, of course. Geena was just muttering that her elder sister really need to loosen up a little, when the doorbell rang.

'Hi!' She opened the front door and shivered in the draught of cold air. 'Come on in.'

The young couple introduced themselves as Phil and Jess and paused in the hallway, looking around but not speaking.

'OK,' Geena said as she tried to recall if she'd removed her make-up before going to bed the night before, or whether she now resembled a panda with personal hygiene issues, 'I've never shown anyone around a house before, so what would you like to see first?'

Phil looked up from the Union Jack doormat and glanced at Jess. 'Well,' he said, 'to be honest, this is the first house we've ever looked at as well. So, whatever you think best, I guess.'

'Come this way then.' Geena led the way into the living room and licked her teeth before she spoke again. She could taste that she had morning breath and wished she'd found a second to clean her own teeth and not just the bathroom sink.

Phil and Jess stood just inside the doorway and looked around the room. They didn't seem much older than Geena herself and she swallowed her bitterness that they were in the position to consider this house as their first step on the property ladder. She glanced at Jess's left hand as she talked about the size of the room, mentioning how the sun came in every morning before moving round to light the patio in the back garden by the afternoon. Jess wore both a wedding ring and a tiny diamond solitaire. Cheap, high street stuff, but it gave Geena an insight into what she should tell them and she adapted her sales pitch.

'I grew up in this house,' she said. 'And I loved playing in this room when I was little. My sister and I made dens from the sofa cushions and imagined the seat here in the bay window was the deck of a ship.'

She paused. That was a happy memory. Tanya used to be full of big ideas.

'If you want to come through to the dining room,' she said, and led them back through the hall to open the door of the room they no longer used, 'My mum made us eat all our meals in here. It would be great for kids' parties too.'

It had been unspoken agreement between her, Tanya and Dadda that they'd eaten every meal since her mum's death in the kitchen. To be without mum at the head of the dining table was unthinkable.

'I know the decor must look dated to you, but everything's clean and just think how you'd be able to stamp your personalities on it. Imagine how bright the room will look with a fresh coat of paint.'

As she witnessed the strangers scrutinise her home, Geena realised that she hadn't really thought through the concept of the house being sold. She hadn't believed Dadda would go through with it. Until now.

She steered them into the kitchen, automatically playing the role of saleswoman. All those hours letting property programmes wash over her glazed eyes had turned out to be some use after all.

'Now this is both practical and spacious,' she said, gesturing around the room and let her hand drop to cover one of the many chips in the granite-effect work surface. The desirable kitchens on those programmes were generally fitted with high-gloss flat fronted units, stainless steel splash backs and high-tech coffee making equipment. Not faux-rustic oak cupboards and rag-rolled walls. 'My sister and I do lots of cooking and you can see there's tons of storage and workspace.' Geena opened a cupboard door to demonstrate, only to immediately close it again as the jumble of old ice cream and margarine tubs being kept to store leftovers threatened to topple out onto the floor.

She pressed her lips together and only nodded when Jess asked if they'd be leaving the appliances. The idea that she might not be cooking with or for Tanya much longer made Geena hug her arms around herself. Maybe her sister's offer to find a flat for them both hadn't been patronising. It had been validation that being close to her sister mattered to Tanya as well. Dadda was right. They should be together.

'No space for a dishwasher though,' Phil said.

Geena shook her head. 'We never needed one. You just get into the routine of washing up straight away.'

'Perhaps we could knock through,' Jess said. 'Make a bigger kitchen-diner?'

Geena choked down a protest. Knock through? Her mum would never have wanted the dining room spoiled, or her territory in the kitchen opened up for everyone to live in. Perhaps the kitchen could be extended somehow, but it wouldn't be right. It wouldn't be her family home.

'Come and see upstairs,' she said.

She let them look into the three bedrooms and the bathroom by themselves, there was nothing she could say to convince them anyway. The rooms held so much history for Geena but must look in need of a revamp to anyone else.

Phil pointed to the collection of royal wedding commemorative plates propped up on the landing windowsill. 'Someone's patriotic.'

'Yeah. My dad's lived in Britain for about thirty years now. He really loves this country. My sister and I were born here so I guess it's less of a big deal to us.'

Geena wondered why she'd bothered to explain. OK, she thought those plates ridiculous too, but Phil's comment annoyed her. Was he suggesting the Gill family weren't Asian enough for him? What was it to him if Dadda wanted to wear his allegiance on his sleeve? As for the look on Jess's face when she'd come out of the bathroom, well, if it wasn't good enough for her, she didn't have to buy it, did she?

'I'll let you come down in your own time,' Geena said and turned to go back down the stairs.

As she leant against the warmth of the radiator in the living room while she waited for them, she considered her reaction. The house was only bricks and mortar, but the reality of leaving it had shocked her like a slap as she watched strangers judge the spaces which meant so much to her.

Could Dadda really walk away from it after so many years of mostly happy family life there? Just because some idiots on a bus had upset him? The idea of moving into the flat above the shop had seemed a good solution, but really, she couldn't leave the only home she'd ever known. She wasn't ready.

She replaced her frown with a bright smile as Phil leant around the door frame and said, 'Thanks for showing us around. We'll have a think about it and let the estate agent know.'

Geena showed them out and waited at the front door while they walked down the driveway. She heard Dadda come back into the house as she closed the door.

'How did it go?' he asked.

Geena screwed up her nose. 'I'm not sure it's quite what they're after.' Her own failings during the viewing didn't matter. That Jess clearly had ideas above her station and the Gill family home would never match her aspirations. 'Anyway, what time do we need to go out?'

'Quite soon,' he replied.

'I'll just grab something to eat.'

She surveyed the kitchen as she scoffed a bowl of cereal. As though a bit of washing up would kill that bloke, she thought, conveniently forgetting that she'd been nagging Tanya about the fact they should get a dishwasher for years. Ever practical, Tanya kept pointing out that unless they refitted the kitchen, there was nowhere for it to go.

The room could do with a refit really. It had last been done out when Geena was little. She could remember how proud her mum had been to see the new cabinets and appliances of what had been, to her, a dream kitchen. Sure, the world changed, but it was a shame that one woman's "dream come true" was now deemed "not good enough". Geena dumped her bowl in the sink and went to get ready.

She waited as Dadda paused at the front door before taking his first step into the street since the incident on the bus and let him set the pace as they walked together towards the surgery, aware of his uncharacteristically shuffling footsteps. They paused to cross the road in front of the gates to the crematorium and she broke the silence between them to say, 'You must have missed coming up here recently.'

He nodded. In recent weeks he hadn't even made his regular visit to the rose bush they'd adopted in the crematorium grounds. Geena frowned. That was more significant than any of the other changes since his incident: to say he wasn't well enough to work or to make excuses to get her and Tanya to run errands for him were minor in comparison to him abandoning his Sunday morning trips to the rose bush memorial to his wife.

Geena slipped her hand into the crook of his arm as they crossed the road. 'I'll come with you this week,' she said.

Inside the surgery they waited on the slippery plastic seats surrounded by coughing toddlers, mothers with wailing babies and an elderly woman so frail Geena didn't think she'd be able to stand up again once she sat down. Eventually Dadda's name was called over the intercom and he glanced at Geena as he stood up.

'I'll wait here, shall I?' she said.

He seemed uncertain, but nodded.

She grabbed an ancient copy of Good Housekeeping from the table to her side and was reading a torn page describing a recipe that had caught her eye when the door to the consulting rooms opened.

'Miss Gill, would you come through, please?' the doctor said.

Geena threw the magazine aside. 'Is something wrong?' she asked as she followed their GP down the corridor.

'Your dad's quite upset,' the woman replied. 'I'll give you a few moments alone together.'

Already worried, Geena rushed into the room where Dadda sat beside the doctor's desk. He glanced up and wiped his eyes, his expression anguished.

She reached for his hand. 'What is it?' she asked.

'Geena, my precious girl,' he said. 'You have to understand that I have only ever wanted to protect my family.'

'I know,' she said, but her mouth dropped open and she froze in place while he told her the story of why he'd left India, how he'd never wanted to speak of it and the trauma caused by recent events.

'Oh,' she said once he'd finished talking. She rubbed at her hands and arms to ease the tension which had grown in her body as she'd listened. She didn't want to react too fast because this was important, possibly the most difficult thing she'd been faced with. If only she could think what was the right thing to do. It was time to take control of something; this was the time to make a change.

*

As she met the gaze of the little boy standing in front of her, Tanya's heart twinged. He stared at her wide-eyed with a trust and acceptance she found moving and she wondered how much of what was happening he understood. He followed her instructions with total obedience, but it was obvious without the help of X-rays that he was very ill.

The world was unfair, it was cruel and random, but this innocent boy did not deserve to be suffering like this. He coughed, a weak, shallow sound, but the twist in his forehead as he frowned at the pain made Tanya want to bear his agony for him. Instead she turned him to face the cassette holding the X-ray film and gestured that his mother should follow her into the adjoining room.

'Stay very still, Arun,' she said. 'I'll be as quick as I can.'

She double-checked his notes before taking the chest X-ray he'd been sent for. His mother, whose English was poor, had presented with him at A&E a few hours earlier. The cough had worsened, he had a fever and samples of blood and sputum had been sent for testing. It seemed the doctor suspected pneumonia and Tanya knew if that were the case she'd expect to see opacity in the image of his lungs.

She spoke calmly to Arun, then fired the beam of radiation and indicated that his mother could go back to him while she reviewed the image.

There was no opacity. She squinted and looked carefully. Her other main experience with chest X-rays was in identifying the cloudy mass of a tumour in a patient's lungs, but she didn't see that here either. She knew what she was actually looking at was still common across the world but less so in Britain where, in most cases, any local patients found themselves referred directly to Birmingham's central Chest Clinic. The fluid of pleural effusions, a prime indicator of tuberculosis, had only appeared in front of her in Arun's case because he'd been brought straight to A&E.

She typed up the notes on her findings and returned to the main room, hardly able to look at Arun's pained face. He'd only recently come to Britain to join family over here and must have been exposed to the illness while in his home country.

For a disease which had been supposedly eradicated in the UK, TB cases were growing. Arun might be one of very few Tanya had seen, but he wouldn't be the last. She sent him and his mum back to A&E. He was actually one of the lucky ones, to be diagnosed in Britain where the disease could be treated, but he had a struggle ahead.

She glanced at her watch which had now become a constant reminder of her own mum's sacrifices. At least by coming here she'd given her daughters access to better healthcare than they might have had back in Delhi. And better working conditions. Tanya's shift was finally over for the day so she tidied the room and went to collect her belongings from her locker.

'Hi,' she said to her boss, Colin, who was already in the staffroom.

'Ah, I was hoping to see you,' he said.

'What's up?'

'It's about your training application.'

Tanya straightened her tired shoulders and prepared to pitch the idea to him. 'Yes, I'd really like to go on that course and expand into MRI work. It'd be an asset to the team to have more of us able to work across techniques, don't you think?'

He frowned. 'Yes and no. You see, you're not the only one whose development I have to think of.'

'I realise that, but I haven't been on any training courses for a couple of years now.'

'No, well we had the team reorganisation and other strategic priorities to focus on.'

Tanya remained silent. This wasn't going how she'd hoped.

Colin cleared his throat. 'I'm afraid I can't nominate you for the course, Tanya. It just doesn't fit with our current requirements and I've got no flexibility in the budget.'

'I see,' Tanya said and grabbed her jacket and bag from her locker. 'Thanks for letting me know.'

Despite knowing she should immediately go and find out how Dadda had got on at his doctor's appointment, Tanya couldn't face going straight home. She turned off her normal route and drove towards the grand red-brick buildings of the University of Birmingham, aiming for the city centre. At a pedestrian crossing she had to stop for ages as a stream of students crossed from the campus back towards their rented houses or student flats in Bournbrook.

All were engrossed in their conversations with friends, or absorbed in the music being fed via earphones from mobile phones. Utterly confident of their right to be there, they carried on crossing even once the green man had winked out.

Tanya shook her head and inched her car forward until the crowd became aware that it was no longer their right of way. Their arrogance annoyed her. Why did everyone else get to go before her? What gave these students the confidence to be so certain of their place in the world?

She crunched the gears as she slowed down towards another red light where more students crossed the road. With their bags containing computers and books, sports equipment and musical instruments, they were all busy achieving things, on their way to bright futures.

Colin's refusal to fund her training meant she was going nowhere. Even now she had no real destination in mind. Realising she was doing nothing more than wasting petrol, she turned off the main road and pulled in at the kerb. With hands over her eyes she took a series of deep breaths. She needed a new plan, a better purpose. Shifting the car into gear again, she indicated, turned right at the next junction and right again to head back towards what was still, for now, her home.

*

Geena heard Tanya return from work and stormed into her bedroom. 'How could you not tell me about what happened to Dadda back in India?' she said.

'He asked me not to,' Tanya replied and sat up from her prone position on the bed. 'He wanted to protect you. I take it he's told you now though.'

Geena folded her arms. 'I don't need protecting. You know that. I could have talked to him too.'

'You're hardly ever in, Gee. It's always me who has to take responsibility.'

'If you'd take your head out the clouds for five minutes you might have noticed that I have actually been in for weeks now.'

Tanya sucked her lips in and Geena waited for her to respond.

'Oh. Um, sorry. I take it you haven't made things up with Jude then?'

The sigh in Tanya's voice as she said this riled Geena. This was typical of how both Tanya and Dadda treated her. 'She's still refusing to speak to me actually. Totally unjustified.'

Tanya frowned but Geena carried on before she could speak. 'Anyway, the point is that I am here and I do know and I want to help. Dadda said the doctor's going to refer him to a specialist but surely thinking about moving is way too stressful for him at the moment?'

'I hope the referral comes through quickly,' Tanya said, 'and, you're right, moving probably is too much. But I also don't think it's a good idea to try and push him into anything. I think he needs to feel he's got some control in his life.'

'Yeah, well I'm not letting him sell this house. It's not the right thing for any of us to do.'

Tanya's raised eyebrows suggested she was unconvinced.

'This is our home,' Geena went on. 'We should stay here. All of us. I want to carry on working for Mr Davis, but I also want to keep living here. So you can leave it with me. This house is not for sale.' She turned and opened the door.

'Gee?' Tanya called after her. 'Be gentle with him.'

'I know. I get it.'

'OK. And, hey, this thing with Jude - anything I can do?'

Geena smiled back at her sister. 'No, thanks. Her loss. I'm going to be a bit busy from now on anyway.'

She closed the door behind her and paused. Tanya had seemed a bit quiet considering Will got back to Birmingham the next day. She ought to be glad of her sister's help in supporting their dad. Typical Tanya to not be able to say thank you.

Geena marched down the stairs to lay some groundwork with Dadda. Not that she was too concerned. If he wouldn't agree to take the house off the market, she could always offer to handle all the viewings and sabotage them. Better for Dadda to be disappointed than to make a terrible mistake.

Chapter Eighteen

Though she was excited about collecting Will from Birmingham Airport the next day, Tanya was also anxious about seeing him again. He'd tried to insist that the airport was too far from the city, that he could catch the train, or charge a cab to his expenses, but she couldn't wait to see him. She was desperate to hug him, to receive some reassurance that what she was feeling wasn't one sided and to be sure as soon as possible that he'd landed safely.

Besides, she spent so much time looking at the airport code BHX on her computer screen, that an actual trip there was a treat. This would be one of only a very few visits she'd made there. Her first, to drop Mary from next door off for a holiday flight many years ago when Tanya had just passed her driving test and was keen to drive anywhere, had sparked her interest in the adventurous potential of air travel, despite the concept of flying herself being a source of terror. Now, even seeing the aeroplane symbol printed on road signs on the long drive out of Birmingham, quickened her pulse.

She switched on the radio and turned up the volume. While Dadda had been quiet in response to her questioning about how things had gone with the doctor, he had at least left the house without any drama yesterday and seemed less fretful. Even Geena was being uncharacteristically sensible. In retrospect, Tanya couldn't believe how calmly she'd handled the revelation about what had happened to their family in the past. Perhaps time away from Jude's frivolous influence was all Geena had ever needed to develop a little maturity. Only a little though. She hadn't bothered to ask how things were with Tanya herself.

Tanya indicated to turn into the approach road to the airport. Of course she'd already checked that the plane was on time so she pulled into the short stay parking reserved for picking up passengers and only glanced long enough at a plane on its descent to the runway to identify it as a Ryanair flight, probably the one she'd seen online coming in from Derry, before she hurried into the terminal. She glanced at the arrivals screens to confirm that Will's plane was among those from a variety of other exotic and domestic destinations which had already landed and that he should at that moment be collecting his baggage, unless ...

'Tanya!'

Will had approached when she was looking at the screen and grabbed her so tightly she didn't feel she was supporting her own weight. She staggered as he let go and put a hand to his chest to steady herself. She looked up at him but had temporarily lost the ability to speak.

'God, it's good to see you again,' he said and kissed her.

The overwhelming sensation of his mouth on hers and the warmth and pressure of his arms holding her to him blanked Tanya's mind.

'You too,' she eventually managed to reply. 'It's felt a lot longer than two weeks and you appear to have two working arms again.'

'The wrist's still strapped up, doc. Don't panic,' he said and bent to rub his nose against hers. 'I sense we have a lot to catch up on. So what say we head to my hotel to drop this,' he indicated the bag dumped by his feet, 'and make a start on that?'

She nodded, shy to be back in his company after the closeness they'd built up before he left had dissipated over emails and the awkwardness of a single online video call. Their relationship had seemed to be slipping away; now she had to remember how to be with him.

'That sounds good,' she said and clung on to his hand as they walked to her car.

'Uh huh,' he replied. 'And, we should go out for a celebratory dinner.'

'We should?'

'I'll try not to take offence at your lack of enthusiasm. Not only am I back in Birmingham, not only do I finally have my wrist out of plaster, but it's Thanksgiving. What kind of American would I be if I let that pass without celebration just because I've been in transit?'

Tanya shrugged. Whatever Thanksgiving was, its significance had passed her by. She opened the car boot and watched him load his case in. He only had the small bag which he'd carried as hand luggage and she swallowed the disappointment that he clearly wasn't staying long enough to need anything more.

'What's Thanksgiving?' she asked.

'You don't know? Jeez, what do they teach you in British schools? It's when we celebrate the good stuff - American independence, being with family and friends, anything you like. For most people it's a day off work, for one thing.'

She settled into the driver's seat and clipped her seatbelt into place. 'If it's in honour of American independence it wouldn't exactly be top of the British list of things to celebrate. You used to belong to us, after all.'

He reached across and squeezed her knee as she pulled out of the car park. 'OK, OK, but the first Thanksgiving was like a harvest festival after the Pilgrim Fathers' crops were successful.'

She couldn't help grinning. 'The Pilgrim Fathers? Are we talking about the weird folk who decided to leave Britain? Again, I fail to see its relevance.'

'Ouch. Weird? Because they wanted to be left in peace to follow their own religion in their own way? America the free - it's what the rest of the world admire us for. Anyway,' he stretched his legs out in the foot well, 'nowadays it's about recognising what you're thankful for. And I am thankful to be back in Birmingham, with you.'

Tanya pulled up at a red light and turned to look at him. 'I'm thankful for that too.' She didn't argue with his confidence that the rest of the world admired the United States. Instead, she listened to him talk about what he'd been up to in Chicago since they'd last met.

It was strange to hear him talk about his parents and sisters in so much detail and his relatives became real to her as he repeated their words, mimicking voices to make her laugh. Getting back to America had obviously been a big thrill. But as she considered every phrase he uttered, she began to recognise an unspoken subtext. His family were such a huge part of his life, she'd never be able to compete.

'They must be pleased your new job will mean you're in Chicago more,' she said.

'Hmm, they might be. Not sure I am. I'd have liked more time over here, to bed in the new procedures. The project I'm on Stateside isn't so interesting.'

'You've been noticed by your bosses though, that's a good thing.' She pressed her lips hard together. The contrast with her own situation of being overlooked at work dipped her mood. Apart from Will's actual presence in her car at that moment, she felt she had little to be thankful for. Even he was talking about his family and his work rather than asking anything about her. He had a much greater importance in her life than she did in his.

'Tell you what else has been noticed - how often I mention you.' He nodded. 'Mom, the girls and Emma all picked me up on it. I took a lot of teasing on your behalf.'

She glanced at him. 'Really?' There was that name again: Emma. She had to ask. 'Um, who is Emma, by the way?'

'Didn't I say? She's my roommate.'

Tanya swallowed hard. 'Roommate? Oh, I see.' She didn't see.

'Uh huh. Apparently I've never been so enthusiastic about a girl before.'

'But you live with Emma?'

'Yeah, but not "with" her. She's a friend. She rents the spare room in my condo.'

'Ah.' Tanya blushed and shook her head.

Will laughed. 'I guess I should have made that clear. What did you think was going on here, with me and you? Wasn't it obvious how I feel about you? Emma is just a friend.' He reached across to stroke her cheek.

Tanya crunched the gears as she slowed down for a junction. 'I'm an idiot,' she said. 'I just couldn't quite believe you'd really be so interested in me.'

'Believe me,' he replied and dropped his hand to squeeze her thigh, 'I'm interested.'

Maybe she did feature on his priorities list, after all. But what did that really mean? Realistically, what future could the two of them have? They were from such different backgrounds. She had obligations and problems, he had a big, warm, supportive family and a world of opportunities. She spotted a parking space on a meter round the corner from the city centre hotel his company had booked for him and pulled in.

'You go and check in, I'll feed the meter and come and find you in a minute.'

'OK,' he said but frowned as he lifted his case out and turned to cross the road.

Tanya scrabbled in her purse for change and mentally kicked herself for failing to respond positively to his admission. His reference to the enthusiasm he'd shown when he told his family and friends about her could have been him expressing how important she was to him, or

193

might have just been more information about the dynamics within his family - that he was the one they always teased. She should have said something: something encouraging, something to let him know how she felt, where he stood. Anything else was just playing games. Games where she wasn't sure of the rules. But his dismissal of Emma hadn't entirely reassured her.

She stuck the ticket inside the car windscreen and went into the hotel foyer where Will was talking to the receptionist, a young man with an Eastern European accent. From the plate glass of the automatic doors to the high gloss of the marble floor, the whole area reflected too much light. She attempted to adopt a relaxed posture as she stood behind Will, but felt utterly self-conscious. She moved away from the reception desk to study a rack of leaflets about local tourist attractions, but couldn't focus on any of them.

'Come on, I'm on the third floor,' Will said.

'Um, OK,' she said and followed him to the lift. He'd mentioned dinner, but going into his hotel room suggested something more intimate first. Not that she wasn't interested, only that their time apart had left her unsure how to behave with him and she stared around the lift as it ascended rather than looking at him. Its floor was laid with plush carpet and as she glanced around the mirrored walls she could see that Will was watching her.

'Nice elevator,' he said.

'Fancy hotel,' she replied.

Once they were inside his room, he put his bag down and turned to her. 'OK, what's wrong?'

She opened her mouth, took a breath, but didn't speak.

'Let me go first then,' he said and reached out to hold her hands. 'We're in a crappy situation here. When I arrived last time I was thinking only about the job. I didn't expect to meet someone who'd matter to me, but I did. I met you. And I've missed you while I've been back in the States. But you live here, I live there and we aren't going to get the chance to take our time over getting to know each other.'

He put a finger to her lips to stop her interrupting. 'I'll level with you. I don't truly need to be in the UK right now, but I convinced my boss here it was essential. I told her a whole pack of lies about how no-one else could do this job. For you. Because I needed to see you and you weren't jumping at the idea of making the trip to Chicago.'

Tanya couldn't meet his eyes. She squeezed his warm hands and tried to think of a way to communicate how she was feeling. Of course she wanted to go to Chicago, but how could she express how alarming that journey seemed? Not just the flight, but the freedom. The irresponsibility of leaving her obligations behind. She didn't even want to put in words the fear that, should she escape the demands of her own life, she might keep running. She pressed her lips together and blinked as tears spilt down her cheeks.

'I'm genuinely crazy about you, Tanya,' Will said and lifted a hand to stroke the tears off her face as he stepped closer. 'I love that you challenge me, the things you think and say just blow my mind, and,' he paused until she looked up and met his eyes, 'right from that first moment when I saw you in your uniform, surrounded by terrifying machines, I knew you were the most gorgeous woman I'd ever met.'

'Wow,' she said and took a deep, shaky breath.

He let go of her other hand and put his arms around her to hold her tight against him. 'Yeah, I'm a smooth operator. Now, unless you've got anything to add to my analysis of our situation, give me a kiss and relax, why don't you?'

*

Later, as they curled together in the soft nest of the hotel bed, she told him all the things she hadn't felt able to put into emails about what Dadda had revealed, about her disappointment at work, about her concern for Geena. He stroked her back and listened in silence as she spoke. She didn't cry and she didn't leave out any details. Being able to share everything that had been running around her head for the past few days helped her see it all in context. Her problems were overwhelming, but talking calmly about them made her realise something else.

'The thing which really hurts is that I want to grab your offer to visit you in Chicago. I want to be the kind of impulsive, romantic, adventurous person who'd drop everything and get on the next plane, but that's just not who I am. I'm the one who studies things from every angle, analyses every possible outcome. I could spend my whole life thinking and never doing.'

He stopped stroking and laid his palm flat against her shoulder blade. 'Those traits are what make you good at your job. No wonder your boss doesn't want to risk losing you.'

'To be fair, he's probably the least of my problems. Making sure Dadda gets the support he needs has to come first.'

Will nodded. 'Your dad sounds amazing.'

She twisted to frown at him.

'I mean it,' he said. 'Think about what he and your mom did - having the balls to escape all that violence, being pioneers and committing to creating a new life for themselves here, raising two incredible daughters - who've both inherited that bravery from what I can see.'

'I'm not brave,' she said. 'I'm even being pathetic about saying I'll visit you in Chicago and I promise you I really do want to do that. I'd love to meet your family.'

'So what's actually stopping you?'

She paused. How could she verbalise the mass of conflicting thoughts crowding her mind? Everything from her responsibilities to her family, to her insecurity about the relationship with him bothered her. She stroked a hand down his arm towards his wrist, still bandaged but almost fully healed from the fracture which had brought them together. As her fingers passed over the stars and stripes tattoo which had been the first thing she noticed about him, she realised the biggest problem might actually be that: home, where it was and what it meant.

She hid her face against his chest and mumbled, 'I've never even been on a plane. My entire life has been here. What if, once I left Britain, I caught the bug and decided I didn't really want to return? Coming back once I'd been away might be too hard. And then what would Dadda and Geena do?'

She didn't admit her fear of flying to him. In comparison to what he'd done in tricking his boss to travel back to Britain, her phobia seemed ridiculous, if still very real.

'Hey, you'd always come back,' he said. 'There's no place like home.'

He squeezed her but she sat up and shivered as the warmth of the duvet fell away from her. 'But Birmingham has never felt like home. I don't know where home is.' She scrambled out of bed and picked her clothes up from the floor. 'I'm on an early shift tomorrow. I should go.'

'When can I see you again?' he asked and pulled himself up into a sitting position on the bed. 'Are you free tomorrow evening?'

'I should spend some time with Dadda. I don't trust Geena to handle it if he's still upset.'

'When, then? The day after? I'm only here for five days, Tanya. I understand you have a lot going on, I'm hugely sympathetic about all that, but please, give us a chance. Especially if this might be the only chance we get.'

She couldn't look at him. 'I'll call you,' she said. 'I promise.'

She almost ran from his room and closed her eyes as the lift carried her back down to the foyer. She couldn't risk catching sight of her reflection. The volume of her swift footsteps across the marble floor made her certain that all the staff at the reception desk were watching as she had to pause for the automatic door to open wide enough to release her back to the street. She didn't look at them. She couldn't bear the scrutiny.

The roads were clear for her drive home and the front door double-locked as usual. Dadda and Geena were in the living room, but she didn't stop to speak to them, just called a greeting and hurried up to her room. There, she booted up the laptop and clicked straight to the image of planes currently in the skies around Birmingham hoping it would calm her.

Each symbol flickered silently, making incremental progress towards its destination. She zoomed the image out and it refreshed to show hundreds more symbols across Europe and out to sea as far from land as the radar images could detect. All those journeys, all those people in transit - to Chicago, to Delhi, to airports across the globe.

She sat back and tried to imagine herself up there in the air, travelling. The temptation drew her, the idea of travelling hopefully, of the journey as a destination in itself. What she couldn't imagine was ever arriving anywhere.

Chapter Nineteen

Tanya slid Dadda's favourite meal of shepherd's pie with a hint of added chilli out of the oven. It was done to perfection with a crisp, browned top and the rich, meaty sauce oozed over mounds of creamy mash as she served it out. Both Dadda and Geena tucked in, while Tanya picked at her own portion. Even though Dadda was going to be getting the professional help he needed and now had the support of both his daughters, Tanya was still concerned.

He'd mentioned that he'd called his boss at the shoe repair firm to discuss potentially going back to work and, while Tanya peeled the potatoes, Geena had sat at the kitchen table and bubbled over with her ideas for developing Mr Davis's business. Giving up the idea of moving into the flat above the shop wasn't troubling her at all.

'I'd rather stay here with you, Tan,' she'd said. 'I'll think of the right thing to convince Dadda, don't you worry.'

Tanya had been flattered, but at the same time dismayed. While Dadda was saying the right things and Geena's recent actions showed uncharacteristic maturity, they both wanted things to stay the same. They both still needed her so much.

'The estate agent called,' Dadda said, 'another viewing, tomorrow morning.'

Tanya and Geena looked at each other and Geena shifted in her seat. 'Tomorrow? OK, well I can handle that for you, no problem. It's my day off,' she said.

'Thank you,' he said. 'I hoped you would.'

'Tan, I totally forgot to ask.' Geena put her knife and fork down with a clatter on her plate. 'You saw Will last night, didn't you? How is he?'

Tanya was aware that Dadda had also turned to look at her.

'Will?' he asked. 'Is he the American man you met?'

Tanya nodded. 'Yes, and he's fine, thanks. It was nice to see him again.'

'Nice?' Geena snorted. 'He comes all the way over here from America; the first thing he wants to do when he gets off the plane is see you and all you can say about it is that it was "nice"?'

'We can't all be as exuberant as you,' Tanya replied. 'It was lovely to see him again but, let's face facts, he lives in America; I live here. It's not going to come to anything.'

Geena sighed. 'Well it won't if you take that attitude.'

Tanya finished eating and carefully aligned her cutlery on her plate. 'What choice do I have?' she said.

'This man,' Dadda said, 'do you like him a lot?'

Tanya bit her lip and eventually managed to look up at him. She nodded.

'Perhaps I should meet him,' Dadda said.

The sisters exchanged a surprised glance as Geena reached out to gather up their plates. 'That is a brilliant idea,' she said. 'Invite him over so we can all get to know him. I'll cook, maybe a roast dinner, something totally British anyway.'

'Shepherd's pie is totally British,' Tanya said, aware she was avoiding the subject.

'Nowhere near special enough for a guest though,' Geena replied.

Tanya turned to Dadda. She sighed and said, 'It's lovely that you'd like to meet him, but I don't want to put any pressure on you. You weren't really up to meeting Deb, were you?'

The legs of his chair scraped against the kitchen floor as he pushed back from the table. 'This is different. This man seems to be important to you. I only want you to be happy, both of you girls. That's all your mother and I ever wanted.'

Tanya smiled at him but she was faking it. For all Will's enthusiasm for her to meet his family, she'd never considered bringing him into her home. What would he think of them? Even the house didn't match up to the rented house he'd been living in down in Bournville and he'd been disparaging enough about that. No average house in Birmingham was going to match up to American standards.

And while it was great that Dadda seemed to be facing his problem, and that was the first step on the road towards fixing it, would he really be able to handle meeting a confident, even slightly brash, young, white man? Wouldn't it be better to protect him from anything new, from any change?

Geena looked over her shoulder as she filled the kettle at the sink. 'You'll like him, Dadda. Not that it'll come to anything with Tan here playing it so cool.'

Tanya raised her eyebrows at her sister. 'I'm just not sure about inviting him here. It's a big step.'

'No. It's not,' Geena replied. 'How many boyfriends have I brought back here?'

'Too many,' Dadda said with a shake of his head. 'Too many, Geena.'

Tanya couldn't help smiling as the two of them debated this. It was good to have the focus shifted off her and to see Dadda behaving more normally again, chastising his youngest daughter when they all knew he would eventually indulge her every whim and support her in every endeavour.

Except now, when Geena's campaign to get him to take the house off the market hadn't yet seen any success.

Despite all her current protestations about the importance of an active and varied social life though, Tanya realised that Geena hadn't just not been out with Jude lately, she hadn't been out at all.

'Haven't you been seeing anyone recently?' Tanya asked her. The guilt of having failed to keep in touch with her sister's life joined all the other concerns running around Tanya's mind.

'Completely off the scene. Don't worry, I know neither of you will lose any sleep over that.' Geena put mugs of tea down in front of each of them. 'I'm going to be busy with this new business development plan, anyway. Won't have time for romance.'

Tanya sipped at her tea and watched her sister as she took off into further flights of innovation. She feared that Geena would be committed to supporting Dadda only until her social life recovered, but Dadda smiled and encouraged Geena's ideas and Tanya was grateful that he'd stayed at the table to talk, that he even was talking to them. The longer she watched though, the more she became aware that the role she was filling really belonged to her mum. She choked on her drink as a wave of grief hit her. The person she most wanted to be able to introduce Will to, the person whose opinion of him she most craved, would never meet him. Instead, Tanya was stuck trying to fill her shoes and unable to see a way out of the situation.

She thought about Arun, the little boy in whose lungs she'd seen the symptoms of tuberculosis, and his mother's obvious concern about their situation. Like Tanya's own mother, she'd left her home country hoping for a better life for her family. And it would work out for them: Arun was well placed to get the care he needed, to recover and live a happy and healthy life. Just like things were working out for Geena: she could get over whatever had happened with Sami without a backward glance because, with Geena's luck, another man would be along the moment Geena decided that was what she wanted.

That wasn't how things happened in Tanya's life. She didn't attract attention and she shouldn't have to be the maternal figure in this family. She wished she knew what her mum would have said about Will. Would a woman who'd left her own family and home to be with a man advise another woman to do the same? Or would a woman who followed her own vocation to be a nurse, even when it made her own life difficult, have understood that actually Tanya needed her own source of satisfaction as well? It was a question to which Tanya knew she'd have to find her own answer.

She stood up and interrupted the story Geena was telling Dadda about a woman who'd been into the shop to ask them to value her jewellery collection when it was all obviously made from gilt and paste.

'Can you manage to clear up without me, Gee? I think I need an early night.'

Geena frowned as she glanced up. 'Of course, but ...'

'Night then,' Tanya said before Geena could voice her objection.

She closed the door behind her and trudged up the stairs.

*

Geena watched the two women who'd been over to view the house walk down the path. They'd been hard to discourage, both talking like property experts although Geena suspected their knowledge, like much of her own, had been gleaned from the television rather than practical experience.

They'd brushed off her comments about the awkwardness of the bathroom layout, limitations of the size of the kitchen and the tendency for puddles to form in the uneven surface of the drive. Anything could be fixed, they'd said. For a price, she'd replied, but it hadn't deterred them.

Even the cortege of funeral cars crawling up the road towards the cemetery at the top of the hill hadn't dampened their enthusiasm. The sight of the convoy of grief made Geena's eyes prick with tears as they'd always done since a similar procession had started from their own door and taken her beloved mum away for the final time.

These women didn't appear deterred either by proximity to the cemetery or the frequent buses rumbling past. There was a very real possibility that they'd put in an offer. She'd have to work on Dadda instead.

'All done?' he asked as she joined him in the living room. 'They seemed nice.'

'Hmm,' she replied, and sat down on the sofa near him rather than taking her usual position across the room. 'They had lots of ideas, wanted to change everything.'

'Change? What's wrong with it as it is?'

She latched on to his comment. 'You're right. This house is ideal really, isn't it? Perfect for us.' It could work; all she needed to do was to stay positive, keep his focus on all the good things about living there. 'It entirely suits our lifestyle, doesn't it?'

He didn't reply and Geena turned to the television to see what had captured his attention. The reporter on the lunchtime local news bulletin stood in front of a line of police tape and something about his surroundings seemed familiar. 'Isn't that ..?'

'Yes,' he said.

She nodded. It was a road perhaps a couple of miles away from them, a road with a parade of shops which included a branch of the same shoe repair firm that Dadda worked for. She tuned in to what the reporter was saying. The content of his report made stark contrast with the Christmas decoration hanging from the lamppost behind him.

'The attack took place at 10:45 this morning and police are appealing for anyone who was in the area at the time to come forward with information about anything they might have seen.'

Geena turned to Dadda, about to observe that it seemed so early in the day for something to have happened, not late enough to be under the cover of darkness or the influence of alcohol, but the look on his face stopped her from speaking. She moved instead to crouch beside him and put a hand on his shoulder. He flinched.

'Turn it off, Geena,' he said. 'Turn it off.'

She grabbed the remote and aimed it at the screen which died into blackness.

'It's OK,' she said. 'Sounds like it was just something random, not anything we need to worry about.'

He pushed himself up from his chair and she straightened to stand in front of him. His eyes, although downcast, darted from side to side and he took gasping breaths through his mouth.

'It's OK,' she repeated, beginning to wonder if it really was.

'Yes,' he said and reached out to pat her arm. 'Yes. Were you about to make us some lunch now those women have gone? I'll come and sit in the kitchen with you.'

'That would be great,' she replied, aware that her voice sounded falsely bright. She turned and led the way to the kitchen cursing the news bulletin. It had only given him more evidence for why they should move away from Birmingham. She couldn't attempt to manipulate him about the house now. She was going to need a better idea.

*

'I was meant to invite you to dinner at our place,' Tanya said to Will when she picked him up from work.

'Meant to? What, is it the law or something? Every sixth date must be in the company of the woman's family?' He grinned and leant across the car to kiss her.

'Six dates? Is that all?'

He mimed counting on his fingers. 'Yep, six times we've actually been together. A lot of texts, emails and phone calls as well, of course.' He paused. 'Feels like more, doesn't it? I sure feel I know you better than that.'

She turned the key in the ignition. 'Would you actually like to meet my dad? I mean, you've already met Geena.'

He touched the back of the hand she'd clenched around the gear lever. 'Of course I'd like to meet him. And see where you grew up, and hear him tell me stories of what a naughty girl you were when you were a kid.'

She laughed. 'I wasn't.'

'Bet you were. Listen, I'd love it, but if it's not what you want, then what I really, really want from this evening is to spend time with you. Anywhere. Doing anything.'

The suggestive tone in his voice sent a thrill through her, but she took a breath and focused on driving. 'Maybe we could just pop in for a cuppa later. Let's go to that pub you were interested in.'

Will had messaged her earlier that day with a link to the website for a pub he'd been told about which was known for stocking drinks from local breweries. He was keen to try a couple of the beers they had on tap there and the place looked cool and quirky, which probably explained why Tanya had never been. She knew where it was though so drove them into town against the queues of rush hour traffic clogging the roads heading out of the city and found a parking space nearby.

As soon as they walked in, Will began to beam. 'Man, this is so cool!'

Tanya took in the details she'd have expected to see in any traditional British pub: the wooden bar, fireplaces, stained glass and upholstered benches around the walls. But those original details had all been overlain with what appeared to her as a self-conscious gloss of funky design with cartoons painted as murals across the walls, weird artwork and staff who all seemed to be many times trendier than she was. Even the Christmas decorations they'd put up seemed stylishly ironic. Will was already at the bar asking about the beers on offer though, so she joined him and agreed to try a half pint of the pub's resident ale.

Most of the other customers had obviously come straight from work so Will wasn't out of place in his suit and tie. Tanya's black jeans and a slightly dressy jumper didn't give her confidence though. All the other women were wearing outfits which reflected their interesting personalities. Yet again, Tanya didn't fit in. If this was really the kind of place where Will felt at home, then she would never measure up.

Most of their other dates had been lower key somehow. There'd always been more emphasis on talking to each other, even if they were in a crowd or doing something which required attention. Now he was acting more like a tourist wanting to experience Britain rather than concentrate on getting to know her. She mentally kicked herself for being critical. Why shouldn't he?

'What do you think?' Will asked, pointing at her beer.

She took a sip and wiped away the line of foam that remained on her top lip. 'Mmm, nice,' she said.

'May I?' he reached for her glass and drank some himself to compare with his own choice from their list of guest ales. 'Hmm, very interesting flavours going on here. We may need to try a couple more.'

'Shall we sit down?' Tanya pointed to a spare space on the bench and they squeezed in between two groups on adjacent tables. Will smiled at the people he passed and even greeted a few. Tanya noticed how other women looked at him and then at her, as though to assess his relationship status. She felt immediately inadequate, but Will chose to sit next to her rather than on the stool opposite and rested a hand on her knee.

'So,' he said, 'how was work?'

He was definitely behaving differently. He obviously expected that their relationship had moved on from the early stages. She wasn't sure she was ready for that, but smiled and said, 'Not too bad, the usual mix of broken and damaged limbs with a side helping of disease.'

He smiled. 'You do it cos you love it though.'

'I suppose I do. I like feeling that I achieve something practical and useful, help people feel better.' She paused. 'Um, not that what you do isn't, um, useful, I mean ...'

'It's OK. I'm well aware my job is far from essential to society. Doesn't mean I don't get a buzz from it though.'

She smiled and tried to regain the sense of ease in his company she'd enjoyed before. 'Of course. I wouldn't say I got a buzz from mine. More that I know I'm good at it, you know? There's a sense of satisfaction, although, it does feel a bit wasted when it's just some idiot who fell over because he wasn't looking where he was going.'

He let his mouth drop open in a parody of taking offence. 'I was looking! I was just confused because I'd been nearly killed crossing the street. You guys insist on driving on the wrong side, so when I got to the sidewalk I was understandably disoriented.'

She nodded. 'Understandable.'

He nudged her and smiled. 'As long as there are enough times when you feel the patient was worth your attention, then I guess it's OK.'

'Yeah. There's plenty of annoying patients, but then there'll be one or two where you know you were the right person at the right time. Like, I saw a little boy with TB the other day. Can't get him out of my mind. I'm sure he'll be fine now it's diagnosed, but I just can't stop thinking about what would have happened if his mum hadn't brought him to us.' She felt a dry ache grow in her throat and abruptly cut off what she was going to say next. She didn't want to be a downer on their evening.

He frowned at her though. 'Hey,' he said and put an arm around her shoulders, 'she did bring him to you. So everything's good. You helped save him, but you know you can't save everyone.'

'Doesn't stop me wanting to do more though,' she said, annoyed she couldn't cover the crack in her voice as she spoke. She was so used to burying her emotions, but lately didn't seem able to keep them in.

'I understand,' Will said. 'This city is lucky to have you. You should do more though, if that's what would inspire you. Find a new challenge, maybe. I know you'd be brilliant at anything you turned your hand to. You've got that vibe about you.'

'Hmm,' she said. Being knocked back in her training application had prompted her to think again about what other opportunities there might be. Friends from college were doing well in private hospitals or working for other health authorities. There were definitely options out there if she was going to be held back in her current position. Any move she made would have to take into account what Dadda needed though.

The thought of him made her reach for her phone. 'Sorry,' she said, 'can I just check I haven't got any messages?'

'Go ahead.'

As the screen illuminated under her touch she could see that in the noise of the pub she had missed a call from Geena, who'd left a voicemail.

'I need to get this,' she explained and squeezed out of the seat to go and stand on the street where it would be quiet enough to hear.

After a frustrating delay while the network connected her to the voicemail, Geena said, 'I didn't know if you were going to bring Will over but listen, Dadda doesn't seem too good this evening. He's gone very quiet, a bit shaky. I'm sure it's fine, you don't need to rush home, but you know, he probably isn't up to meeting someone new. Don't worry though. We'll see you later. Have fun.'

The queasy panic which had stirred Tanya's stomach as soon as she saw the call was from Geena, threatened to overwhelm her. Geena didn't sound too worried, but then

Geena was not equipped to judge things accurately. She was likely to make the wrong assumptions. Tanya slumped against the wall of the pub and a man standing out on the pavement to smoke looked at her and asked, 'You OK, bab?'

She nodded and made her way back inside. As she sat down next to Will he turned from where he'd struck up a conversation with the man sitting next to him, touched her arm and said, 'Hey, what's wrong?'

'Geena says Dadda's not too good this evening. Not worse than before, but not right. He'd been seeming better so, I'm worried.'

He reached to take her hand and squeezed her fingers. 'Would you like to go home and see him?'

Tanya took a deep breath. Geena hadn't said that was necessary, she'd said Tanya should stay out and have fun. Tanya wanted to stay out and be with Will. And she ought to be able to let Geena handle things. She'd call again if there was really a problem, wouldn't she?

'No, it's fine,' Tanya said and placed her phone face up on the table in front of her. 'I just probably shouldn't stay out too late is all.'

'OK.' He took his hand away. 'Want to go somewhere quieter and get some food?'

'No, this is fine. Let me get you that other beer you wanted to try.' She went to the bar and ordered, seeing that while she was away, Will immediately resumed his conversation with the man beside him. She envied his social ease and began to feel jealous until she remembered that, unless he'd been so forward about talking to strangers, if he hadn't possessed that confidence and charisma, she wouldn't be here with him now.

By the time she took their drinks back, the party at the table next to theirs were preparing to leave. 'Something you said?' she asked Will.

'A prior engagement at the theatre, thank you very much,' he said. 'Should get a bit quieter in here now if a few folk are going to that.'

As predicted a number of people did glance at their phones or watches and begin downing their drinks. Instead of taking advantage of the extra space available, Will moved closer to her on their bench and put his arms around her.

'You know that idea I had, about you coming to Chicago for a visit? Well, I've had a better idea. The fact you were a bit cagey about whether I should meet your dad made me realise maybe Chicago feels like too much pressure to you. So how about we go on a holiday together? Somewhere different. I'd love to show you some of America though - we could go to New England, I'm sure you'd love it.'

Tanya looked at him. 'A holiday?'

He nodded. 'I get the impression you could do with one.'

She took a sip from her drink. Holidays were what she dreamt of, travel was her greatest fantasy, but it had always been just that - a fantasy. Whenever friends had invited her away with them before, her fear of flying had been behind her excuses. Now, when she really wanted to say yes, she actually had a non-negotiable reason why she'd have to say no.

'I don't think I can leave Dadda at the moment,' she said, unable to look at him.

'Hey,' Will said and touched her chin to tilt her face back towards his. 'You know you do get to put yourself first sometimes? Geena can handle it, can't she?'

Tanya frowned. How could Geena be trusted, how could Will be expected to understand? Neither of them had ever needed to take responsibility the way she had. 'I don't know if Geena's up to it,' she said.

He raised his eyebrows. 'I don't doubt it. Listen, I go back to the States the day after tomorrow. There won't be any more excuses I can give as reasons to be sent back over here, but I don't want us to just fizzle out. And we both know that's what'll happen if we try to make this a long distance thing. We were rubbish on that Internet call, weren't we?'

She nodded and sniffed. 'Maybe you can come back here for a holiday though? See some more of Old England?'

He moved even closer to her and rested his forehead against hers. 'I could do that.' he said. 'Or, I never got that trip to Ireland I wanted. But the thing is that I already know I could never leave the States, not permanently. Being close to my family is too important to me. You understand that, right? So even if I met the woman of my dreams, a woman I wanted to spend the rest of my life with, if she didn't want to move to the States then it wouldn't work between us.'

Tanya tensed as the meaning of his words sank in. She opened her mouth to speak but he put a finger against her lips.

'I'm not saying that I'm sure I feel that for you right now, we don't know each other well enough. But I do know that I could feel that, that you're special enough, that being apart from you feels wrong. So I want you to come over just to see the States firstly so we can have more time together and find out if we're right for each other, but also so you know what you'd be letting yourself in for if, you know, things did get serious.'

Tanya gulped and despite blinking fast wasn't able to stop tears running down her cheeks. His words sounded like an ultimatum and one she was in no position to respond to even if she did know how she felt about it. Her first reaction wasn't good. The presumption of his expectations made him sound immature and demanding. Yet another person who wanted their own needs put first, even if his desires did align with her own.

She pulled away.

'I have to go home and check on Dadda for myself,' she said.

Chapter Twenty

Three days had passed since Tanya had taken Will back to the airport and then stood dwarfed beside a floor to ceiling window looking at the expanse of land needed for the runway. She'd waited and watched until his plane left the tarmac.

While they'd seen each other again since his invitation to holiday in America, he hadn't mentioned it until just before he went through the security check and into the departure lounge.

'Come and see me?' he'd whispered into her ear as he held her tight. 'Don't let this be the last time we're together.'

She'd nodded against his shoulder but made no verbal commitment. Since then they'd emailed each other and his last message had included a wonderfully encouraging passage about how she should definitely stretch her wings at work and not let her talents be overlooked.

He obviously wanted the best for her, even if she didn't ever make it across the Atlantic to visit his home. And she liked him. A lot. The ultimatum about how he could never leave Chicago permanently only showed he was equally committed to his family as she was to hers. Surely, if it came to it, everything was negotiable?

Geena had been asking questions in a variety of ways in an attempt to get Tanya to reveal the current status of her relationship with Will. Everything from the direct, 'So do you consider yourself single or are you in a relationship?' to the trick nature of, 'Have you got particular plans for Christmas?' which could have been as much a query about whether Tanya would be working as about whether there might be an extra guest at the table.

Tanya didn't take the bait. Geena was not someone she'd currently choose to confide in. Geena was part of the problem.

After Tanya had run away from Will's ultimatum in the pub, she'd got home to find Dadda quiet and anxious. The local news report about a man being attacked in a road he'd recognised had included graphic photos of the man's injuries as police appealed for those with any information to come forward. Tanya accused Geena of handling it inadequately.

'How was I to know?' Geena whined. 'I mean, you have to keep that kind of stuff in perspective. Otherwise you'd never leave the house.'

'Get a grip, Gee,' Tanya replied. 'He isn't leaving the house. It's obvious he's not up to any kind of distress. You know when they say "contains images which may offend some viewers"? He's the "some viewers".'

'Well I know now, all right? And it's fine. Me and him were OK together.'

Tanya shook her head. Nothing was all right. Things were mostly all wrong. 'We need to be with him more, talk to him. Make sure he talks to us.'

'I get it, Tan,' Geena said. 'I'll be better able to handle it next time. We're actually getting on really well since he told me everything. We're talking loads. Don't stress about us.'

Which, Tanya had thought at the time, was easy for Geena to say.

Now, as she parked the car and walked up to the front door, Tanya prepared herself to fend off whatever gossip-gathering approach Geena had devised today and tried not to get her hopes up that she'd find a new email from Will waiting in her inbox.

'Is that you, Tanya?' Dadda called from the living room as she closed the door.

'Yes,' she called back as she kicked her shoes under the hall table and went to join him. 'How are you?'

He was holding an envelope out towards her. 'I'm fine, but I had to have my photograph taken before I was allowed this.'

Tanya frowned and took the envelope from him. It was addressed to her. 'Your photo? What do you mean?'

'The delivery driver said I could sign for it but he had to take a photograph of where it had been delivered. What is it?'

She shrugged, turned the brown envelope over and tore into it. Inside she found a few sheets of folded paper wrapped around a slim booklet whose burgundy cover was embossed with a gilt crest. Her passport had arrived.

'Oh,' she said and sat down on the sofa. She dropped the envelope and papers into her lap and held the passport in both hands, staring at the lion and unicorn motif on the front. 'I'm sorry, Dadda. I guess the photo was part of the security arrangements for the delivery.'

'That's a British passport,' he said.

'Yes, I've never had one.'

He paused before saying, 'You never needed one before.'

The word "before" hung in the air between them. Tanya ignored it and just said, 'No.'

Neither of them spoke as she opened the passport to see the page from which her digitally-rendered image looked back at her alongside the words "British Citizen". Tanya swallowed and flipped through the pages adorned with weather symbols drawn in coloured ink. That enduring British obsession: the weather, with all its unpredictability and extremes, was the symbol the country had chosen to send its people into the world bearing. That, and the redundant language of a long gone empire inside the front cover requesting and requiring "in the Name of Her Majesty all those whom it may concern to allow the bearer to pass freely without let or hindrance". That wasn't how Tanya had heard it worked at border controls these days.

She turned to the back. There were thirty-one pages. Thirty-one unstamped pages taunting her with their images of British wildlife and geographical features as though they knew she'd never seen anything more exotic. Watermarks glinted in the texture of the paper, revealing a thistle, rose, daffodil and shamrock against the light as she riffled the pages. Icons almost devalued by their ubiquity.

The design team had refrained from printing a Union Jack on the passport, but they had wound red, white and blue threads into the string which stitched the pages together. This slim book with its old-fashioned ideas and quaint decoration was as British as could be and that meant so was Tanya Gill.

She could now both leave the country and return to it. The thought terrified her.

'Does this mean,' Dadda said carefully, 'that you are planning to go somewhere?'

Tanya put the passport down and looked at him. 'I honestly don't know, Dadda. It's just that, well, I've always wanted to, you know that.'

'And now maybe you have the opportunity? I imagine your American friend would like you to go and see him.'

She couldn't read anything from Dadda's tone of voice. There was no obvious disapproval, or disappointment. She looked up at him.

'Will did ask me to visit him. But I haven't said yes or no yet.' She ran her finger over the texture of the word "passport" stamped on the shiny cover. It brought Chicago a little closer.

He nodded, sat back in his chair and opened his newspaper. 'Then perhaps you should go,' he said.

She raised her eyebrows.

'I was wrong to judge him without meeting him. He might be different from us, but I seemed different to your mother's family. They still took me in, looked after me.'

Tanya smiled, but he was glossing over an important fact. 'Right up to the point where you wanted to marry her,' she said.

He nodded. 'Yes. You're not planning on marrying this man, are you?' He grinned.

She couldn't believe it. Was Dadda actually teasing her?

'Go. Go on your holiday,' he said.

Tanya looked at the passport and sighed. Its arrival might have unlocked doors, but it couldn't release her. 'I'm not sure I want to leave you.'

'Leave me? Tanya I am an adult and, yes, I accept I am not feeling entirely myself lately, but Geena is here. Between us we will survive while you have a holiday.' He put the paper down and looked at her. 'Geena and I have been talking. We agreed that it would be best to stay here for the time being. I've taken the house off the market.'

Tanya gasped. 'That's, um, that's a good decision,' she said, wondering what Geena could have said to bring about that change of heart. 'But I'm not sure ...'

Dadda shook his head. 'I know that your mother would have told you to go,' he said.

Tanya pursed her lips. He wasn't reacting at all as she'd have anticipated. She stared at the front of her passport again. A British passport. It was the goal of so many immigrants but hers by right and ridiculous that she'd never even touched one until now.

As she looked at it though, that flimsy, lightweight symbol of all it meant to be British and to have the right to move freely anywhere in the European Union and many other countries besides, she didn't feel borders opening. There was still the matter of her fear of flying to address, as well as her responsibilities.

'Do you really think that's what Mum would have wanted?' she asked.

'Yes. I do. Her greatest wish was for her daughters to be happy and I know you have had to carry too many burdens. And that Geena,' he gestured towards the kitchen where they could hear Geena singing along to pop songs on the radio, 'has enjoyed freedoms you chose not to exploit.'

Tanya pressed her lips together. Everything he'd said sounded plausible, if the opposite of some of his recent attitudes. Everything Deb had said about Will advised her in the same direction, while her advice about Dadda was that he needed to find his own pace of recovery. Perhaps he was getting better, and maybe her mum would have told her to go to America.

She thought again over those words her mum had left her with, "be my daughter but, most of all, be yourself". Maybe it didn't have to mean she should only fill her mum's role and live by the decisions she'd made. It could also mean she could truly inherit her mum's bravery. She could make her own decisions.

'Will you be putting the kettle on?' Dadda asked.

'Of course,' she said and went through to the kitchen where Geena grinned at her.

Tanya held up a hand to indicate she shouldn't speak. 'Before you say anything,' she said, 'I want a straight answer to this. What have you done to Dadda? Something's changed.'

Geena tutted. 'I thought you'd be pleased,' she said. 'I've done something to help him, just like you said. I've offered him a job.'

*

Upstairs, Tanya placed the passport on her desk before reaching into the top drawer to retrieve Will's atlas. She turned the pages and looked at each of the pictures he'd chosen, from a pride of lions to the Taj Mahal, knowing each landmark, each experience was now closer to being reality rather than dreams.

The passport plus Dadda's improvement and Geena's new ideas meant maybe it was possible for her to take a trip soon. Maybe she could think of what she wanted for herself, rather than putting her family first. She smiled and stroked the map of the UK, labelled as a treasure map with the X marking Birmingham, then turned to the final page: the map of North America and its plea for her to visit.

She grabbed her laptop and clicked into her emails. There was no new message from Will, but she opened a blank email and typed 'I'll come to see you. When's good?' She paused before pressing send though. While many of the barriers had gone, the concept of the flight itself remained a problem. She opened up more browser tabs to check the cost of flying to Chicago, knowing it was a diversionary tactic to avoid confronting her real concerns.

As she scrolled down the first website the search engine retrieved, adverts appeared in the sidebar, their random subjects obviously inspired by cookies from her recent browsing history. A scrolling feed of job adverts distracted her eye away from the flight timings she'd been looking for and the word "tuberculosis" jumped out at her from the blurb about one in particular. She moved the mouse and clicked through to read the details.

She'd downloaded the application form before she'd even finished reading the person specification and began to complete it electronically, cutting and pasting details in from the recent training application she'd put together. By the time Geena shouted that dinner was ready, the form was nearly complete. She clicked to save it and closed the laptop. The email to Will remained in her drafts folder.

Chapter Twenty-One

Geena hummed along to the Christmas music on the radio as she clicked on the wedding ring image she'd selected and dragged it onto the website template she was setting up. This was just a first draft, a mock-up to help Mr Davis understand the type of thing she'd like them to develop. She'd been working in her new role for nearly a month now and felt certain his lack of computer skills meant he'd agree to anything she suggested for the firm's online presence.

While her plans didn't involve a large proportion of their business moving online, after all, it was personal service that was her prime selling point, the website was needed to make sure potential customers could find out they existed, see example products and get a feel for the character of the shop. Enough to tempt them to visit.

The new job meant she was working harder than ever before, even on her days off, like today. But she felt no inclination to complain about the workload.

A professional web designer would be needed though. While she was enjoying playing with the visuals, all the jargon about search engine optimisation, bounce rates and payment transactions had her confused.

'Geena,' Dadda called, 'come and tell me where you want this fixed.'

She jumped up from her seat at the kitchen table and joined him in the hall. He'd laid a dust sheet over the carpet and was poised with a cordless drill in one hand. She stood back to survey their project.

The fresh pale green paint on the walls transformed the feel of the space and the white-washed wooden shoe rack Dadda had built to her own design would be a finishing touch to reorganise the way they used it. It was a test really. Now that Mr Davis allowed her to work on her own jewellery designs at her desk in his workroom, she'd encouraged Dadda to turn the garage back into what it had originally been - a workshop for him.

In the weeks since she'd suggested he could do some work for her while he built up to going back out to work in the shoe repair shop, he'd embraced the project. He'd reorganised the garage and got his long-disused tools back into working order. He'd also started seeing a therapist and, while she had to travel to and from every appointment with him, the effects so far were positive.

The shoe rack fitted exactly under the old console table, which he'd sanded and varnished and to which she'd attached a curtain made from an off-cut of vintage fabric.

'Here, let's come slightly to the left. Then we can cluster the framed photos above it and it'll be central to the gap from the front door to the start of the stairs,' she said.

He nodded, repositioned things as she'd directed and began to fix the rack to the wall.

She patted his shoulder. 'We make a great team, Dadda.'

'Thirsty work, though,' he replied.

She laughed and went back to the kitchen to put the kettle on.

*

For the second day running, Tanya opened the front door and wondered if she was in the right house. The day before she'd been greeted by paint fumes and found the hallway empty of furniture and with walls an entirely new colour.

'I like it,' she'd said in response to Geena and Dadda's questioning, but they wouldn't reveal the rest of their plans.

Now she could almost have believed herself in a boutique hotel. The Union Jack doormat and clutter of abandoned shoes and bags were banished and the house was silent. She closed the front door and stepped forward to look at the pictures on the wall. They weren't new, but she hadn't seen them in years. Snapshots from her childhood showing her and Geena on beaches, riding bikes and with faces smeared with ice cream were grouped around a central photograph in which the sisters each held one of their mum's hands while Dadda stood behind her, chin held high and one arm across his wife's shoulders. Tanya smiled: it was a collection of happy memories.

She bent to take off her shoes and, unable to just kick them under the table as she usually did, pulled the new curtain aside to investigate. Three rows of shelves across half the space had been designed to accommodate their shoes, with Geena's high heels and brightly coloured trainers across the top, her own mostly black shoes on the middle shelf, and Dadda's two pairs, one black, one brown, at the bottom. The other half of the space was open to the full height of the table and made space for Geena's knee high boots. Tanya placed her shoes into the obvious space and turned to see what they had planned for her coat and bag. As she hung them on the new hooks on the opposite wall she saw Dadda and Geena peeking at her from the living room.

Geena threw the door open. 'Well?' she said.

'It's brilliant, Gee,' Tanya said. 'I love it.'

'I figured that the entrance hall sets the tone of a house and the clash of the old-fashioned wallpaper and Dadda's kitsch patriotic stuff did not give us a great welcome. I wanted our home to say something about us.'

Tanya glanced at Dadda to see his reaction to Geena's dismissal of his taste, but he was just smiling at his younger daughter.

'I love seeing the old photos there,' Tanya said, nodding towards the display. 'Where did you find matching frames for all the different sizes?'

'Dadda made them.'

'To Geena's design,' he added. 'She thought it was time we put them on display. I hope you agree, Tanya?'

'Yes,' she said, 'I completely agree. So this is what the two of you have been whispering about for the past few weeks.'

They grinned at each other. 'Well, we've got a few things on the go,' Geena said. 'Dadda's coming with me to the craft fair tomorrow where we'll unveil some of our other designs.'

Tanya frowned. 'Are you sure, Dadda? It'll be quite crowded, won't it?'

'Yes, but Geena will be there too. I'm looking forward to it.' He turned, went back into the living room and put the television on.

'We'll be OK, Tan. I promise,' Geena said. 'You can see how much he's improved recently. We loved doing that photo project. We wanted it to be a surprise for you, but I wish you could have heard him chatting about those holidays we had when we were kids, all the funny things mum said.'

Tanya followed Geena into the kitchen. 'We haven't talked about those things in years.'

'No,' Geena replied. 'About time, wasn't it?'

Tanya nodded.

'Anyway,' Geena went on, 'you should come down and see us at the fair tomorrow. It'll set your mind at rest to see that we can cope without you. I mean, we'll have to, won't we? Not long now until you're off on your travels.'

'No,' Tanya said. 'It's coming round terrifyingly soon.'

*

As she stood behind her stall in the church hall the next morning, Geena smoothed down the tunic she'd made from fabric she'd salvaged from one of her mum's old dresses and

223

tucked her hair behind her ears. Everything was ready and Dadda's custom-made display racks meant their table was presented more professionally than most of the others surrounding them.

The craft market aimed at last minute Christmas gift shoppers wasn't the ideal event for her to unveil her jewellery designs, but could be considered a safe, soft launch for a new product range. Yes, it was fine if she thought of it like that. If she didn't sell a single piece, she'd be able to blame the customers and it was unlikely any of her former friends would be seen dead in this church hall. What did they know about anything which mattered, anyway?

The doors had opened half an hour ago and a few people had already passed the table without stopping to look more closely. But they were the early risers, elderly women more likely to buy a crocheted Santa Claus from the stall next to hers. Not Geena's target market at all.

Dadda had been for a look around at the other stalls while it was quiet and returned with polystyrene cups of tea for them. He seemed to be coping with being out and among strangers. She'd accompanied him on almost every expedition in recent months: to the DIY superstore, to meet with his old boss to discuss when he might return to work, even a couple of walks in the park. Only the worry that the room may become crowded and too claustrophobic for him bothered her today. But they weren't far from home. She could call Tanya to come and meet him if it became too much.

'OK, Dadda?' she asked and he nodded in response.

'Oh, how lovely!'

Geena turned to find a woman had stopped at her stall and had lifted a pair of earrings to examine them closer.

'Thank you,' Geena said. 'There's a matching pendant as well. Just ask if you have any questions.'

She stepped back, not wanting to intimidate the woman or make her feel awkward if she only wanted to browse, but really Geena longed to give the woman a huge hug. The first independent person to look at the collection actually liked it.

The stall did look fantastic, the varied colours of the wires she'd used in each piece glinting as the light caught them, the racks and stands Dadda had made to her specifications displayed everything to great effect, and the whole table was covered with a layer of emerald-green silk to add a sense of luxury and hint at the exotic.

Geena reached out and squeezed Dadda's arm. He looked at her and smiled, but the smile immediately left his face as his eyes shifted to something over her shoulder. She turned to see what he'd noticed.

A man with cropped hair and a roaring lion tattoo on the side of his neck limped along the row of stalls towards them. He paused to look at the products on each table, which gave Geena the chance to take in the crutch he used to help him balance and his "Help For Heroes" sweatshirt with its empty left sleeve pinned to his side. He was obviously still adjusting to walking with one prosthetic leg, its metal post flashed beneath his trouser leg as he lifted his thigh unnaturally high to move forwards. As she watched, an older man approached and patted the injured man on his back, saying something to which he responded with a nod and a grim smile. He moved closer to their table.

Geena turned back to Dadda, who had put his cup down and folded his arms tight across his chest.

'It's OK,' she said.

'He's a soldier,' he replied.

'Yes, probably one of the ones Tanya's friend Deb treats up at the hospital.' She was uncertain what would be best to say or do. 'Looks like he was hurt pretty badly. Do you want to pop out for a bit?'

Dadda shook his head and Geena turned back to the front of the stall.

'I'll leave it for now,' the woman who'd been browsing said, 'but I might pop back in a bit.'

'Of course,' Geena said. 'Here, take my card.' She passed her contact details over and by the time she'd turned back, the soldier had arrived at her stall.

He gave her a quick smile, which she returned but she immediately stepped back to stand shoulder to shoulder with Dadda. She could feel a slight tremor in his arm. The soldier looked from side to side across the table, examining all the items in their display. Eventually he looked up with a frown.

'Um, could I ask for your help, please?' he said.

Geena stepped forward. 'Of course.' She realised that with his remaining hand clinging to the crutch, he was unable to do anything other than look. 'Is there something I can show you?'

He smiled, a quick, shy smile. 'Please. Those earrings - could you hold them up? Maybe near your ear so I can see how it works?'

Geena obliged and also selected a matching pendant which she held near her neck. 'They'd make a lovely set. Are you looking to buy a present?'

He nodded but his eyes dropped back to the other items on the table. Keen not to lose a customer, Geena put the earrings and pendant down and asked, 'Are you shopping for a girlfriend? What kind of jewellery does she wear?'

He pursed his lips. 'Um, kind of quirky stuff, you know. That's why this caught my eye, I guess. And we went on holiday to India once, I thought maybe your stuff might be a nice reminder of, well, things are a bit different now.' He shuffled the crutch awkwardly, pivoting on his good foot.

'It's OK,' Geena said. 'I understand.' She glanced behind her to where Dadda had unfolded his arms and was looking at the man more kindly.

'May I ask what happened?' Dadda said.

The soldier looked at him and was silent for a tense moment before he replied, 'Roadside IED. Afghanistan. Killed a kid and my mate. I'm the lucky one.' He shrugged with his intact shoulder.

Dadda nodded. 'Better to survive. Better to remember.'

'Yeah. And my girlfriend's been great. Really supportive. Hence the present. It's been months but I've still got to stay near the hospital for the rehab and physio. She can't get over here too often.'

'I'm sure she'll love anything you send,' Geena said.

He nodded. 'But will she want to be reminded of a holiday we took when I was, you know, able-bodied? I'm sorry, maybe this isn't the right thing at all.'

Geena bit her lip. She reached for a different pendant, one on which the Indian-influenced design was more abstract with its cerise wire curling across a tiny polished silver lozenge.

'Happy memories are important,' she said as she held it up. 'They're what you build a happy future on. Please, will you take this for her? On the house. I'd like her to have it.'

'I couldn't,' he said, beginning to back away.

'I kind of insist,' Geena replied and snipped off the price tag, wrapped the pendant in purple tissue and dropped it into one of the paper bags she'd decorated with stickers.

'Um, OK,' he replied and leant his elbow on the crutch so he could take the bag from her to slip into his pocket. 'Thank you.'

'Have my card as well. Let us know what she thinks of it, won't you?'

He nodded. 'I will. Thank you. You're very kind.'

Geena slipped her arm through Dadda's as they watched the soldier limp away.

'OK?' she asked him.

He reached for the discarded price tag. 'Ten pounds you wanted for that, Geena. And you told me you were a proper businesswoman.'

'Yeah,' she replied. 'But I'm also a sucker for romance.' She reached forward to rearrange the display.

'I'm glad you gave him the necklace. I had forgotten how important tokens can be.' He touched the bangles clustered at Geena's wrist. 'Your mum valued these much higher than their worth. We would have left India with nothing, but her mum, your grandmother, gave her these. She refused to sell them though. Said they were worth more on her arm than in the bank.'

Geena blinked until the tears cleared from her eyes. 'Oh, Dadda. They're worth that much to me too. Thank you for telling me their story.' She reached out to hug him.

He patted her back. 'Perhaps I should have told you before, not waited until a soldier showed me the right thing to do.'

'He was all right, wasn't he?' Geena said.

Dadda nodded. 'Yes. It was nice to speak to him, to find that he's as human as us. I'm glad I came.'

'I'm glad you came,' she replied. 'Now, come on, let's get selling.'

Chapter Twenty-Two

Tanya stepped through the automatic doors and hoisted the strap of her handbag higher on her shoulder, knocking awry one of the dangling earrings Geena had given her as a going away present. She straightened it to make sure it still hung securely and smiled.

Geena's collection had sold well at the craft fairs she'd taken it to in recent months, especially over Christmas, and the work Dadda was doing to build new cabinets for Mr Davis's shop meant she'd soon have it prominently displayed there too. Tanya finally felt confident they'd be OK without her.

What she didn't feel confident about was what she was doing herself. But, after all the changes sparked by a few idiots on a bus the previous autumn, spring represented a new start for the Gill family. Geena and Dadda had settled into new roles. Now it was Tanya's turn.

She dragged her case over to look up at the screen which listed departures until she picked the flight code she was looking for out from others to destinations as diverse as Milan, Shanghai and Casablanca. Things had certainly changed in the six months since Will had walked into her clinic and interrupted her daydreams about travelling overseas.

She'd arrived at the airport well in advance of the suggested check-in time, but was pleased to see a desk number was already displayed so she could drop off her heavy suitcase and adjust to being at Heathrow. It was one of the world's busiest airports, and the reality of being there to travel on her first ever flight threatened to overwhelm her. Her fear had been building over the past few days as the point came closer when she'd step onto a plane before leaving the ground to travel abroad. Now anxiety contracted her throat and she sniffed and hurried towards the baggage drop counter.

She'd set an alarm for the early hours of the previous morning so she could complete the online check-in details as soon as the flight was available. Will had advised her to get a window seat away from the wing for the best view. Tanya had actually chosen an aisle seat, knowing she'd probably spend the entire flight with her eyelids screwed shut. Now she joined the queue to drop off her hold luggage (yes, she'd packed it herself, no, no one could have tampered with it) and made her way towards the security check point.

She was disappointed that no one took much interest in her passport and, unfamiliar with the procedures, she copied the passengers in front of her, first presenting her boarding pass to an official who ignored her polite "hello", then loading her hand baggage, jacket, belt, shoes and clear plastic bag containing liquids and gels into a tray to pass through the X-ray scanner. She took a brief professional interest in this machine, but once beckoned to walk through the metal detector and given the all clear to pick up her possessions, all thoughts of X-rays left her mind. The only technology she was interested in now was the engineering and laws of physics which would keep her plane in the sky.

She thought about the message Deb had scrawled into the Bon Voyage card one of her children had made for Tanya. 'Fly high,' Deb had written. 'The sky is not a limit.' That was all Tanya had to remember, that planes carried passengers safely around the globe on a daily basis. There was nothing to fear.

She bypassed the branches of shops she could have visited in Birmingham to find the thing she knew she could find only at Heathrow's Terminal 4.

Since her ticket on this flight was booked, she hadn't even looked at the online reports of planes flying over Birmingham. She no longer considered herself a plane geek; for her it had never been about the planes themselves, it was the destinations which caught her imagination, the potential offered by travel. But, having spent so much time on the flight tracking website, reading the forum posts, and aware that the planes were what attracted the interest of many other people, she couldn't miss the opportunity to visit the airside observation deck from which she'd seen so many photographs. She also wanted to spend some time watching planes take off, just to reassure herself how easy it was.

She found the room near the end of a long corridor and, as she stepped inside, was struck by how light it was. Unlike the tinted glass at the windows of the rest of the terminal, the panoramic windows here were designed to give the best possible view of everything happening on the tarmac in front of her.

To her left, where she'd noticed a crowd of passengers waiting at their gate, the hold of an American Airways jet was being loaded with pallets piled with luggage. Trucks towing crates looked like toys beside the scale of the airliner and the workers could be picked out of the confusion only because of their high-visibility jackets.

She stepped close to the window, where a man looked out through binoculars towards the runway. On a desk in front of her was a touch screen logged into the familiar website on which symbols representing the actual aircraft in front of her blinked but remained fixed in place. For now. She grinned. The world which had seemed virtual or remote was finally real.

The man turned as the plane he was watching began to accelerate along the runway, tilting his head upwards as it lifted into the sky. Once it was airborne, he lowered the binoculars and said, 'There goes another one.'

Tanya smiled, unsure how to respond. This man obviously had all the knowledge and experience she lacked. 'It's my first visit,' she said.

'Didn't think you seemed our usual type,' he said. 'Only the die-hard aviation fans make it here.'

She nodded, and glanced at the screen to see where the plane which had just taken off was headed. Paris, not exciting enough for her.

'Where are you travelling to?' she asked the man.

He'd lifted the binoculars again and didn't look at her as he replied, 'Amsterdam. KLM. Fokker 70. Whereas that,' she looked in the direction he was pointing, 'that is the A380 off to Singapore. Look at her. Fabulous bird.'

Tanya was glad he didn't ask for her flight details; she'd have been embarrassed to admit her ignorance when she'd spent so long immersed in flight data. Looking up the type of plane hadn't even occurred to her. 'I hope you have a good trip,' she said.

He was silent as the A380 turned onto the runway and paused there before a burst of acceleration propelled the plane into the air trailing a plume of hot air which distorted the scenery behind it. Tanya's stomach lurched.

'Thanks, it's only business,' he said. 'How about you, are you travelling on business or for pleasure?'

'Bit of both,' Tanya replied.

She left the observation lounge and strolled back along the carpeted walkway towards the gate number listed for her own departure. The diversity of the crowd gathering there immediately indicated that her destination was more exotic than Amsterdam.

Women swathed in bright fabrics with matching headdresses shepherded hordes of grinning children into a queue that was more like a rugby scrum, while their menfolk lounged on nearby chairs. No-one seemed to be speaking English.

Tanya took her phone from her bag and typed a message to Will, "Just boarding the plane. Can you imagine how terrified I am? Excited as well, though." She hesitated, realising that the time difference meant he wouldn't see the message for hours. She'd have arrived by the time she picked up any response from him.

Instead she sent a text to Geena, "Getting on plane! This is actually happening. Take care and I'll see you soon."

She gripped her phone as the queue inched forwards, determined not to switch it off until the last moment. Geena responded quickly though, "Disagree with your definition of 'soon'. Have a safe flight and be sure to tell me everything. Love you, G x".

Tanya smiled. She would be away quite a while, but knew the time would race by. And the experience was going to be well worth facing her fear of flying. It wasn't a fear, she reminded herself, thinking of Deb's advice, only apprehension and completely manageable as long as she remained calm. She took a deep breath and consciously forced the muscles in her neck and shoulders to relax.

'Excuse me,' a male voice behind her said.

She turned to find an elderly, white man who looked as out of place in the crowd as she did. He was holding out a slip of paper.

'You dropped this' he said.

'Oops, thank you.' She took back her boarding pass, unable to believe she'd managed to drop it. 'There's a bit too much to think about here.'

He nodded. 'They'll want to see your passport too, check you are who you say you are.'

'Of course.' She delved in her bag to retrieve it.

Obviously pleased to find a fellow English-speaker, the man kept talking as the queue moved forward. 'Is this your first trip to Nairobi?'

'Yes, but I'll only see the airport there, I'm making a connection on to Ethiopia.' She smiled. 'If I sound as though I know what I'm doing, I don't. It's not only my first trip to Africa, this is the first time I've ever even been on a plane. I'm a little nervous, to be honest.'

The man raised his eyebrows. 'It's brave of you to travel so far. What takes you to Ethiopia?'

'Tuberculosis.' The smile left Tanya's face and she forgot her fears. 'I've volunteered to help set up a new screening clinic. I'm a radiographer.'

The moment that advert had appeared on her computer screen, it replaced all other ambitions and desires. Not only would the job help develop her professional skills and make a difference to the community she'd be serving, it was also the ideal chance to do something just for her. To travel, to see something of the world, to do something entirely new.

Will understood that she needed to follow her instinct to do something worthwhile. She'd be in Africa for three months, then travel on to Chicago and into his arms. Who knew how the African experience would change her though, who she'd meet, and what she'd learn about herself?

The thought of Will was a temptation, but she didn't intend to wish away her time in Ethiopia, not when adventure had been what she'd dreamt of all her life. And she couldn't think yet about his ultimatum that any partner of his needed to live in the States. She put her family high up her priorities list too. But, right now, the job came first.

That was who she was, and this was what she was going to do.

The End

<<<<>>>>

Author's Note

Thank you for reading. I hope you've enjoyed Tanya and Geena's story. If so, please do tell a friend about the book or consider writing an online review — word of mouth is the best advertising there is! I'd be very grateful for any support.

While I am inspired by Birmingham, the city I'm fortunate to live in, I have used artistic licence with the settings for this book. There are lovely gift shops and jewellers in Bournville, but Mr Davis's shop doesn't exist and the chocolate factory and hospital of the book are fictionalised versions of reality whose procedures I'm sure vary hugely from those depicted here. There are sensitive, warm-hearted people like Tanya, Geena, Jagtar and Deb in Birmingham though. I've been lucky enough to meet some.

Thanks to: Chris Randall, William Gallagher and Titania Krimpas for their feedback on early drafts of this novel; to Andy Killeen and the members of the Pow-Wow Writers' Group for their critique sessions; to Claire Johnson-Creek of Twenty7 Books for editorial notes when No Place won a competition run by the company; to John Findlay, Mary Ellen Flynn and Peter Lewis who indulged me by answering some oddly specific questions; and to Kirsten Lacey, Anne D'Souza and Clair Hughes for being supportive early readers. Also, many thanks to Jane Dixon-Smith for the cover design. All mistakes and inaccuracies are my own.

If, like Tanya, you're wondering where that plane is going, or fancy some armchair travelling ideas, take a look at flightradar24.com to find out what's happening above you.

Or, if you're inspired to support a tuberculosis project, Médecins Sans Frontièrs (Doctors Without Borders) are doing important work around the world. Find out more at msf.org.uk.

For more about me and my books, do visit my website at katharinedsouza.co.uk or find me on Twitter as @KatharineDS.

Other books by the same author:

Park Life
by
Katharine D'Souza

A tale of neighbours, cafés and cake in Birmingham.

Craig's ambitious. He wants promotion, recognition and to be one of the lads. Relationships and family don't feature in the plan; until he's given no alternative.

Susan's taken a huge step. She's walked away from the oppressive security of her marriage and moved to Birmingham for a fresh start – in the flat next door to Craig.

They're not friends. But maybe a neighbour can do more than keep an emergency spare key.

Life isn't a walk in the park. Perhaps taking one might help.

Deeds Not Words
by
Katharine D'Souza

Museum curator Caroline thinks history is safely in the
past, until a century-old family secret collides with
problems at work and upsets her plans for a quiet life in
Birmingham.

Why has nobody mentioned Great Aunt Susannah
before?
What does Caroline's old flame want from her?
And are any of the paintings really what they appear to
be?

As she battles professional rivalries, attempts to contain
family dramas, and searches for historical treasure amongst
the clutter, Caroline is forced to decide what she holds
most valuable and exactly what she's going to do to
protect it.

Deeds Not Words.
Because actions speak louder.

59294283R00145

Made in the USA
Charleston, SC
03 August 2016